Beautiful Secrets

Clairie Saunders

Published by Clairie Saunders, 2024.

BEAUTIFUL SECRETS

First edition. April 12, 2024.

ISBN: 979-8224717675

Written by Clairie Saunders.

Table of Contents

Beautiful Secrets

By
Clairie Saunders

Existen

Chapter 1

"Mr. Kalogerou, your car is waiting for you, sir." The voice of his secretary didn't interrupt his thoughts as Dimitris Kalogerou ignored her once more.

It was Tuesday night, early January, in New York City. Dimitris Kalogerou lived there almost for a month. He had decided on staying in America permanently– for the rest of his life - if Manos' housekeeper didn't inform him about the horrible accident that Manos had the night before.

Staying in New York for good, after the last fight he had with Manos, was a difficult decision he made, as Manos was not only his co – partner but also his best friend. Kalogerou couldn't understand the reason why he should be the *one* sending to the factories in Ioannina and Thessaloniki – always during Christmas, Easter and summer - for a financial and legal control. *When everyone was on vacation, I had to work even harder,* Kalogerou thought.

He had tolerated enough from Manos' strange behavior. For ten years. He was a grown man and had his own life and his own work. He couldn't obey to Manos, whenever Manos wanted to as if he was one of his clerks.

This Christmas he had arranged to spend his vacation away from work. "I deserve it", he had explained to Manos and he was going to do that, despite Manos' 'orders'. This was the last time when Dimitris Kalogerou saw Manos alive.

He suffered agonies of remorse. Terrible remorse. He groaned.

Enough, thought Kalogerou. An awful feeling hit his heart. Again. He felt sad when remembering Manos and how he had stood to him after his father's death. *Oh, no, not that remorse again,* soliloquized

Kalogerou. He lit up a cigarette after the third phone call of Maria from Athens.

Bringing back in his mind the last fight he had with Manos, he wondered who was behind those strange requests. *A chick, who else,* he murmured. Kalogerou was one hundred percent sure that behind Manos' strange behavior was a woman. That pisses Kalogerou off, even more.

Kalogerou used to say that one woman is a big problem, although, many women wouldn't be any problem. Manos was of a different opinion.

And by keeping this woman secret from him was a matter of trust, he thought. That was what hurt him most. There was a silent arrangement between them. They will never quarrel for the same woman. Period. They were adults. They were friends. Best friends. Why couldn't Manos understand that?

Kalogerou was pissed off again while he was thinking these things. Why did he remember all that things? He was having a very good time in New York, forgetting all that irritated stuff until Maria informed him about the accident.

He put some papers in his briefcase. "Let's see", he said looking out of the window of his office, "is this chick going to appear now that Manos is in such bad condition?" *She is not going to show up, you know that,* a little malice voice said inside him.

This woman must be so...., he couldn't think of the appropriate word to describe her absurd claims. He thought of it more clearly. *Perhaps, she is married,* an idea passed his mind. *That was out of question,* he thought, *due to practical reasons,* he smiled.

This 'secret girlfriend' of Manos was free to travel all over Greece and all over the rest countries of the Mediterranean Sea or Europe every Christmas, every Easter and for, at least, three whole months every summer.

How she could do that if she was married? And there is also the jet. Something is missing here, he said to himself.

And it wasn't only that. It was also another thing, which was more serious and more annoying, at least for Kalogerou. When this bimbo left, Manos used to behave like a monk. As if there was the only beautiful woman in Athens.

A faint smile formed in his shapely mouth. The women in Athens are also very beautiful. The only thing you need is to know where to look for. He wouldn't leave Manos alone. They would go out together. But no, no, no, Manos preferred to sit in his huge living room, drinking wine and remembering the days and the nights he spent with this bimbo.

All this stupid romance. Kalogerou hated romance. He kicked the chair in front of him. He wasn't like Manos. If he found a beautiful woman he was straight to the point without a lot of talking or romancing. He frowned. He has put this sort of sport on ice for several weeks.

All women he saw during last few weeks didn't excite him, although they were objectively gorgeous. He had some very serious negotiations which led nowhere and that bothered him a lot. "Perhaps that was the problem," he said murmuring, as whenever he was in America he used to lead an active life dating a lot of women.

The phone in his office rang again. His secretary informed him that the car was waiting for him. Kalogerou extinguished his cigarette in an ashtray in front of him. He took his briefcase and left the office without saying anything to anyone. He was about to visit Greece to see how serious was Manos' condition. Then he could fly back to New York. He had decided to live in New York for the rest of his life and he would leave Greece as soon as Manos' condition permitted.

Sitting in the car, he was staring abstract out of the window. It was true that the accident of Manos Alexiou had shocked him. Maria said to him that Manos was returning from the factory late that night, as usual, and somehow he lost the control of his car and crashed into a wall.

That's strange, because Manos is a very good driver. How did he lose the control of his car?

Apostolou, Manos' doctor, wasn't very optimistic, Maria had told him.

The heart of Kalogerou tightened. "If Apostolou said such a thing," he left his sentence unfinished. Apostolou was a mutual friend of both of them and also an experienced and exceptional doctor, with his own private clinic.

He felt his heart heavy. He didn't want Manos to die. He was furious with Manos' behavior, but he wanted his friend kick and alive for sure. Manos Alexiou and Costas Apostolou were his best friends all these years. The three of them were the most confirmed bachelors of Athens.

Perhaps, I own to Manos an apology. Now he could understand how childish he had behaved. *It wasn't my fault,* he told himself and tossed his newspaper on the seat of the car.

Again remorse caught him.

At least, I could be a little bit friendlier when Manos called me last time, he said to himself. *Nonsense, Manos spoke to him with such an arrogant style that he decided to be as typical as he could.* Nothing more than typical. Like all famous lawyers used to do. Typical, stringent and without any trace of humanity. He punched the car seat beside him.

He glared out the car window. Apart from all that, it was also the factory. Manos' accident created many problems to the proper work of the factory, which if Manos had heard him, they would have overcome those problems long ago. But no! Above all, was Manos' stubbornness.

Kalogerou knew that very well as a Vice President and a Legal Counsel of the greatest dairy – factory in Greece, and he was trying for years to make Manos wise. Without any success.

He looking at the papers he had in his hands. "So big problems", he said aloud, unconsciously, lost in his thoughts, looking out at the wet road, "and who the hell is this Alina Johnson?" questioned himself while he was reading the factory papers once more.

THE BLACK LIMOUSINE crossed the area of the New York airport in torrential rain. The sky was sparkled and thundered. The rain beat against the car windows. As soon as Manos becomes healthy, he would leave for America. His decision was final.

The car stopped in front of the staircase of his jet. For a moment, he flinched to get out. This trip to Greece would be much different as Manos wouldn't be at the airport in order to meet him and annoy him, like he used to do. He hesitated for a while when he opened the door and went out. Heavy and cloudy, like the weather, he climbed the stairs of the jet in a rush.

Inside the jet, a figure of a very beautiful woman arrests his attention. She smiled at him. He looked at her with a seducing gaze from top to bottom. As he observed her a smile came on his lips. *It's time for a little fun. Factory issues could wait,* he thought as he saw her.

His dark blue eyes sparkled looking at her nice long legs as outlined below the short brown suede skirt. Her breasts followed her breath going up and down under her silk shirt in skin color. *A very aesthetic figure, indeed.* Tall, with the right curves, big green eyes, brown hair with unruly curls that fell to her shoulders. *Yes*, his male parts celebrated.

Watching the woman standing opposite him, he smiled. His gaze darkened for a moment while taking a look at those exquisite legs. His eyes took a sly light shade. This evening, high in the skies, it would acquire another dimension. He lost no more time. He walked to his seat and he approached the woman.

"Sweetheart, will you bring me a glass of whiskey?" he said by stroking her hair. The woman went away without saying a word. He followed her sensual figure with his gaze.

He looked at his watch. He had enough time to throw her on the bed. He settled in his seat waiting for his whiskey. He saw her as she was directed toward him by rocking her body. *Her body is pure hell*, a voice cried in his head, *pure hell*. He felt a tingling from top to the bottom of his body.

The beautiful woman leaned provocatively toward him and said, "Mr. Kalogerou, your whiskey, sir," she smiled at him and as he stretched out his hand to take the glass, she threw it in his face.

That was a big surprise. An unpleasant one! And it wasn't just that. She defiantly turned her back and sat on the seat directly opposite him. He stood up distracted from the wrath of seeking a towel to wipe his shirt.

The woman looked at him ironically from top to bottom. A smug smile showed to her beautiful lips which had the color of cherry and then turned her head to the window of the jet ignoring him while Kalogerou was screaming at her.

Peter, the pilot of the jet, showed up. "Oh, Mr. Kalogerou, you came at last." The two men greeted each other with a hearty handshake. "What happened to you, sir?" he said pointing to Kalogerou's shirt.

"Thanks to the new flight attendant," said to Peter as he was staring at the woman, "she is so helpful. Yet, I don't see how she could stay on this jet or on any other plane."

The woman turned her head and grimace to him. *Oh, I surely choke this one.* After that, he turned to Peter and told him with anger, "I don't want her on my jet. Throw her out." His voice was heard so angry that if there was another woman she would have run away without any question. However, this one watched him relaxed, and that made a great impression to him.

Peter, who realized what had happened, laughed.

"Peter, could you please tell me why are you laughing?" Kalogerou growled through his teeth, "the thing is that I was the one that had the whiskey in the face, not you and believe me I don't find it funny."

Peter tried to get serious and undertook to solve the misunderstanding, "Mr. Kalogerou, how could you possibly think that this lady over here is an air – hostess, sir?"

"What can I tell you, Peter, if there isn't a flight attendant who the hell is she and what is she doing in my jet?" Kalogerou was furious as he looked once at Peter and once at the beautiful woman.

Peter took a deep breath. "Mr. Kalogerou, this is a great misunderstanding. The lady here isn't a flight attendant. She is the daughter of Mr. Alexiou. This is Miss Alexiou, sir."

She turned and gave him a murderous look, "Well, well, well, Mr. Kalogerou, what can I say? That I am glad to meet you? That would be a terrible lie." She made no attempt to hide her feelings of antipathy. Her smile was one of those ironical ones, he was usually hanging out at his rivals when he won a trial or succeed a merger.

Kalogerou collapsed in his seat. He looked better at her and realized that Peter was right. How couldn't he recognize those big green eyes of Manos? She was tall like Manos, she had Manos' eyes, but she was incomparably more beautiful than her father. This was true. How didn't he notice that earlier?

Because you gave all your attention to her curves, said the male voice inside him.

Kalogerou glanced at Peter. "Oh, Mr. Kalogerou, don't look at me. The young lady here is Mr. Alexiou's daughter, not mine. Well, I leave you two alone to know each other better. I also have a plane to fly."

When Kalogerou left alone with Manos' daughter he was furious. "Miss Alexiou, are you always so perverse?" He was still trying to clean up the whiskey from his shirt.

"It depends on whom I have before me. By the way, this is my own jet," she emphasized the words by lifting her eyebrow.

Yes, this journey would be interesting enough, not the way he had in mind when he first saw her.

"As I see, you speak Greek fluently. As for the jet that belongs more to the company than to you or to me or to your father," he answered back to her with clenched teeth.

"As well as other five languages and this is my jet," she confirmed with all that nerve, before turning her gaze to the runway. They were about to take off.

Be calm Dimitris, he advised himself, "Miss Alexiou, have you been informed of you father's condition after the car crash?" Kalogerou couldn't take his eyes off her.

"Comprehensively." Her eyes were still stuck out of the window.

Her attitude was further irritated him.

"I presume that you are also Alina Johnson, am I right?" Alina didn't answer his question. "Have you been informed of your responsibilities at the factory?" He asked her trying to remain calm, although his rage had taken off like the airplane, successfully.

After a while, Peter lighted the lights to unfasten their belts. Kalogerou unfastened his belt in order to feel more comfortable. Alina didn't.

"Mr. Kalogerou, I'm here, because of my father. I don't give a damn for the factory," she frowned upon him.

This made Kalogerou even angrier as he wasn't one of those men who could tolerate such a behavior. Even though that awful behavior came from a beautiful woman and daughter of his best friend and his partner.

He had to give to this spoiled young lady a good lesson. He knew rich girls very well, especially daughters who are making their fathers whatever they want.

A flash came to his mind. *This was the bimbo. For her sake, Manos sent him away to their factories every Christmas, Easter, and summer. This trust problem again,* murmured looking at her. He knew how fathers are in all over the world. So protective of their daughters. Why Manos would be an exception?

That's ridiculous. He looked better at her. *Yes, that was Manos afraid of. For sure*, he murmured to himself. He hates that.

Apart from being Manos' daughter, her behavior was unacceptable. So he stood up from his seat and came over her. Miss Alexiou was taken aback. She didn't expect such a reaction. "First of all, when I'm talking to you, you have to look at me straight in the eyes, and secondly, you have to deal with the factory, at least at the percentage that belongs to you, sweetie."

The green of her big eyes made his heart beat like crazy in his chest. *Damn her*, he thought. Her aroma dominated his whole body. A delicate, aesthetic and romantic sense of roses and lemon hit his nostrils making him feel a little bit dizzy. He removed from her and sat heavy in his seat again.

Alexiou looked at him. "Mr. Kalogerou, what's your problem?"

This time, she was looking at him deep in his dark blue eyes. She felt a shiver. Those dark blue eyes created strong emotions to her heart. *Concentrate,* she scolded herself. She gave him a fabulous smile, although the tone of her voice was chilly as she spoke.

Kalogerou decided to spend a counterattack to her. "Miss Alexiou, could you please tell me how long ago did you find out that you're the daughter of Manos Alexiou?" His tone was offensive.

Alina was determined not to play his game. "For the last 28 years," she responded in a harsh and sharp acerbic tone.

A muffled giggle full of irony escaped from his mouth. She was very good. *She has learned her lesson very well this little Missy over here.* However, he won't be caught like a sucker, "I don't mean that." The rigorous style and clenched teeth made him irresistible.

She nailed him with her big green eyes. "And what exactly do you mean, Mr. Kalogerou?" She won't make any favor to him and be annoyed by his offended comment.

"What I mean is when do you discover that you are the one and only daughter, I presume, of Manos Alexiou, who is the owner of the first and biggest dairy factory of Greece?" His remarks were rather acid.

As Kalogerou spoke out these words one by one she would like to slap him. She hesitated. She was so confident that she would restore that opportunity later, so she looked at him defiantly. It was the first time in her whole life, that someone questioned the fact that she was the daughter of Manos Alexiou. She raised her hand and took a curl from her eyes.

"My answer is the same, Mr. Kalogerou. During the last 28 years," she said emphasizing every single word, as he had done earlier. "If it makes you feel more comfortable, I'm willing to do a DNA – test." Her smile was so sophisticated. She knew also very well how to mock people. That wasn't an exclusive asset of Kalogerou.

Well, this was the first thing that went through my mind, thought Kalogerou, *but it will be useless,* as he observed her once more from top to bottom. She looks like her father. She even had that annoying and irritating look that Manos used to have. Arrogant and authoritarian like Manos. *Damn these genes,* Kalogerou puffed.

Miss Alexiou was best settled into her seat, putting one foot on the other. Kalogerou passed his fingers through his hair, trying not to be disruptive by her irresistible legs.

She had the opportunity to watch him better. Dark brown hair with dark blue eyes and his age - must be around 40 – perfectly shaped and fit as she could see through his shirt, when he bent over her. She shuddered. The suit that he wore, it must be sewn on him. Same shade of his eyes, in order to cast women.

Be careful, the female voice inside her shouted at her again. *He is handsome, very handsome and because he knows how handsome he is, he takes his advantage every time he wants to. Not with me,* she shouting in her mind.

They just stared at each other like enemies before the battle.

Kalogerou spoke first, "However, Miss Alexiou, it is weird that we haven't met before, I mean all these years because you see I use this jet often enough," Kalogerou lifted his eyebrow.

His style continued to be arrogant, offensive, ironic, and ... ugh, what is this other Greek word that isn't coming to my mind right now? She murmured and clenched her fists.

She didn't answer, she just shrugged her shoulders indifferently. She was of no concern to his queries. She unfastened her belt and stood up. As she was passing in front of him she unwittingly landed in his arms.

"How I hate these air gaps!" she muttered.

Kalogerou laughed. "Why? Don't you enjoy yourself in my arms?" he said as he tightened her in his arms.

She flushed, "No," she answered back turning her face to his. *Big, big, big mistake,* she thought as her mouth was too close to his. "Can you let me go now?"

Instead of answering to her question Kalogerou tightened her even more in his arms. He satiated the scent of her hair. His lips touched her neck. The silk of her shirt rose at the height of her breasts. A lace of a skin color bra appeared. He glanced at it admiring the content.

I cannot stay in his arms for so long, she thought, "Well, Mr. Kalogerou, will you let me go or not?" She was trying to sound as calm as she could, though, inside her, she was boiling not with anger, but by passion. She didn't like this.

"Miss Alexiou, I don't hold you," he said pointing to his hands, which were away from her. It was strange because she had the feeling that his masculine hands were around her.

"May I ask where are you going?"

"In the kitchen with your permission, sir." She said annoyed as soon as she gets up.

"Could you please bring me ... oh, no, leave it, don't bring me anything. I will get up and get it on my own. The last time I asked something, I cannot say that I enjoyed it."

Miss Alexiou growled. She went first to the kitchen

"Miss Alexiou, you haven't told me your first name."

She was leaning in front of the fridge. She bent. Dimitris bent too in order to admire the back view of her. She stood up as if something was burning her. She was holding a bottle of mineral water in her hand. Kalogerou also stood up smiling.

She turned toward him. "Mr. Kalogerou, my first name is Alina, but to you, I will be Miss Alexiou." She opened the bottle and brought it into her mouth. Another air gap shook her and half of the mineral water dropped onto her shirt. "Oh, Peter please, leave some air gaps for other airplanes," she cried.

Kalogerou approached her laughing aloud, "Now we're even," Kalogerou said by trapping her with his hands in the kitchen. He bent down and looked through her shirt provocatively. "As I see, Miss Alexiou, you are more beautiful in wet." Some drops glittered on the curve of her breasts. He wanted to lick them so hard. He retained. Instead, his hand touched her neck.

"Mr. Kalogerou, I'm sorry, I don't understand you." Her voice was even heard.

He leaned into her ear, "Miss Alexiou, in Greece what had just happened we call it 'Nemesis.'" His husky voice combined with his hot breath was enough for her to feel chilly throughout her body.

Kalogerou understood her shivering and enjoyed it. He brought his body closer to hers. One finger caressed the curve of her breasts, just where the drops had fallen, which were rolling in her bra. With his other hand, he holds her, making Alina freezing.

"Miss Alexiou, I think that we could find a way of communication." He lifted his eyebrows and Alina grimace with irony.

"Mr. Kalogerou, your communication is synonymous of the bed. And no thank you, I don't want to 'communicate' with you."

He came closer to her. "Oh, Miss Alexiou, don't be so narrow-minded. There are so many other places, like sofas, or kitchens, where we could 'communicate', and there are many possibilities in 'communication' today. It's up to you. Whatever you choose I'm in," he winked without moving an inch from her.

"I haven't got any doubt about that, and I am going to upset you and that's make me feel marvelous, you know," her ironic comment didn't bother him.

"Oh, is that so. Let's hear what it is going to afflict me so much," he came even closer to her.

Alina tried to look as calmer as she could, so Kalogerou couldn't understand that he had put her body on fire. She said in cold blood. "You see, Mr. Kalogerou, you're not my type, and you don't know how much that frets myself about," her voice was icy. Kalogerou didn't seem to be fazed.

"I see," he leaned closer and his lips were near to her ear, "just because I'm not your type you're squeezing my jacket with your hands. That's very convenience."

Alina looked at her hands which literally tightened to the lapels of his jacket. She hadn't realized that she had hooked so shamelessly over him. She loosened her hands and straightening his lapels.

Kalogerou laughed with her move. "Besides, I think you're in a hurry to reach to such a conclusion, so wrongly in my opinion," he continued whispering in her ear.

"Excuse me?"

"How do you know that I'm not your type? Will you try me and not being pleased?" His smooth voice drove her crazy.

She was right as she had her opportunity to slap him, so she lifted her hand. Dimitris grabbed her hand and immobilized her wrist. Alina didn't miss the chance and lifted her other hand. That move of hers ended like the previous one. Kalogerou smiled with her reaction. Her both hands were immobilized behind her back.

"Miss Alexiou," his lips were drawn from her ear to her neck, "I think that we will, eventually, 'communicate,'" and he stuck his lips to hers demandingly.

She found her breath when Kalogerou was away from her and magically was sitting in his seat enjoying his whiskey.

Oh, how I hate this man, how much I hate him, she whispered. With all vexation, she went and sat in her seat. He winked her. She took the computer out of her bag typing furiously.

"Do you always have so many nerves?" She avoided to answer or look at him. "Miss Alexiou, I forgot to ask you. Are you working or just spending your daddy's money?" And, for one more time, his tone was provocative, offensive and ironic and he didn't lift up his head to look at her. His turn, deliberately, to lessen her.

Alina stopped typing at once. A deathly silence spread in the cabin of the jet. She looked at him with a murdered eye. *Oh, yes I hate this man for good*, she said with a not so soft voice inside her.

"I work," she replied trying to be calm.

Kalogerou raised his eyes from a document. "Oh, I see, and what do you do for a living?" He adored her pissed-off look, her blush cheeks and tightened cherry – colored lips.

Alina won't allow him to irritate her, "I am a writer." The tone of her voice was deadly serious.

This was something that Kalogerou didn't expect to ever hear it. He waited to hear something else. That she had studied business administration or had a university degree in Economics, as her father was the owner of the first dairy factory in Greece and instead of that, he heard what? That Manos' daughter is a writer. This was beyond fantasy. He couldn't stand it.

His laughter was so loud that he had nearly fallen out of his seat. Alina remained calm. After the Homeric fight she had ten years ago with her father, when she announced him her decision, the laughter of Kalogerou, was just a smooth hearing to her ears. She had learned not to react to such pettiness.

She waited patiently, till Kalogerou calmed down from his laughing explosion. "Mr. Kalogerou, take your time," she said.

In the meanwhile, she was typing something on her computer and waited until to appear it on the screen. Her nails beating rhythmically the table in front of her. After a few minutes, she turned her computer toward him.

Kalogerou tried to recover. "Miss Alexiou, what do you want me to see?" he said trying to stop laughing.

"This is the number which is corresponding to my fortune from my writing work, my books' rights, from movies based on my books. Mr. Kalogerou, could you, please count the zeros, or due to your age, it's difficult for you?"

He took a short look and became very serious, as the number on the computer screen was an awful lot of money. Kalogerou couldn't believe his eyes. *Manos' daughter has reached the acme of success soon enough*, he thought. He watched her agape.

He sucked a solid sip of his whiskey. "Well, Miss Alexiou, you made your point," he said and continued, "Congratulations!" What else he could say after what he saw. Kalogerou regained his composure and went to counterattack once more. "Since you can manage all this amount of money, take a look at these papers and when I wake up I will 'examine' you."

He leaned back in his seat trying to arrange his 190 cm of his body. Alina ignored his slyly commentary and stretched out her hand to get her computer. Kalogerou took her laptop. "Oh, no, this is confiscated, sweetie," and he put her laptop on the left side of his seat.

She didn't know either to get pissed off for calling her 'sweetie' for the second time or that he's got her computer and gave her some financial papers to read it, instead of writing her book.

She threw a stern gaze to him. These papers were full of numbers and tables. She dropped the pack before her. She glared Kalogerou, who seemed to sleep for good. *Such a caveman he was. I wonder how my father could cooperate with him*, thought Alina. Then she looked at her computer and back to Kalogerou.

She decided that she could take her computer back. *If I get up without making the slightest noise*, Kalogerou moved a little bit in his seat. *Let's wait for a little longer...*, she murmured. She gave a glance back on the papers that were in front of her and she felt dizzy. She looked back at Kalogerou. *Hmm... he sounds like sleeping more deeply*, she said to herself.

Her plan was simple and perfect. Just perfect. *I get up, I stretch, and reached out my hand on the laptop and quietly I returned to my seat. Simple,* she thought.

She took a deep breath. She stretched over the table that stood between them, and it would succeed catching her laptop if Kalogerou hadn't caught her hand and pulled her towards him.

"Miss Alexiou, you are a very disobedient young lady," his lips pressed the lobe of her ear. His voice was hoarse slow-moving and made her heart beating crazy. She swallowed. "For you own good, sit back in your seat," he said severely, "and read the papers I gave you."

She grimaced and collapsed in her seat. She got back the papers in her hands and started looking at them page by page, and by turning them making too much noise. He watched her, enjoying the spectacle. Her green eyes had darkened.

I'm pretty much sure that she cannot understand anything, Kalogerou spoke to himself. Alina made her hair in a ponytail. Her face brightened.

Oh, my God, how beautiful she is, a sly voice said inside him. He saw her as she was turning the pages front and back, understanding nothing of what it was written in there. She looked totally helpless.

A faint smile was shaped in the corner of his mouth. *Never mind, let's chasten her a bit longer before I offer my help as a great gentleman as I am. I like the way she is lost in numbers, she looks so beautiful when she is angry*, Kalogerou decided.

All this time Alina was blowing and huffing. "Damn you, I don't understand anything. I'm an author, not an economist freak," and threw all the papers in his chest. Kalogerou brought back his chair to the upright position.

"Miss Alexiou, tell me something, if you don't throw anything to anybody, will ruin your day?" His ironic smile exasperates her once more.

She glared him. "Mr. Kalogerou, what happened to you? Did you enjoy your nap?"

"You didn't let me sleep, and from what I can see you must be a real scrappy in economics. So, I decided to show magnanimity and give you some private lessons."

He came towards her. He took the papers in his hands and without delay began to explain the numbers, the columns and all those inconceivable tables full of some, not understandable parameters.

After an hour, she started to understand a little bit of what it was written on the papers paying superhuman efforts, since her mind was running elsewhere, like to his mouth, which she preferred kissing her than talking and filling her head with numerical gibberish. His mouth tasted very good, as she can remember from his kiss in the kitchen.

Oh, Alina concentrate, ordered herself. She managed to concentrate for a few seconds before his aftershave passed through her delicate nostrils and made her heart leap. *I cannot continue like that,* Alina thought.

Kalogerou continued by explaining and explaining everything to her, page by page. How far could she go with this torment? It turned out that these were the three most terrible hours of her life. In so many different ways.

On the contrary, for Kalogerou, these were the most amazing three hours of his life. Law and finance were his two biggest passions. Women came third and during these three hours, he managed to combine all his three passions together. Did he want anything else? *Apart from Alina to his bed, no,* he thought, *he wanted nothing more for the time being.* He looked at her while she was studying some papers.

He acknowledged that she had an advantage that other women didn't have. Alina was Manos' daughter. *That's the problem. That's a very serious problem,* a voice shouted in his mind.

He tried thinking something else without success. He couldn't forget how wonderful her lips tasted and he wanted to taste more. He tasted her neck and he wanted the rest of her body. He liked touching her breasts, he wanted to make love to her. How will he even withstand without touching her?

This journey was a neat severe suffering not only for his body but also for his mind. His best friend, Manos, was between life and death, and he was sitting next to his beautiful secret daughter and although he wanted bad to make love to her he had just explained her some economic facts about the factory. He swore through his teeth. Alina looked at him reproachfully. Kalogerou lifted his eyebrow without any apology.

He had to go somewhere away from her. To be away from her, even for several minutes, to catch his breath and to calm his heart. He left her reading and went to the kitchen. When he returned he was holding two glasses of whiskey and a couple of sandwiches. Alina drank a large sip of whiskey he offered her. Dimitris sat down again beside her.

She had to admit it. If her mind wasn't to Kalogerou she could understand some things. It seemed that Kalogerou was a very good teacher. She lost her mind again, as it was traveling to his eyes, to his magnificent blue eyes.

This particular blue I liked it, thought Alina. *Oh, they are so blue like the Aegean Sea seeing it up from the sky while she was looking out the jet window. His hands, strong and stable, very erotic,* she thought, as he caught her in his arms when they were in the kitchen. How could she possibly concentrate under these circumstances? She was a woman, not made out of steel.

"Enough, Mr. Kalogerou, I cannot stand any longer this torture. My head hurts me. Please let's stop."

He threw her a glance as she was tilted back in her chair, looking even more beautiful.

She drank the rest gulp of whiskey in one ship. "I want to sleep for a while if you allow me," she took a pillow and leaned into her seat closing her eyes.

He watched her breasts rising and falling down rhythmically while she was breathing. Her skirt had risen to dangerous heights. He found a blanket and he covered her. He sat beside her and continued reading at a more leisurely pace. He decided to lean briefly on his seat, too.

With Alina sleeping, a serenity of aura had spread in the cabin. He was also very tired, so he didn't take long for him to fall asleep.

Chapter 2

Kalogerou couldn't realize how long he was sleeping. He must have slept enough when he felt in his sleep that his hand was touching something very - very soft which was on his chest. Who was sleeping on his arm? He opened his eyes and saw her.

Miss Alexiou was sleeping peacefully in his arms. He stroked her hair gently and she stuck even more on him. He enjoyed it so much. Manos' daughter was sleeping in his arms. A smile froze on his lips.

He tried to expel her, without much success. Alina's hand caressed his neck and dragged her foot up and down a couple of times in his thigh. He muttered something incomprehensible, as her toes stopped just below his sex. Dimitris couldn't even think to make the slightest move.

And then it would be my fault if ..., but he didn't complete his thought. He held his breath while remaining still. It was the only thing he could do. Just to bear her while she was sleeping in his chest. How harmful could that be? It wasn't harmful. He could bear her. For how long? It doesn't matter for how long. The only thing that matters, was that she was in his arms without screaming or complaining.

On the one hand, he liked that Alina was sleeping in his arms, but then if he doesn't do something, the responsibility wouldn't be only his. He decided that he couldn't stand anymore. He nudged by saying her name. Alina instead of waking up, she hugged his neck and raised her leg above his thigh. Her lips were drawn from one side of his neck and felt her hand caressing his ear. Kalogerou was pissed off.

It was obvious that Miss Alexiou had a love dream with someone else and she caressed him. He didn't like that thought. This time, he nudged louder her name. "Miss Alexiou!" His voice sounded strict. She mumbled something as she opened her eyes a little. She saw him and she smiled at him. A huge smile animated his face.

Alina jumped up like a spring when she realized who had embraced. She tried to scrape together her shirt, which had left from its place, leaving her breasts in full view. Her skirt had also climbed halfway up her toned thighs. Kalogerou watched her, trying to restrain his passion.

"Miss Alexiou, did you sleep well?"

His smile was so offensive and so embarrassing that drove her crazy. What did he expect to tell him, that she slept well, as a matter of fact, that she slept too well? "I had a very good sleep, Mr. Kalogerou, and," she cleared her throat, "I'm sorry if I cornered you in any way."

"Nah, it was my pleasure to serve you."

Alina nodded to Kalogerou's mocking. "Can I have my laptop back, please?" Dimitris gave her the laptop. She opened it and begun to work. Her eyes escaped to Kalogerou several times, she rammed deeper in her seat in order to be hiding behind her computer screen.

Kalogerou was engrossed in his own paper, but in every chance, he threw furtive glances at her. Alina was ruddy. *Where did my composure get?* She wondered. For the next few hours, she devoted to her work trying to forget Kalogerou.

Peter lit the indicator to tie their belts, as they were about to land to Greece National Airport. They were in Athens. It was the longest and the most agonizing journey of her life. *Oh, dad,* she thought, recollecting all the previous times when her father was waiting for her at the airport and she was running straight into his arms.

This time, no hugs to her father. Once they landed she gathered her things hastily. Peter got out of the cockpit and welcomed both of them to Greece. Alina gave him a kiss on the cheek and she ran down the stairs.

After that Peter greeted Kalogerou, "Mr. Kalogerou, I hope that you had a good trip. I know that Miss Alexiou isn't the easiest - going woman in the world. That must be Mr. Manos fault", he smiled, "at the end, I think that you are going to like her, sir."

Dimitris laughed, "Peter, I have one question for you. Why she kissed you and she threw me a glass of whiskey?" He touched his shirt which was still smelling whiskey.

"Oh, sir, please, don't complain. From now on, you will be with her all the time, and that sounds much better to me than a fleeting kiss on my cheek," and he beat Kalogerou friendly on his shoulder, "I wish that Mr. Manos overcome his injuries and be with us as soon as possible, sir."

"Me too Peter, that is the only thing I truly hope and wish for Manos, in order to take care of her," he said pointing to Alina. They both laughed.

"Mr. Kalogerou, I'll always be at your disposal," Peter said as Dimitris was going downstairs.

Alina was near to the car. *Oh please, this woman is going from hug to hug. Only my hug doesn't like, yet,* he thought as he saw her in Stelios arms.

"Oh, Stelios how are you?" Alina kissed him also on the cheek.

Stelios, the traitor, was worth her kiss, not I, Dimitris continued his thought.

"Miss Alina, I'm very well, thank you very much. I'm very glad seeing you again so soon, although the circumstances." Alina nodded distressed and she entered the car.

Kalogerou cleared his throat before he spoke to Stelios. "Hello Stelios, how are you?" Stelios turned and looked at him.

"Mr. Kalogerou, I'm very well. How are you, sir? I hope that you had a very good flight." Stelios got serious and spoke with a professional style.

"Stelios, I'm going to tell you that only once. You are the greatest traitor in the whole Greek history. Congratulations." Stelios could easily understand, that Alina had managed to turn Kalogerou's journey into a nightmare.

"Mr. Kalogerou, I'm very pleased, that you come to Greece. To the hospital, sir?"

"Yes, to the hospital," Kalogerou answered through his teeth, and he entered the car. Dimitris pulled his phone from his pocket and phoned Apostolou.

AT THE ENTRANCE OF the hospital, Costas Apostolou was there to welcome them. Apostolou was Manos' doctor for many years and also a close friend of Manos Alexiou. When he saw Dimitris he hugged him. Then he saw the girl coming out of the limousine. "I don't believe you. Manos' life is at a great risk in Intensive Care and you showed up with this gorgeous chick in the hospital? The same old Dimitris."

Dimitris pulled out from his jacket a pack of cigarettes and lit one. After having a couple of puffs he looked Apostolou. "Costas, as I see, you're floating in the same sea of ignorance like me. Good, that's good. That makes two of us." He turned his head toward to Alina Alexiou.

"I don't understand what you mean."

"This 'chick' as you called her, please take a better look at her."

Apostolou looked at her from top to bottom as she was pacing toward them. "As I can see, she is a masterpiece. I'm speaking as a doctor my friend," Apostolou laughed slyly.

"Yes, you do, like always. As you observe, Manos' daughter is flawless." Apostolou was about to fall from the stairs. Kalogerou offered him a cigarette. "Do you want one?" he asked sarcastically. Apostolou took the cigarette because he couldn't believe what Dimitris just told him.

Alina was standing next to Dimitris, and as she saw that Kalogerou didn't make any move to recommend her to the man near him, she pulled Kalogerou's sleeve. Dimitris made the recommendations. "Costas, this is Miss Alexiou, Manos' daughter," said dried.

"Miss Alexiou, I'm fascinated!" Apostolou said without taking his eyes off her.

"You are because you weren't closed for ten hours in a plane with her," Kalogerou growled and blew out his cigarette. Alina glared at him.

Apostolou tried not to laugh. They began to climb the stairs. "What happened Dimitris, so many hours with such a goddess and you failed to go to bed with her? That's why you are like that? I think that you are getting old my friend, perhaps too old."

"Costas, stop joking and please get us to Manos." They entered the elevator. Alina stood awkward between them.

"Oh, wait a minute." Apostolou pulled out a card from the pocket of his medicine shirt and gave it to Dimitris.

"What's this?" Kalogerou asked as he was taking the card in his hand.

"Police, just routine as the police officer told me. He made several questions about Manos. About his family, his relatives. I told him that his closest person is you. I didn't know that he had such a beautiful and secret daughter. I spoke to this police officer about you and he is waiting for you. Call him first thing." Alina looked back at Dimitris. Dimitris took the card from Apostolou and put it in the pocket of his jacket, without telling anything to her.

"I will call him as soon as possible," Dimitris said to him.

They had reached the top floor which was the Intensive Care Unit. Apostolou gave them a sterile outfit and when they wore it, they went inside. He led them to a bed where on top of it there was a man lying down full of cables and hoses.

That man couldn't be my father, Alina thought and fainted. Dimitris caught her in his arms before Alina collapsed on the floor. Together with Apostolou moved her into another room which was empty. Kalogerou had become white as he gave her an agonized look. Apostolou pitied him.

"Don't worry, my friend," Apostolou beat him amicably on the back, "there are many people who cannot afford to see their beloved ones in such a bad condition ... with all these wires coming out of their bodies. She will recover soon." They were both over her bed. "However," said Apostolou, "she was a big surprise to you when you first saw her, don't deny it. I saw you how you look at her. She looks just like Manos. Even her eyes are the same like Manos."

"And believe me, Costas, also her temperament is the same like Manos', believe me," added Kalogerou. "She talks to me only to talk me back. Isn't it perfect? Just like her father," Kalogerou was murmuring.

"Yes, indeed," agreed on Apostolou, "but she is much more beautiful than Manos, don't you think?" Both men laughed. Dimitris threw a glance at her as she was lying on the bed. "At least, we will calm down for a while," murmured Dimitris.

"What happened on the jet, man?" asked Costas, "How she has managed to piss you off?" Dimitris shrugged his shoulders and Apostolou noticed that. "Perhaps you fell in love with her." Dimitris blasphemed through his teeth. "Ok, I don't talk anymore, stay here with her. I'll send a nurse to make an injection to her," and he left the room.

Dimitris stayed there looking at her astonished. "What a lovely evening I spent here in Greece," he murmured, "Manos is in the Intensive Care between life and death and his daughter, who kept her secret from me for the last twenty - eight years, unconscious in the bed. Just perfect. Not exactly what I had in mind." He got up and went to the window.

Shortly after the injection, Alina began to come together. She opened her eyes and looked around the room with fear. Everything seemed unknown to her, although the man who was looking out of the window was very well known. She tried to get off the bed. Dimitris saw her reflection in the window and went towards her.

"Miss Alexiou, I think it's better for you to lie down for a while." As she didn't manage to get up, she was forced to lie down and stay still in bed. Dimitris was sitting in front of her when she burst out crying. She fell into his arms.

"I don't want my father died," she says through her sobs.

Kalogerou understood her. When his own father died, his whole world shattered, even though they were striking all the time. She hugged him strongly while she was continued to speak and weeping at the same time. "I don't spend a long time with my dad. I need time in order to know him, and ...," she couldn't finish her sentence without crying.

Kalogerou stroked her hair. "I understand you," he said and he meant it.

"Oh, no you don't understand," her hands were clenched on his shoulder, "You were seeing your father every day, you had him every single day. It isn't the same." Alina cried between her sobs. It wasn't any chance that Manos' daughter would ever agree with him, wasn't it? Not a chance. Even now.

He spoke to her. "I had the opportunity to have my father every day, as you put it, and he also had the opportunity to drive me crazy all day long, every day." He held her in his arms and caressed her hair. He loved to hold her in his arm. She smelled so elegant. An aroma of roses, sensual and romantic, at the same time, awaken his senses. He didn't know that his senses were sleeping all these years.

"Neither mine is an easy one. I don't mind that. I prefer to have him alive and shouting at me. I don't want him to die, can you understand that," she wiped her nose on his jacket at the level of his shoulder, "As a matter of fact, I don't mind shouting at me all the time. Like ten years ago when I told him that I like to be a writer and he became so furious that he shouted at me for two hours. Oh, it was a disaster, but I preferred that from being like he is now," she pointing to the Intensive Care. "Ten years ago, when I told him that I was going to be a famous writer, I was here in Greece. When I got back to America I used to call him every day and the only thing I was telling him was: 'Hey, dad, I will be a famous writer you see and nothing or nobody could change my mind.' He shouted at me as a hell, you know my father how he is when he is shouting, and just before I hung up the phone I used to say to him, 'oh dad, I love you so much,' and he sent me a kiss through the phone. I want my dad back. I don't want him to die. Do you understand that? I don't want him to die." She was blubbing in his arms. Kalogerou let her break out.

After half an hour Apostolou came in the room. Alina had calmed down enough, although her eyes were red from crying.

"Oh, Miss Alexiou, as I see you are much better. That's good, very good. Well, Dimitris, take her and go home. She had too many emotions for one day. On one hand she saw her father in this condition and, on the other hand, she spent so many hours with you on the jet, hmm, Dimitris you aren't the easiest - going person, as we all know."

Alina laughed. Dimitris glared at them both. Apostolou didn't pay attention to the murderous look of Kalogerou and continued his instructions, "take her and go home in order to calm down and relax and when, Miss Alexiou, you feel ready you can come back to see your father. Manos isn't going anywhere, hopefully, you could allow me a medical sense of humor," Apostolou told to Alina, who smiled, "That's it, I'll keep you informed about everything, don't worry." Apostolou helped her to get up, "take a good sleep and a good rest."

Dimitris gathered her things and they left the hospital.

AS THEY BOARDED THE car, he threw her a look of inquiry. "How are you? How do you feel?" Kalogerou asked her with interest.

"Much better, thank you." She wasn't in a mood for any discussion, especially with Kalogerou. Kalogerou didn't bother by her bad manner.

"Good to hear it, Miss Alexiou, because there are some issues which are urgent. Now that Manos is in this condition I suppose you could ..."

Oh, this man is intolerable, yes, this was the word I was looking for. She clenched her fists looking him angrily. "You suppose what, Mr. Kalogerou?" Although her eyes were green, they were throwing deep red flames to him.

Dimitris took a deep breath, "You must, without further delay, take the control over the factory," he said pompously.

"Mr. Kalogerou, do you know something? We have just ten hours to be met and I have a very strong feeling of killing you. It is so difficult for you to understand that I do not intend to replace my father, as I have told you on my jet," she said through her teeth.

Kalogerou had come closer to her. She felt her heart ready to come out of her breasts. "And, I, Miss Alexiou, do not intend to release all these employees of our fathers because of you." Her eyes sparkled. "Oh, yes sweetie, we are partners, fifty - fifty. Also, I would like to inform you that this factory, which degrades you, gives jobs to almost 10,000 families all over Greece. I do not intend to fire them because of you and your emotional womanly thing. Also, I think that 'job therapy' is the best you can do in order to forget your father's bad condition. So, listen to me and don't you dare to interrupt me ...", he put his finger in her mouth, "... you are going to get rest today and tomorrow first thing in the morning we will go together to the factory whether you like it or not, I don't care. So, at 8 o' clock you'll be ready for work," Kalogerou cornered her in her own side of the car.

He always managed to corner her since they first met. This must stop, Alina thought. She tried to push him away with her hands, instead of that, he came closer to her. She gathered all her courage she had left.

"Mr. Kalogerou, you are the most unbearable and most obnoxious man in the world."

Kalogerou flinched at her words. He stuck more on her, "Miss Alexiou, I really like you and believe me tomorrow morning at eight

I'd rather do other things with you than struggling with factory affairs. You can count on that."

Before Kalogerou removed from her his lips lightly touched hers. With the edge of her eye, she saw that they arrived home. She came out of the car and running to Maria, the housekeeper of her father, who waited them on the steps. Alina fell into her arms.

"Oh, Alina, how are you doing, my dear?" Maria kissed her on her cheeks.

Dimitris approached them. "Maria, I would never expect such a treachery from you. Traitor number two."

Maria looked at him. "Who is traitor number one?"

"I am," Stelios cried as he was carrying Alina's baggage out of the car.

Maria and Stelios were bursting into laughter. Kalogerou growled from his nerves. After that, Maria spoke to Alina again. "Oh, leave this caveman alone, and tell me, my little girl, did you have a good flight?" Alina didn't answer because Kalogerou interrupted her.

"The best ever," cried Kalogerou with vexation, "she threw me a whole glass of whiskey at my face. My shirt smells awful."

Maria looked at Alina, who looked like an angel on earth.

Maria stood her up. "Perhaps you say something to her and upset her. I know you."

Alina smiled smugly and defiantly to Kalogerou. The lovely angel face just disappeared.

"Maria, be careful because I'm pretty aware what you two are trying to do with me."

"Are you?" said Maria. Alina was an angel again. "And what are we trying to do to you?"

"To piss me off with the full support of her," he pointed to Alina. "Watch out!" He screamed. Although he spoke to Maria his gaze was pinned on Alina.

Maria ignored him and she returned to Alina. "Please, tell me. Did you see your father? How is he?"

They had got into the house. The house looked different, although nothing had changed from her last visit.

"To see what?" growled Kalogerou, "As soon as she saw Manos she fainted."

Maria looked at her and Alina burst into tears.

"I had to pick her up before hitting the floor. Now enough with her. I'm hungry! What did you cook?"

"Do you want breakfast?" Maria asked Dimitris, who was in the kitchen, too.

"No, I don't want breakfast. I want something to eat. What did you cook for lunch?"

"It's twelve o'clock at noon. Are you going to eat lunch?"

"Yes, and I'm asking you for the third time. What did you cook?"

"Moussaka. Do you want moussaka at twelve o'clock in the morning?"

"Yes, and a salad, and then a cup of strong, very strong coffee and I hope that you made some delicious dessert, Maria."

Alina followed them to the kitchen. This could be the most tolerant thing in the world. Kalogerou was hungry after seeing her father in such horrible condition. How could he? It was unbelievable. He was so cold, so indifferent. Her father was in the hospital and he wanted to eat. Kalogerou was waiting eagerly for Maria to serve him, 'the emperor', ugh.

"Do you want to eat something?" Maria asked Alina.

"I'm not a pig to eat like him when my father is trying to stay alive and for God's sake he eats moussaka for breakfast, what is he pregnant? No, thank you, and apart from that I don't know how moussaka is getting off the clothes, so it's better for me to go upstairs to sleep," she looked Kalogerou who had eaten the first piece of moussaka and asked for one more.

Kalogerou glared her. When Alina left, Maria stayed in the kitchen to hang out to Dimitris, who had devoured in between the third piece of moussaka.

"Is Manos so bad?" Dimitris shook his head because his mouth was stuffed with moussaka.

"Oh, stop eating like that. You are about to explode," said Maria, "I'm going to make you a cup of coffee and you are going to tell me everything about Manos."

Dimitris lit a cigarette. "Do you know, however, that I won't forgive you for not telling me about Manos' beautiful secret daughter. Never! And don't you dare to ask me to bring you anything, because you will get absolute nothing." Dimitris behaved like a small child who lost his toys.

"Oh, come on. I know that you love me. So tell me, did you have a good journey first time flying with Alina?"

Dimitris sighed. "Traveling with her was just beyond me. It was a nightmare. Believe me," and he recited to Maria everything except the juicy things. He lies to Maria showing that he was Alina's victim.

"Oh, whiskey is that what stinks," Maria laughed with her heart and stroked his cheek. "Okay, I know, that Alina is a little bit whimsical, like her father..."

"Yes, but she is more beautiful than Manos," he murmured and laughed unconsciously.

She gave him a nudge, "to your information, Manos in his youth was a very handsome man and he is even now. So, Dimitris, stay away from her. I recognize this wicked look of you."

Dimitris laughed, "well, could you please tell me how you two or should I say the three of you manage to hide the 'little princess' from me?"

"It was like a 'mission impossible'. However, we've managed it, till today ..." Maria answered his question. "Due to Manos' command. He knew that you were jumping to her as soon as you saw her so Mr. Manos decided to protect his daughter like a proper father he was."

Dimitris grimace.

"Don't make faces at me. Manos is the most proper father I've ever know."

"Yes. So every time Alina was about to come to Greece, I had to travel all over Greece just to stay away from her. Well done, amazing plan, congratulations to all of you. Fucked, though, and now she is here and Manos not. What are you going to do?"

Maria looked him reproachfully, "oh my poor boy, you were so bruised by traveling around Greece in a private plane. What can I tell you! I'm sympathizing you deeply. Stop making fun of me Dimitris. You were photographed in every tabloid all over Greece. Beware, nobody knows that Manos has a daughter. Don't look at me, her parents arranged it and if you ask me I agree with them."

"Why?" He devoured the third piece of a chocolate cake that Maria served him in order to drink his coffee.

"I think that you could imagine what would happen if Manos Alexiou, the owner of the biggest dairy factory in Greece, had a seventeen – year - old daughter from nowhere. Because Alina was only a seventeen – year - old girl when she first came to Greece. She was tall and graceless, as I can remember her. She was ashamed to even to speak. Poor girl."

Dimitris smiled. "Well, I can assure you that she can speak fluently and not only speaks, she can also speak back to me every single second of her life," he said by gripping his shirt, "she is so beautiful!" Maria looked at him suspiciously. "Why are you looking at me like that? I speak objectively."

"Dimitris, I'm going to watch you closely. Alina is a serious girl, I repeat that to you..."

"What do you mean? That I'm not serious?"

Maria looked at him with the edge of her eye. Always the same Maria, so he took his coffee fretful and went to Manos' office. He sat on the chair and from his pocket, he pulled out a card that Apostolou gave him. He called the number of the mobile number he saw.

"How can I help you?" a female voice on the other side of the line spoke to him.

"I would like to speak with Mr. Georgiou, please."

"What's your name, sir?"

"Dimitris Kalogerou for the case of Manos Alexiou."

"Wait a minute, please, I put you through, sir."

After some seconds, Kalogerou heard a booming voice. "Mr. Kalogerou, thank you for calling me."

"Mr. Georgiou, don't mention it. What can I do for you?"

"Mr. Kalogerou, if it's possible I would like to meet you in person."

"I just got back from America and ..."

"I know. Mr. Apostolou informed me thoroughly, but it's urgent."

Kalogerou puffed cheerless. These police officers always become so burdensome. "Mr. Georgiou, how about in my office in an hour?" proposed Kalogerou after some thought. He never digested policemen.

"Give me your address, sir." Georgiou wrote down the address. "Very well. I will be in your office in an hour."

Dimitris came out from Manos' office. He found Maria in the kitchen. "Maria, I have to go to my office. I won't be late". He took the car keys and left.

THE STREETS OF ATHENS were flooded by cars. Nothing has changed. Traffic, traffic, and nothing but traffic. He had missed the chaos of Athens and its traffic, although New York was also full of traffic. When he arrived at the office his secretary didn't show much happy seeing him.

"Christina, I'm glad to see you."

"Oh, give me a break, I thought you would come to the office tomorrow. When did you land ... and I think that you need rest and what's that smell." Christina opened the closet behind her and gave him a fresh shirt. "Go to your office and change and ...um ... I would like to leave a little bit earlier tonight, that's all. I'm glad to see you." She had scraped together her office and had her computer turned off.

"I have an urgent appointment," he told her, as he changed his shirt, "his name is Georgiou. As soon as he comes in, you may leave."

"Oh, thank you, that's why I'm telling to everybody that you are the best boss ever," said Christina so cute and polite.

Dimitris shut the door of his office, which was full of unfinished law business, unfinished factory business and a daughter who sprang from nowhere. At least, she is beautiful because work isn't beautiful.

He looked at the stack of the files on his desk. He wasn't in any mood for work. He leaned back in his chair and brought Alina in his mind, when he kissed her or as she was hugging him while she was sleeping or in the hospital bed when she was crying.

He smiled. This was the first time he slept with a woman in his arms without touching her. He got up from his chair and lit a cigarette. "I think that I'm rusted enough," he admitted. He paced up and down in his office, recollecting this journey, which was an interesting one. His thoughts were interrupted by Christina, who cried out his name. "Oh, Dimitris, come on, wake up, I'm speaking to you for five minutes. Concentrate."

Oh, what happened with women today and shouting to him for another reason than that he was accustomed to? "What's going on, Christina?" he said defeated.

"Mr. Georgiou is here. He is waiting in the living room," she beckoned with her eyes.

"All right, let him come in, please." Christina gave him her most brilliant smile. "And yes, you may go now," he told her.

ALINA WENT TO HER ROOM and lying down on her bed she burst into tears. If her father doesn't become well, there was no way to endure in Greece with Kalogerou to swell her every now and then with the factory.

Going to the bathroom she saw Kalogerou entering his car. A deep sigh came out from her chest. *It was about time for him to go home*, she thought and went into the shower.

The hot water calms her down enough. She was unable to forget her father in bed with all those cables and all those machines. *This will be my father's life from now on?* She wondered and frowned. She couldn't bear with this thought.

Her father was an alive man. He was cheerful and happy. She had also understood during the last two years that he would like to see her mother again. He wanted to try to gain her mother's heart again, although her mother stubbornly refused. *Oh, mother, your opportunity just flew away.*

And don't forget Kalogerou, she said silently. In the thought of Kalogerou, her whole body shivered. She caught with her fingers her lips where Kalogerou had kissed her. A faint smile formed at the edge of her lips. She pissed off with this thought. What was going on? She knew his type. He was after every woman, every single woman in the world. *Ugh, he is so irresistible,* she thought. *Alina, concentrate please,* scolded herself.

She came out of the bathroom in a bathrobe pacing in her room up and down. Then she put on her black silk pajamas. After rammed beneath the bed's cover she was trying to calm her mind, which was running to Kalogerou.

Okay, she admitted, he is a very handsome man and he knows that. That's bad. She sat up in her bed supporting her back on a pillow. "That's has nothing to do with me," said Alina aloud. She turned on her computer, in order to work her last book, as she was far behind. She scrolled the pages one after another without any particular purpose.

"He is to blame," she said again, "that I cannot work." She stopped scrolling the pages and let the computer on the bedside table. She got up and paced barefoot on the thick carpet with her hands on her waist.

She reached the window of her room. Outside the darkness was thick and snow had covered all the flowers of her father. She thought her father's garden with roses and she felt depressed. Again Kalogerou invaded uninvited at her thought. She turned on the other side of the room muttering. *Alina, get him out of your mind. This man is not your type*, she heard a voice advising her.

"Oh, I know that," said Alina aloud. "Ugh, just perfect, I'm speaking to myself, like a lunatic one," and fell back on her bed. Being covered with the warm duvet over her head, she tightly closed her eyes trying to fall asleep. In vain. She growled and threw the duvet away.

She sat cross-legged in meditation posture. "Oh, Mr. Kalogerou, get out of my mind as you get out of my home." She closed her eyes and took a deep breath and then many small breaths. She tried to empty her mind, empty her mind, empty her mind. Nothing could empty her mind.

Her whole mind was flooded by Kalogerou, his smell, as remembering his chest while she was sleeping on him. His scent came in her mind, in her nose. A smell of black amber, red pepper, and a sea breeze filled the room. Yes, this last thought didn't help. She abandoned yoga. *They say that you could empty your mind with yoga. They don't know Kalogerou that's why they say such bullshits*, said Alina furious.

She took her computer again and entered the internet googling the name 'Kalogerou'. Her mouth opened. Such many results and all with women. So many women. *How he didn't lose control*, she wondered. She had a relationship once and she was always out of control. But Kalogerou no.

Every week he was photographed with different women in two or three different magazines every day. So, Mr. Kalogerou knew very well that all those women would 'died' for him.

"Well, until now," said Alina aloud. *Because there is one woman in this world that she is going to make his life a real torment and without dying in his view, which is a very good view… concentrate again, Alina. Make his life a torment, stay to that statement*, and she smiled complacently.

She liked this idea. She turned off the computer and put it to charge. She lowered her pillows and lay down on them with happiness. She had found a solution to her problem and that was to make Kalogerou's life a torment. Now she could sleep with a big smile on her lips.

Chapter 3

When Georgiou opened the door, Kalogerou saw a man of average height, dark hair with two small intelligent eyes. "Mr. Kalogerou, how nice meeting you." Georgiou tended his hand to Kalogerou, who responded immediately.

"Mr. Georgiou, please have a sit. Do you smoke?" Kalogerou asked him while Mr. Georgiou was sitting in the chair in front of the desk.

"No, thanks, I haven't smoked for years."

Georgiou didn't expect Kalogerou to be so young. He thought that he was in the age group of Alexiou and Apostolou. That was a very silly mistake of him, he blamed himself.

"You don't mind if I smoke, right?" Kalogerou was comfortable as all great lawyers used to be. *How not to be,* thought Georgiou.

Dimitris Kalogerou was a third generation lawyer and one of the most expensive lawyers in Athens. If someone would like an appointment with him, he must wait five to six months, and paid a very large amount of money, just to see him. His law firm was located in the most expensive street in downtown of Athens, in a modern building with glass windows outside. This building was the first modern building in Athens and the first law firm due to Kalogerou's father.

"Please, this is your office," Georgiou replied.

Kalogerou lit a cigarette and leaned back in his chair. "Well, Mr. Georgiou, I'm listening to you. Why such a rush?"

Kalogerou listened to the police officer, trying to understand what kind of person he has in front of him. He dislikes police officers a lot. Why? Because they always involved into his business.

"Mr. Kalogerou, I will come straight to the point. How well did you know Mr. Alexiou?"

"First of all, I don't like past tense. So, I know Manos since I was born. My father was also his friend and I am his best friend for years. Also, they were partners at the factory. After my father's death, I took over his place at the law office and at the factory."

"When did your father die?" Georgiou was sitting more comfortably in the armchair, which was quite large for his body.

"Twelve years ago."

"Yes, and in what percentage did your father participate in the factory?"

This kind of police questions didn't like Kalogerou, but he answered it.

"Fifty percent, Mr. Georgiou." After my father's death, his fifty percent split it into two of 25%. The first 25% went to my mother and the other 25% split it to my sister me. Recently, I bought the 25% of my mother and the percentage of my sister so at the present time I have the 50% of the factory. Manos has the other 50%."

Georgiou was no exception, thought Kalogerou. Another policeman who tried to find something, anything and for what? For an ordinary car crash.

"I understand. So, I would like to ask you another question. Who gets the share of Mr. Alexiou, supposing that Mr. Alexiou died? I assume that he has descendants, hasn't he?"

Kalogerou hesitated to answer that question and Georgiou noticed that. In order to earn some time Dimitris extinguished his cigarette. "Mr. Georgiou, Manos Alexiou has no children," he said severely. And with suspicion.

"Sorry, I didn't know that." Then he cleared his throat. "How long have you been in America?" There was a hint of accusation in his voice. Kalogerou never misunderstand things.

Dimitris looked him straight in the eyes. "Are you interrogating me? Because if so I must call my lawyer."

Georgiou laughed. "Mr. Kalogerou, I like your sense of humor." Georgiou hates lawyers. Police do the dirty work and arrest bad guys and lawyers set them free all the time.

"Thank you," Kalogerou replied in a dried way.

"You're welcome, but you didn't ask my question," said Georgiou, demanding a clearer answer.

Kalogerou looked at his watch. This discussion with this police officer was going too far, "I went to America just before Christmas. Could you please tell me why are you asking me all these questions?"

Georgiou decided to put all his cards on the table. He couldn't bear lawyers, and Kalogerou was no exception to this rule. But this man in front of him wasn't a murderer. If he wanted to take over the factory from Alexiou he could do that with some lawyers' tricks and no one could understand anything.

Georgiou was an experienced police officer, "Mr. Kalogerou, I'll be honest with you. After a thorough inspection of Mr. Alexiou's vehicle, after the accident, the Forensic concluded that the accident wasn't an accident. How can I put it? The car of Mr. Alexiou was tweaked a little." Georgiou realized that Kalogerou was worried about something.

Kalogerou's eyes darkened. He lit a second cigarette, "And judging by your visit and the tone of your voice you think that I'm the one that tweaked Manos' car, isn't it?" Dimitris had risen from his chair and stared out the window of his office.

"Mr. Kalogerou, I won't lie to you. At first, this thought came to my mind, although after some research about you, I think I can trust you."

"Thank you, Mr. Georgiou, you're so kind," Kalogerou said to him in an ironic style.

"No, I'm not, Mr. Kalogerou, believe me. I insist on the question about Mr. Alexiou's children and I'm asking you again. Are you sure that Mr. Alexiou has no children? Because you can realize too that if someone caused the accident of Mr. Alexiou, he could do the same thing with Alexiou's children. Even an illegitimate one?"

Kalogerou sat heavy in his chair, "I can assure you, sir. Manos is childless." Kalogerou's voice was cold even when he was lying. He was exercised in this 'sport' for years and he was unreachable.

"That's good," said Georgiou relieved, "At least, whoever wants to murder Alexiou, for any reason, he had to stop to Alexiou."

"I guess you're right, Mr. Georgiou." His voice sounded heavy.

"So, all I have to do is to find who did it." Georgiou was most spoken to himself than to Kalogerou. "Well, Mr. Kalogerou, thank you very much for your time. It was an interesting and enlighten discussion." Georgiou got up from his chair.

"Mr. Georgiou, I remain at your disposal," and accompanied him to the elevator.

As Georgiou was going down the sidewalk he looked once right and then once left before crossing the street. To the right side of the street, he saw a man – one of his best policemen - on a motorcycle in order to become the shadow of Kalogerou. He was sure that Kalogerou was hiding something, although he didn't know what it was. Instinctively, he knew that Kalogerou wasn't so honest to him and he wanted to know why. And as Georgiou used to say, only suspects have something to hide.

Kalogerou was sitting on hot coals. "Oh, my God. What was that?" He was speaking to himself aloud. "Perfect! What am I going to do with her?"

He paced up and down in his office and then he sat down weary in his chair. He bent over his desk skeptical. A thousand thoughts invaded in his mind and all had to do with Manos' daughter. He passed his fingers through his hair. He sighed. He was very tired to do anything. He couldn't work after that. He locked his office and left.

Going down to his car Kalogerou continued to talk to himself aloud. "I don't know how I could come to an understanding with her for the factory matters, how can I ever tell her that there is somebody who wants to kill your father and perhaps he succeeded and - guess what - perhaps he wants to kill you, too!"

Kalogerou was trying to figure out how he could turn this situation to his advantage. He thought it once more. There is no way to tell Alina something like that. That was final. It would be better for her not to know anything. He descended to the sidewalk. He breathed the night breeze before entered his car. A motorbike followed him. When he arrived home, Maria was ready to leave.

"Where is she?" Kalogerou asked Maria looking lost in his thoughts.

"She sleeps and don't you dare to wake her up. Is everything all right?"

"Well, no one is allowed to bother the 'princess'. Is there anybody thinking of me in this world? And, no, nothing is all right," he cried out to Maria.

"Whatever it bothers you I'm sure that you can fix it. And, my dear, all women with whom you slept with all these years are thinking of you somehow." Maria answered him mocking as she was leaving.

"Good night, Maria," he said cheerlessly.

He went up the stairs and entered her room. He saw her sleeping and she was like an angel. So beautiful, so calm. Irritatingly beautiful and in great danger. Dimitris sighed. "Great!" he said. Alina changed side muttering. The duvet came down to her abdomen, exposing her breasts. He covered her and he went out on his toes.

In his room, he went straight to the bathroom. When he finished showering, his mind was clearer. He arrived at a decision. The fact that no one knows about Alina and won't know about her it was an advantage. He had an ace up his sleeve.

First of all, he must take more precautions around the villa. Additional security was important for keeping the killer outside the house. On the other hand, someone must be close to her just in case. *So, she must be at the factory with Stelios or at home with me, no going out,* thought Kalogerou. *Is Alina going to the factory? A voice said to him. How could you persuade her to do that?*

This wouldn't be easy. Also, it wouldn't be easy to be near her all the time and keep his hands away from her. He laid in his bed. He spun around a table couple of times. How he ended up like this? Such a gorgeous woman was sleeping in the next room and he was on his own. Alone. "Apostolou was right," he muttered and he slept with her thought in his mind.

THE NEXT MORNING, WHEN Alina woke up, Kalogerou had gone for the factory. She went to the kitchen handing her laptop, "Good Morning, Maria."

"Oh, good morning, have a sit and I'll bring your coffee," she brought her a cup full of coffee.

"Where is the 'Devil'?" meaning Kalogerou.

Maria laughed and then she got serious. "You owed me a great deal, missy." Alina drank a sip of her coffee. Warm and strong as she liked. "When the 'Devil' as you called him came down," Maria left her sentence unfinished.

"Maria, where was Mr. Kalogerou and had to come down?" she was smiling although her green eyes had darkened enough.

Maria was anxious, "Oh, we forget to say to you, sweetheart," she said through her teeth. Maria knew this glare of Alina.

"You forget to tell me what?" She felt something boiling inside her.

"That was your dad's idea...," answered Maria by lowering her voice.

Alina was still feeling this boil on her breasts. "What was my dad's idea? You can tell me. There is no need to get out of the kitchen, I'm not going to throw anything. I'm a grown woman and a mature one to do such childish things."

"Yes, but you threw to Dimitris..."

"He has pissed me off ... a lot. But I don't think that you're going to piss me off so much like he did." Alina was sweet again, "Tell me what my dad's idea was? Please," she spoke in a low voice although she was about to explode.

"Dimitris - according to your dad - could sleep here, in the room next to yours. When he asked me I found it a brilliant idea. Isn't it, dear?"

Alina exploded. "And my dad did such a thing, because, I presume, Mr. Kalogerou hasn't any place to stay, or he is an orphan poor boy, isn't that so?"

"Oh, don't be ridiculous. He has a great fortune of his own. He is a wealthy man. As a matter of fact, he has apartments in all over Greece, even in New York, you see his father was also very rich and ..." Maria removed the cup from the new breakfast-ware. She had bought it in September, last September, after Alina's leaving for America.

"Then, I don't understand why?" Alina nailed her with her big green eyes.

"Oh, come on, Alina, just to find a place to eat and sleep and not be alone, to have his clothes ironed, you know how men are, don't you?"

Alina could hardly stay calm. "First of all, as I saw yesterday, Mr. Kalogerou is not limited just to one dish of food only. He ate two pieces of moussaka for breakfast ...," she said.

"Three pieces of moussaka, dear, and three pieces of chocolate cake ...," added Maria, "It's a big boy."

Alina rolled her eyes. "For God's sake, where did he put all this food?" she swore through her teeth and continued, "And if I can recollect correct, I think that his mother is still alive, isn't she?"

"After the death of her husband, she has retired to her estate in north Euboea." Maria also removed the small plate with the cake on it. *This was also brand new and it would be a shame this crazy girl to spoil the set again*, thought Maria.

"He has money, he can hire a housekeeper," said Alina casually.

"What do you say, dear? Who cooks better than me?" retorted Maria offended.

"Yes, that's true. So, we stuck here with Mr. Kalogerou," Alina puffed. "Bring me some more cake, I haven't eaten for two days, due to Mr. Dimitris of yours."

"You know sweetie, Dimitris is staying here just to keep your father company as you stay in America most of the time. Not a big deal."

Alina stared at Maria pissed off. "And he brings also his chicks over here?" Alina looked Maria straight to her eyes. The old woman flushed.

"For God's sake, he respects your father. He has a studio for these things, not far from here, don't worry, my dear."

"Oh thank you, Maria. What a relief. Now I learned that Mr. Kalogerou has a studio not far from here, I feel a better person. Thank you very much for the information." She rammed a big piece of cake into her mouth. "How that slipped my mind," she said with her mouth full of chocolate cake. Her cheeks were red from anger.

Maria was frightened. "Are you ok?"

"I'm fine. Just thinking,"

"What do you think, my little girl?"

"So, as you two become best friends do I have to go and stay in a hotel?"

Maria understood that Alina was angry. "Oh no, of course not, you could stay here, with us. You cannot leave your house, can you?" Maria had recovered her temper and all the breakfast-ware was safe, too. For the time being.

Alina plunged her computer and papers and she rose sharply.

"Where are you going?"

"In dad's office. Bring me a large cup of coffee and three pieces of cake, no, make them four ... and if Mr. Devil asks for me, tell him to get out of here, to go to one of his apartments. I'm staying here and rules have changed. Nobody dares to bother me for anything. Do you hear me? Nobody! I have to finish that book and instead of that I'm here discussing Mr. Kalogerou's chicks."

"You asked for," the imperturbable voice of Maria tore her heart.

"Maria, that's enough," Alina said quite bewildered. "Everyone is about to go to his home and if you don't tell him, I will be very pleased to inform Mr. Kalogerou." She left the kitchen and burst into her father's office by slumping the door.

ALINA WAS ABSORBED for some time when she felt that she wasn't alone in the room. She lifted her eyes and saw Kalogerou. As soon as she saw him the morning anger flared inside her. Kalogerou looked so pissed off. *I cannot imagine why he is so pissed off, as he is the only one having such a good time*, a menacing voice spoke inside her.

"Are you always so focused when you're writing?" he didn't let her answer. "I'm sitting here over half an hour waiting for your 'Highness.'" His reaction pleased her immeasurably. It was so nice that the cause of his frustration was she, and only she.

She first gave him a generous smile, before she spoke to him in cold blood. "Mr. Kalogerou, you could take an advantage of all this time, and collect your things."

Kalogerou was prepared for Alina's attack. Maria had informed him about their morning conversation. He could naturally tell her that some maniac tried to kill her father and perhaps that maniac will try to kill her. Yes, that would be wised, and as a frightening woman she would fell straight to his arms and after that, everything would be a piece of cake.

He decided to be a gentleman.

"Did you see the papers I left for you on the desk?" He was peremptory.

"No, I didn't see anything." Instead of that Alina had taken them and put them on the other side of the desk.

Kalogerou tried to remain calm. "And may I ask you when are you going to see them?" he asked her with a not so calm voice.

"Never!" she said angrily and threw the papers to him.

Kalogerou flared up with anger inside him, but he didn't speak.

"Mr. Kalogerou, I got up just three hours ago and since then I'm occupied with other more urgent issues, such as my book. The factory is currently not my concern."

She started again with all these nonsense, thought Kalogerou, *she is going to drive me crazy.* "Alina,"

She looked at him with a cold glare. "Mr. Kalogerou, for you I'm Miss Alexiou, don't you forget that. Ever."

He unnerved. He recommended patience to himself. *Be patience Dimitris, be patient until Manos becomes well again, and please God,* he prayed, *feel sorry for me and let Manos becoming well soon enough because patience has its limits.*

"Miss Alexiou," he corrected, "do you remember that your father is badly injured, don't you?"

"I haven't suffered from amnesia, Mr. Kalogerou, thank God, and as a matter of speaking, I also remember very well that from the first moment I saw you I have told you how much I disliked you. Do you remember that?" and without letting him answered she continued, "And believe me nothing had changed since yesterday. I still detest you. Every day after day more and more. You have a unique talent to that, Mr. Kalogerou." Kalogerou growled but she didn't pay attention to his growl and continued to speak. "Also, although you think that I'm just another spoiled rich girl I can very well remember when my father once had told me – that must be four or five years ago - that the factory will pass into my hands when I'll be thirty years old, either my father is alive or not. Am I correct, Mr. Kalogerou?" Alina had risen from her chair and sat in front of the desk.

His eyes wandered all over her body. A smile formed on his lips. Her hair, tied in a ponytail, emphasized her eyes which gleamed with little green sparkles, her skinny jeans left nothing to his imagination and her sweater was so small and tight, that left her breasts in his wide and plain view. Well, he liked this view. A lot. He just didn't want other men seeing that view of hers. *Oh, what am I thinking?* He blamed himself.

"Absolutely!" He answered to her question with clenched teeth, and *concentrated*, ordered himself, *to her mouth, to her lovely and hot and wet mouth.* He wanted to kiss her. *Just concentrated*, said to himself again, *not to her mouth, or her breasts, or her hot body. Just concentrate.*

"I am happy! Also, I can remember very well when my father once had told me that I would have the right to sign in my thirties, even my father was alive or not. How am I doing till now, Mr. Kalogerou?"

"Perfect!" he said *and I want to kiss her right now*, he thought. Instead of that, he lit a cigarette. With the cigarette, Kalogerou rediscovered his temper and his arrogant style. Miss Alexiou seemed to know enough about the factory, so this making his job easier. *I cannot stand anymore, I must kiss her*, he thought for the third time.

Alina continued unabated. "So far so good, Mr. Kalogerou. Now I'm coming to my father's present situation and not being thirty yet. I believe that you know, Mr. Kalogerou, who has the right of the first signature, don't you?"

"I didn't know, Miss Alexiou. I had to learn it after Manos' serious injury. I'm the one with this right. What's your point?" Dimitris stood up from the chair.

"Good to know that you know, Mr. Kalogerou. So use your signature and let me out of this till my thirties. Do your job and let me do mine. Simple as that."

"I'm impressed, Miss Alexiou, as you know so many legal thinks about the factory." Dimitris was in front of her and he was huge and *smells so good, and he was so irresistible and fit and handsome.* She was angry with herself.

"Then I cannot understand something, Mr. Kalogerou?"

"What's that, Miss Alexiou?" he cannot stand anymore without kissing her.

"Why don't you use your signature and get over me? Why cannot do your job as my father used to do without bothering me for anything?" Alina flashed and banged. She continued speaking in a more ironic tone, turning ostentatious her back to him in order to go and sit back in her chair, which made Kalogerou an untamable beast. "Be patient, Mr. Kalogerou, in two years I'll be thirty and so you could piss me off all the time. Until then leave me alone," she shouted.

Oh, she is so beautiful when she is angry, he thought, as her cheeks were blushed.

"Be sure, Miss Alexiou, I'll do my best and believe me I'm going to enjoy it. A lot!" He directed towards her behind the desk where she was sitting and blocked her.

"Since you know so much about the factory, could you please tell me something?"

"I'll be delightful to help you as much as I can." Her style wasn't one of his favorites, but he had time for that later.

"Am I your daddy?"

A big surprise covered her eyes. "I beg your pardon?"

"You have analyzed the situation very well, and I'm asking you again. Am I your father?"

She rolled her eyes all over him. "Mr. Kalogerou, I don't understand you."

"Why, Miss Alexiou? It is so difficult," he had come close enough to her. She breathed quicker. Kalogerou's blue eyes deepened. "I'm going to answer this question for you. I'm not your father, thank God."

"You're not," she said by interrupting him, "thank God," she added. A smile showed on his mouth. He wanted to kiss her and he was going about to do it. She wanted to kiss him, but she wasn't about to do anything. This man in front of her was a dangerously charming man and she wanted to protect herself from him.

"So, Miss Alexiou, I'm not Manos. Manos signed without disturbing you because he was, I'm sorry, he still is your father. All that tricks were made from our fathers in order to be transparency in every single transaction. So, once Manos cannot sign any document regarding his present situation, the only way the factory can function is to use our signatures, otherwise, everything is blocked. Can you understand that? It's not very difficult for a smart woman and awarded writer like you." She looked at him speechless. *Now it was about time to kiss her*, he thought. He leaned even closer to her. "Also, Miss Alexiou, there's another problem, more practical."

Alina shallowed. Kalogerou was too close, creating a short hurricane in her mind. "What's the practical problem, Mr. Kalogerou?" She asked exhausted. She couldn't stand to be too close to him. She would lose her control over her mind and her body.

"Let's say that you sign at last, how could you do that as no one in the factory is aware of your existence. Or to be more precise, when nobody in Greece knows that Manos Alexiou has a daughter."

She caught her head with her hand. When talking with her father or with Stelios or with Maria in Greek she could understand them. Talking with Kalogerou was impossible to understand anything of what he was saying.

"Mr. Kalogerou, could you explain to me what do you mean by that? I don't understand you. If I don't sign, you seem that you have trouble with that. If I sign, you have trouble again. I think that it's time for you to visit a psychologist."

Dimitris laughed. "What I'm telling you, is that you cannot sign as Manos' daughter because nobody knows your existence. So, you see, the secrecy of your daddy creates to me such enormous problems." He had cornered her for good, figuratively and literally.

She couldn't escape. "I think that I could sign as Alina Johnson." She put her hands on his chest trying to repel him. She didn't succeed, but she didn't get her hands back.. "All I know is that both of my parents and I, personally, preferred and still prefer not to become a spectacle of the media every time I come to Greece. I think that you can understand the reasons and these reasons are still obvious. I think that it's your problem. Not mine."

"How is my problem? I can sign by myself, thank you very much."

"What I mean, Mr. Kalogerou is that you're the lawyer here, and you must squeeze your mind harder to find a solution when no women occupy you. For every problem, there is a solution Mr. Kalogerou, and normally you should have found one since you were aware of the whole situation years ago."

Kalogerou was taken aback. "Until Manos becomes well or until you'll reach the proper age, we'll have to work in the traditional way, meaning that two signatures of ours are the only solution for the factory. I think I'll answer your question, Miss Alexiou. So from now on, you'll go to the factory every morning. Get it?" he had her with her back against the wall. Literally.

Well, this man was inadmissible. It seemed that Kalogerou had heard nothing from what she had told him. "Mr. Kalogerou, I don't know if you remember - it's your age you see..."

Kalogerou interrupting her with a faint smile. "I'm going to be forty in a few months, Miss Alexiou, and no more jokes about my age because you know what they say for men in my age?"

"No, I don't, Mr. Kalogerou, and I don't care." She was looking him straight in his blue eyes, those beautiful blue eyes.

"Let me enlighten you a little. They say that men in forty are better lovers." His finger touched her neck.

Alina ignored him and continued, "Good for you, but I'm a writer with a contract of thousand dollars. Also, in three months my new book is going to be released. So, as you can see, I have no times for games."

"Neither do I, Miss Alexiou." Kalogerou who had loosened his siege was stuck on her.

Alina was trying to remain calm. And she couldn't go anywhere. To her right side was a little bookcase of her father with all her books. This was a handmade one, a special order of her father when she had brought him her first editions of her books. On the left was his father's office, a heavy piece of furniture of massive proportions. Behind her was a wall and in front of her was – who else - Kalogerou. *No need to panic*, she said to herself, although she was beginning to get dizzy by his magnificent blue eyes and his male scent.

Just don't faint, a voice shouted in her head, *if I faint again and his hands embrace me, I would be ready for everything.*

Her mind ordered her to be cold with him as an iceberg, but her body wanted him desperately. She didn't want to be another 'victim' of Kalogerou's charm, so she must resist to him. How difficult could that be?

Kalogerou had shored up his gaze on her face trying to understand her better. He was trying to understand why this woman magnetized him. She is a very beautiful woman. She has beautiful brown, like chocolate, curly slick hair, although it wasn't only that. Her eyes were so green and so bright like the brightness of the most expensive emerald but weren't only her eyes or her hair or her lips.

Alina was different from the other women he used to go out all these years. She had awakened to him instincts which were sleeping several years now. As he looked into her eyes, he decided that her eyes exercised a strange attraction on him, besides the fact that she has a very beautiful and athletic body, a very sexy body. Her body drives him crazy. Always. Her long legs, her breasts, her flat belly and he wanted desperately to kiss her mouth. He wanted to kiss her and take her breath away.

Alina decided to make the first move. "Mr. Kalogerou," she put her hands on his chest to make him a bit further, "I said on the plane that you're not my type, did you forget it?" She felt his strong body; his muscles of his chest tighten. She could just touch his chest for hours, she decided that it wasn't a clever idea. Also, it would be useful to take her hands from his chest, she didn't do that either.

"Well, Miss Alexiou, I think you're very much my type," he whispered. Her hands repel unconsciously and instead of pulling him away she gets closer to him. Dimitris felt her body tremble. *Hmm, she isn't so cold*, he thought and decided to torture her a little bit. He pulled back a little while stroking her neck. Then he came back close to her touching her lips. She responded. For a while, however, after she repelled. Reluctantly.

Alina decided to surprise him. "Mr. Kalogerou, do you know that you have your father's eyes?"

At the moment, he shocked, but he didn't stop caressing her mouth with his lips. "Did you know my father, Miss Alexiou?" How much he wanted to make love to her over there on the desk.

"I've met him several times when I was in Greece. Yes, you have your father's eyes."

He stuck to her for good. His fingertips caressed her neck and then went down to her sweater. "You knew my father, however, I have to confess that I first saw you on my jet just two days ago. Until then I ignored your existence, Miss Alexiou, and it's a shame because you never stop impressing me."

A sweet warmth had spread all over her body although it was in the heart of the winter and the garden outside had half a meter snow.

"Mr. Kalogerou, you were always occupied." She tried to remove from him once again without success.

Kalogerou approached his face to hers. "However, we are talking for a very long time. So, I cannot accept that we haven't had the opportunity to meet each other only by chance. Or am I wrong?" His warm voice gentle fondled her ear and wiped out the last crumbs of her self-mastery.

"There you are wrong, Mr. Kalogerou. Because you see you were the cause of that. So, I met you at last and I don't think that I lost anything."

Kalogerou laughed with innuendo. She felt his lips at her earlobe. "I like smart women, Miss Alexiou, and you are a very smart woman."

"Oh, really since when?"

He didn't answer as his lips kissed her neck. Alina took a deep breath. "I have a proposal for you, which I think it suits us both." Not saying to unstick over her. What a torment?

"I'm all ears, Miss Alexiou." Alina closed her eyes for a while. His lips descended lower and lower.

"Well, since I have no answer for my signature - issue, and as I think that you are more experienced in dealing with the factory, so, I'm ready to sign whatever you sign without a second thought. Without any objection. In that way, the factory will continue its function and I will be able to work on my book. Don't you think that this is a very fair proposal?" She gave him the brightest smile of hers. It was time to kiss her and he didn't want to miss this opportunity. So he kissed her on the mouth demanded and painfully.

When his lips removed from hers, he said roughly. "No!"

Damn you, she thought. "Why not, Mr. Kalogerou?" Her eyes darkened enough because of lust. *Why did he stop kissing me?* She wondered.

"I would like to inform you that I'm a lawyer and in the mornings, almost every morning I have to say, I have courts which mean that I cannot be in two places at the same time." He couldn't keep his lips from hers and he kissed her again, pressing his lips more. Alina responded to his powerful kiss. When he removed a bit his mouth from hers, she took a deep breath.

"Every single day, Mr. Kalogerou? Lucky you."

He smiled smugly. *She's so good and she smells so nice like the first spring aroma of an almond – tree which it is just blossomed*, thought Kalogerou and kissed her again grasping her waist and bringing her closer to him.

So close that he felt her breasts rising and falling as she leaned on his chest. "You are a hard player, Miss Alexiou, but, yes, to your surprise, I have a court every day, and some days more than one. I'm so sorry about that." His kiss was more passionate and Alina had fully responded. When he left her mouth red from his kiss and his two days beard, Alina felt his lips at her neck.

"Congratulations, Mr. Kalogerou, I'm very glad that you have so many clients," she said biting her lip, trying not to scream from pleasure.

"Thank you," he said as bellowing his lips and sought her longing.

"Again this is not my problem." Alina was trying to be calm as his hand was inside of her sweater making her breasts harden by his touch, something that hasn't gone unnoticed by Kalogerou.

"I think that you want me as much as I do. I'm a very good lover you know." His voice was hoarse from his passion.

"Maybe later," Alina said trying to keep her clothes on.

"What? Why later and not now?" and he took off her sweater before she could react. His lips came down menacingly on her breasts. He heard her groaned. Then he took the other breast by sucking it and Alina groaned louder.

"Shh, Maria is going to hear us."

"So, stop doing that," said Alina and plunged her nails into his jacket in order not to scream.

"Oh, no, that's not going to happen, beautiful." His hand caressed all over her body. He undid her bra and took her breast in his hand. It was so soft and so warm, so he retook her whole breast in his mouth. They sighed both. "Admit it that you like it. Why you make it so difficult to me?" He asked her as his mouth moved to her other breast. Alina begins to groan and Kalogerou kissed her demandingly.

"Because now I'm writing my book and when I'm writing my book I want to be concentrate. Also, although I want to help you, Mr. Kalogerou," she said, trying to regain her composure, realizing that his hand descended to her nature, "I cannot come one day to the factory and say 'hello I'm Manos' daughter'. What do you think about that?" she said through clenched teeth, trying to stifle her own passion that simmered through her jeans. Hearing this Kalogerou thought of Georgiou and froze. He removed from her. She wore her bra and her sweater before Kalogerou gets passionate again. She was a very easy target to Kalogerou's handsomeness.

"So, as you put it, you're right," said Kalogerou thoughtfully while passing his hand in his hair. "But," he continued, and his eyes gleamed strangely, "you can go to the factory ... let's say as my secretary, so why don't you think about that." He turned and took her in his arms ready to kiss her again. Alina boiled in the broth.

"Are you serious?" Alina was preparing an adverse reaction to Kalogerou's peculiar proposal.

He stopped for a moment and looked at her. "Always. Think about it. You are an educated woman, you know these computer things, you look - how can I put it - like an iceberg – don't look at me like that, that was my very first impression, I've changed my mind – you are the secretary of my dreams." He kissed her deep. "Congratulations, Miss Alexiou, the position is yours. As for your salary, we will discuss that matter later, depending on your qualifications", and his mouth sealed hers again.

Alina tried to detach herself from his hands without any success as he was much stronger than her. She responded to his kiss hopefully that he will leave her alone. Kalogerou didn't do anything like that.

This man would send her to prison. For sure. The audacity was bottomless. "Bypassing all these offensive things that just came out of your mouth let me remind you something; first of all, I don't know much about the factory; secondly, my secretarial studies was never my favorite subject; thirdly, I don't even like my own secretary, let alone to be your own secretary; and, fourthly, I have a deadline to catch, which runs at a breakneck speed. So, I'm going to say that once again, Mr. Kalogerou, get out of my sight, as quickly as possible, for your own good," Alina had outraged. Kalogerou enjoys her nerve, even more, so he was still keeping her in his arms.

"There is no reason to panic. You could go to the factory at eight o'clock in the morning, I think this is a very convenient time for you, and there you will pretend that you are my secretary, with another name, don't forget that. Your job at the factory will be too easy for an award-winning writer as you,"- this last comment was ironic, he didn't let her speak as he kissed her lips, "you will accumulate the papers that Emily would give to you, yes, don't goggle your eyes like that – Emily is Manos' best secretary for years - and then you can stay at Manos' office and write undisturbed ... whatever you write,"- the disdainful gesture of him was outrageous - but still, he didn't let her talk, "then at 4 or 5 o'clock in the afternoon, I will be with you, seeing what is urgent and take care of it. As a matter of fact, I will take care of everything. You will sign what I sign without a second thought, as you rightly mentioned a moment ago, and this could be the only way that we can be both happy." He kissed her again in the mouth. "How do you think about my plan?" he said when he detached his lips from hers.

"Mr. Kalogerou, leave the directing and, please do me a favor, limit yourself to your legal science ... only." Her voice was so cold that froze his smile.

"What do you mean?" Trying not to scream from anger.

"You don't understand? I'm just saying a big no to you. Neither will I go to the factory using another name, nor as your secretary. For the last time, as I said before, I have too much work to do ... so leave me alone."

Kalogerou held her by her waist. Her breasts leaned on his. He felt his body burning. He looked hungry for her. He kissed her with all the passion he had and she responded. He was sure that she is crazy about him.

"No," he said without leaving her, "unless you agree to my proposal." He kissed her again and her body reacted as he wanted to react. Her mind was telling her to get out of the room. Her body was melting into his arms as long as he kissed her.

She tried to regain her composure. "Put me down, because if I scream Maria would be here in a second and I don't think that you want that," she whispered in his ear.

Kalogerou put her down and he left the office by slamming the door. Alina flustered by the noise. She couldn't restrain a smile formed on her lips. Men like Kalogerou didn't like to lose. Of course, there is always a first time for everything.

Dimitris came in the kitchen puffing while Maria was cooking.

"Why are you like this? What happened again?" asked Maria.

"The 'princess 'doesn't want to change her precious program and help me to the factory ... and don't even think to take her side. Go to Manos' office to bring me my briefcase that I forgot there because if I saw her again I will strangle her." A few minutes later Maria carried his briefcase and Kalogerou was sitting at the kitchen table trying to work.

"Her majesty is sitting in the office and I'm writing in the kitchen," he muttered.

"Don't you like my company?" asked Maria trying not to laugh. Kalogerou didn't answer her question.

AFTER AN HOUR, ALINA appeared in the kitchen.

As she entered she wasn't even turned to look at him. She bent over Maria's pot to see what she was cooking. Alina whispered something in

Maria's ear and the old lady burst out laughing. Dimitris was sure that the two women were talking about him. Alina took a bottle of water and went back to the office. Dimitris followed her with his angry look.

Once Alina came out from the kitchen Kalogerou glared at Maria. "Did you enjoy so much Miss Alexiou's joke?"

Maria didn't answer him. Dimitris got up from his place and went close to Maria. "Why I have the feeling that she told you something about me."

"Well, Mr. Kalogerou, it doesn't turn the whole world around you, you know."

Dimitris spent a counterattack. "Well done Maria, you betray me for a second time. Congratulations."

"Oh, stop doing like a baby. The girl didn't say anything about you."

"Very good Maria, don't expect me to bring you that coat you saw in the magazine when I go back to New York. Because I will go back to New York when this craziness ends."

Maria glared at him. The truth was that she wanted that coat, which was expensive. She decided to play it for all or nothing. "If I tell you what she said, will you buy me the coat," she shuffled around the roast in the pan with such a mastery, "let's say as a gift?"

All women are the same, thought Kalogerou, *they are all exploiting till to the last cell of their bodies.* "Let's hear what Miss Alexiou told you," and he crossed his arms.

"She said: 'Alexiou - Kalogerou: 1-0' and to tell you the truth I didn't understand what she meant. It just struck me so funny and I laughed. That's all. Will I get my coat?"

"Yes, Maria, you will," and although Maria didn't understand what Alina was meant by that, Kalogerou understood what Miss Alexiou was meant. Turning to Maria who was laughing he told her ostentatiously, "If you continue that behavior you'll have to forget the coat." Maria stopped laughing at once.

Dimitris returned to his papers. So, Miss Alexiou wanted a war? It wasn't so difficult to give her the war she wanted. Starting today. Let alone, that tomorrow at the factory he would have the major opportunity for giving her the best war ever.

Chapter 4

On Friday morning, the clock beat at past half six. Alina tried to shut it down when the clock fell off of the nightstand next to her bed. Maria had persuaded her to go to the factory according to Dimitris' proposition, but waking up so early is the most outrageous thing, *that's why I like being a writer and not a lawyer or an owner of a factory,* thought Alina. Half asleep as she was, she got out of the bed in her pajamas and went down to the kitchen. The smell of the coffee invades her nose.

She entered the kitchen, with messy hair. Kalogerou and Maria spoke in intense. When he saw her his heart went crazy. Even without her makeup and in her pajamas, which were silk showing her toned body, she was gorgeous. Kalogerou sighed.

"A large good morning to the guru of legal science," said Alina passing beside him. Kalogerou instead of a 'hello', he blasphemed.

He drank a sip of coffee and turned all his attention to the newspaper. Alina threw a glance at him hypnotized.

He was wearing a blue suit with a light blue shirt and a tie of a darker shade of grey - blue. *Oh, he is so handsome,* thought Alina *and how he managed to be dressed up so early in the morning?*

She was a bloody mess in her pajamas and half asleep over the kitchen bench until Maria gets her coffee. Several minutes later Maria gets out of the kitchen and Alina couldn't resist asking him, "Mr. Kalogerou, it isn't even seven o' clock in the morning and as I look at you, you are ready for work. Good for you but how could you do that?"

He didn't look at her because as she was spilled on the kitchen bench, her breasts looked marvelous and he wanted to avoid seeing them.

She nudged him in the shoulder. "Hey, I'm talking to you Mr., how do you manage that? I guess you must have slept very long after me," and a sly smile appeared on her lips, "and I wonder how can you be so perfectly dressed up so early in the morning?" She nudged him again.

Kalogerou folded his newspaper while looking to the cup of coffee in front of him when he answered her question. "Miss Alexiou, I didn't come back as late as you think and the truth is that I slept like a birdie. I didn't quarrel with my duvet as you did all night long."

She barely opened her eyes and looked at him with her most honeyed glare. "The truth is that I do a very fickle sleep."

He was trying to look at her eyes instead of her breasts.

Alina closed her eyes again. "I have an aversion to getting up so early, Mr. Kalogerou. Could you find another solution for that factory – thing? Please think of me a little bit." If he doesn't kiss her right here right now he would explode. "Could you please put me some more coffee in case I can open my eyes in a few hours?"

He got up and filled her cup with black coffee. Alina sat up a bit, leaving a full view of her breasts.

Oh my God, he growled and leaving the coffee on the kitchen bench, he took her in his arms. The soft fabric combined with the warmth of her body made him kiss her with all his passion. His fingers passed through the silk pajamas looking for her breast. Two more buttons unbuttoned. His lips conquered her mouth and moved to her neck. She sighed and rammed more in his arms. Her half - naked body over his clothes irritated him even more. He wanted to take her to the kitchen. He undid another button in order to taste her breasts. Her body was so warm and her breasts so soft. Alina responded to his kisses and caresses. Madness conquered her.

His other hand slipped into the bottom of her pajamas in her wet underwear, reaching her nature. The warmth of her body was looking for his own body. He put his hand inside her, making her pull out a strangled voice. He smothered her lips in kisses so as not to be heard.

As she had recovered from her first orgasm she heard Kalogerou telling her that a second one was coming. She made a slight crying as his lips were in hers. "You are so wet for me, I don't understand why do we have to hassle?"

"Because I don't want to be another 'victim' of yours, that's why." Alina was hooked on him as his hand did a great job down there, giving her another orgasm. Her eyes opened wide. Kalogerou smiled and he removed fast from her, as he heard Maria coming down the stairs.

"Miss Alexiou, I see that you woke up, so go upstairs and get dressed. Stelios will take you to the factory." Alina was confused as Kalogerou was drinking his coffee and read his newspaper as if nothing had happened. She came out of the kitchen without saying a word to Maria. *Kalogerou – Alexiou: 1-1*, he thought and smiled because he could drive this woman crazy any time he wants.

Alina wore a knitted brown dress with a V-neck. She put her father's pearl neckless and earrings. A gift when she was twenty. Her shoes were also in the shade of a light brown. She looked herself in the mirror and she found herself just gorgeous. Dimitris couldn't stop watching her as she once passed before him.

Maria was in the kitchen trying to decide what to cook. "Ah, here you are Dimitris. Would you like a fried chicken with potatoes for lunch?"

"Maria, is Mr. Kalogerou going to eat with us again?" She had to get her revenge.

"Yes!"

"Why? As you informed me yesterday he has plenty of places to stay. So, let him eat at one of them."

"He is a man and he doesn't know how to cook. Besides that, all these years he was eating lunch with your father."

"There is a first time for everything, but how can, Mr. Kalogerou, know such small details," Alina continued as if Kalogerou wasn't present, "Ah, I have another great idea. He can eat in a restaurant. What do you think about that?" Alina asked him.

Maria, who enjoyed treating everyone, reacted badly. "What are you saying? My cooking is much better comparing to any restaurant. No, I'm not listening to you. That's not going to change, either you like it or not."

Alina noticed a smile in Kalogerou's shapely mouth.

Kalogerou looked at his watch, "Miss Alexiou, at about 4 o' clock in the afternoon, I'll be in the factory. Have a nice day. You, too, Maria." And without saying another word he left.

What a bonehead, thought Alina. *At every single level, Kalogerou was an annoying, intrusive, handsome man. Oh, forget that last one and stay to annoying and intrusive man*, a voice said inside her.

Alina's eyes brightened mysteriously. As far as Kalogerou's car went out of the gate she asked for Stelios. "Good morning, Stelios, plans had changed for today. At about twelve o' clock you'll go to the factory without me in order to take whatever this Emily gives you and then you will come back here."

Stelios looked strange since he had other orders from Kalogerou. "Mr. Kalogerou told me to escort you to the factory and waited for him there, Miss Alina."

Alina lifted her head and looked at him icily. "And I'm changing my mind so at twelve o' clock you will go to the factory alone and take whatever this Emily gives you. Understood?"

Stelios saw that Alina was getting irritated. "Very well, Miss Alexiou," he said and left.

Well done my girl, she congratulated herself, *now we know who is in charge here*. She walked into the office and sat in the chair. She was smiling as she thought that Kalogerou were about to blow up as soon as he would realize that he was the only one who went to the factory. She was so happy that she started to work with great enthusiasm.

At noon Stelios informed her that he would go to the factory. At three o' clock Alina had a lot of letters in front of her not knowing what to do. She put them aside and get back in her work. It was the two most fruitful hours of her life until the moment that Kalogerou appeared in front of her, closing the door furiously behind him. Alina lifted her eyes from the computer. "I'm sorry that you lose in your court, Mr. Kalogerou, but I need quietness. So, if you don't mind …" and she made a disparaging gesture with her hand.

"I went to the factory and you were not there." He was raging.

And it was about time to take her revenge for the morning airs and graces, which do not come out of her mind not even for a second. "Since I was here. You know, Mr. Kalogerou, I cannot be in two places at the same time." She got up from her chair and went to the table that stood in front of the sofa. "Here is your precious correspondence. Neither a movie star receives so many letters." She took a pack of envelopes of various sizes and gave them furiously to Kalogerou.

She made to leave when Kalogerou caught her by her hand and turned toward him. His eyes pinned to hers. Kalogerou clutched his rage by force. "Miss Alexiou, when I say that you must go to the factory … I mean that you must go to the factory." His tone was beyond negotiation. No objection about that.

"Mr. Kalogerou, when I say that I have three months before releasing my book I mean it, too. Take a look at the correspondence, sign it and then give it to me in order to sign it too and get over me."

His patience was exhausted. Kalogerou wasn't one of those men who could accept such kind of behavior. Even if this attitude came from a very beautiful and attractive woman as Manos' daughter. Kalogerou had used to everyone follows his commands without any delay or any arguments. But no, not her. She was born only to be beautiful and spoke back to him making his life a hell.

"Mr. Kalogerou, is something wrong?" Her eyes were sparkling.

"Miss Alexiou, you think that everything is in order?" His eyes were angry.

"I believe that everything runs very smoothly. You did your court, I worked with my book and the correspondence of the day is in your hands as well, so, yes, I think that everything is in order, Mr. Kalogerou. I don't see a problem, do you?"

"The factory isn't managed from home, Miss Alexiou. Does your dad ever told you that?"

"My dad did a marvelous job with the factory without making my life miserable. He was able to cope with anything on his own. Why can you do the same thing? I think this is ultimately your problem and the solution to your problem isn't for me to stay back to my book and have problems with my publisher."

"Oh, Miss Alexiou, you don't have to worry about that," he looked at her ironically, "if this ever happens to you, you will be represented by the best lawyer of all continents," he said pointing to himself.

The confidence of this man is something else. *Ah, God, what have I done to deserve him*? Alina thought "Mr. Kalogerou, I'm going to tell you once more and this is going to be the last time. This is the only help I can provide until I finished my book. If you want to, Stelios could go to the factory every day bringing the correspondence to the house. There is no other solution for the time being. Otherwise, you're on your own."

Kalogerou couldn't believe what he was hearing. She was so beautiful when she was angry and the only thing he wanted was to finish what he had started in the morning in the kitchen.

Instead of that, he got up and left the room. Alina smiled. "Alexiou - Kalogerou: 2-0," she muttered and returned to her computer screen with more enthusiasm this time.

Chapter 5

The first two months after Manos' accident were very difficult for Kalogerou, as he had a court every day, then he had to go to the factory and very late at night was back to Manos' house. He had settled permanently in the large round kitchen table since 'Her Majesty', as he used to call Alina, had settled more than permanently in the home office. How she had managed that, he couldn't understand it. He had accepted her own way of working, which wasn't very sociable.

They even went to the hospital separately. When Alina went to the hospital Dr. Apostolou was quite attentive with her. When Kalogerou went to the hospital Apostolou couldn't stop teasing him about Alina. His friends had also forgotten him as they had stopped calling him for a late night drink a long ago.

It made sense since he always said no to them. Kalogerou behaved like a monk. The only thing that Kalogerou wanted was to get back home soon every night, just to see her and he was relaxed as Alina not getting out of the house was safe from the maniac that causes Manos' accident.

ANOTHER DAY HAD PASSED when Kalogerou walked into his office without speaking to anyone. He was exhausted in the court, which didn't go so well. His client went to jail because he was thinking of Alina. Who else?

He threw his briefcase on the desk and headed for the window. He lit a cigarette. Down the street was almost full when a well - known figure caught his attention. "I think I'm driving crazy. I see her everywhere", he said loud, but looking better he understood that the woman he saw in the street was very true to be his imagination. He called Maria at home. "Hello, Maria, could you please tell me that Miss Alexiou is writing her book at home?"

"No, Dimitris, I can't tell you that, because she went out ..."

"I suppose she is in the garden?" he asked stuttering.

Maria laughed. "No, she isn't. What could she do in the garden end of February? She finished her book and she told me that she is going out for shopping ... Dimitris?" Maria didn't get any reply.

Kalogerou came out of his office running. Once he arrived at the entrance of the building where his law office located, he sprang out on the road. He didn't, however, see her at once. The blood climbed to his head. He didn't know where to go. He extinguished his cigarette with his foot. He paced up and down searching the street cursing all the time.

How did she think that she could go out of the house? She denied to go to the factory ... and then he saw her. She was coming out of a shop with three - four bags in her hands and a huge smile on her face. "It was about time to cut this smile of hers," growled Kalogerou, although she was so cute. He ran toward her and grabbed her by the arm. She was startled when he saw him.

"Can you tell me what are you doing here?" He growled as he was very angry.

"Mr. Kalogerou, you're hurting me." He dragged her to the entrance of his building. "And I don't need anyone's permission to go shopping," she was glaring at him. "This isn't the first time I go shopping. I know these shops because my father used to bring me here for shopping."

"Let's go to my office." He pulled her by the arm and put her in the elevator.

"I'm not done yet. I want to shop one or two more things," Alina grimaced.

"Oh, yes, you finished your shopping right now," he said full of rage. They were entering the reception of his office growling to Christina, "I'm not here to anyone," pulling Alina behind him.

When they entered his private office he pushed her to the couch. "Sit down over there and do not talk," ordered her. Alina wanted to say something. "Don't talk and let me calm down." He closed her mouth with a kiss and kicked the leg of the table that stood before him.

Kalogerou trembled. He put whiskey in a glass. Alina got up to take off her coat. "Don't do anything. It's so difficult for you?" he said pissed off. Alina made a face to him, and she ostentatiously stood from the couch, took off her coat and sat down again. Dimitris sat on his chair behind his desk watching her as she crossed her legs.

"Well, Mr. Kalogerou, I'm waiting ...," she was waving her foot irritated him.

"And I expect ...," he said angry, "to tell me how you get out of the house alone without Stelios. Everyone had orders not to let you leave the villa without escorting you. Apparently, no one is listening to me."

"Stelios is at the factory. Why you always seem to forget that? And I asked the man at the entrance to open the door of the villa and he did it. What's your problem?"

"Oh, yes, I'm sorry. Stelios is doing your job at the factory, and as I said before no one is listening to me. This man at the entrance had orders not to let you go out."

"Perhaps, but I'm much more beautiful than you, so he didn't argue with me."

And then a thought hit him like a thunderbolt. "How, the hell, did you come down to Athens town center?"

"By taxi." She gave him a wide smile. Dimitris looked dumbfounded. "I suppose that you know those yellow cars that you can phone them and they come to your doorstep, don't you?" she snapped sarcastically.

Dimitris didn't answer her. What to tell her? That a madman out there sent your father to the hospital, and if he learned that Manos has a daughter he might want to do the same to you? He shivered thinking that possibility. Also, he didn't want to scare her. When he spoke again his voice was calm. "Next time you want to shop just inform me. I think that you can do that, don't you?"

"Good," said Alina and stood up, "call me, please, a taxi because I want to go back home, if you don't mind."

Dimitris got up to pick a book from the library. "You won't go home by taxi."

"And how am I suppose going home? On foot?" She was putting her coat.

"I'll take you and take off your coat. I have a lot of work to do. A client of mine is in jail, thanks to you." He approached her and caught her by her waist.

Alina swallowed hard. "And how is that my fault?"

He kissed her on the mouth. "Find something to occupy yourself until I finish my work." Then he went and sat on his chair.

Alina sat on the couch without saying a word. She watched him reading and writing. He was so handsome. His mouth was one of those you want to kiss it all the time. She wets her lips. His taste was on them. His chest was wide. His arms were strong enough. *He must visit a gym*, Alina thought and sighed. Kalogerou looked at her smiling. *Well,* thought Alina, *Kalogerou is a very good looking man and he knows how to take advantage of it.*

Alina couldn't bear anymore sitting doing nothing. She got up and went to his library. She put her hands on her waist and whispered the titles of his books. Dimitris was trying to be focused on his computer screen and not to Alina's body, as were showed through her jeans and silk shirt. "Ugh, all these books are legal ones. I don't have something to read," she said aloud.

A muffled giggle escaped his mouth. "I'm a lawyer, Miss Alexiou, and this is a law office. What did you expect to find in my library? Literature?"

She turned and looked at him. His eyes were fastened on the computer.

She stood behind him and bent over him to have a better view of his computer screen. She mumbled two or three rows of the text that was on the screen. "I don't understand what you're writing."

His heart was going to break "Never mind, Miss Alexiou. Judges will understand what I'm writing." She didn't flinch. She caught the computer mouse and scrolling the text downwards. Her whole body was almost upon him. Her seductive scent clouded his mind. He felt his body stiffen. It was the first time that something like that was happening to him. Usually, he was the one that caused such reactions in women. He had work to do. He should have resisted to her.

He took a deep breath. "Miss Alexiou, could you please let me do my job?"

Alina got up as if she felt the tension in his voice, and she stood behind his chair, watching him writing. She admired his strong hands, his fine and long fingers, as hitting the keyboard.

Kalogerou thought that it was a torture to write with Alina standing so close to him. He wanted to take her to his office. He closed his eyes, he took a deep breath and continued writing, but the letters danced on the computer screen before him. He imagined that he hold her in his arms kissing her passionately. His hands unbuttoned her silk shirt and his mouth voraciously rushes to her breasts. He imagined that he possessed her in his chair. He felt hot. The phone's ringing brought him back to reality. It was Christina. "Mr. Georgiou is on the phone." Christina's voice brought him back to reality, sitting on his chair trying to work while Alina was standing too near to him.

"Yes, Mr. Georgiou, what can I do for you?" Kalogerou listened to him. "It's very easy. No, not need to. I will come to you the day after tomorrow and leave it to your office." He hung up the phone. He got up from his chair. "We are leaving, Miss Alexiou." He had to admit that he couldn't work anymore with this woman beside him

"So, you finished?" She asked him.

"Almost," Kalogerou murmured. He put the papers in his briefcase and wore his coat.

"Do you have any court tomorrow?"

"Yes, Miss Alexiou, I have. Why?"

"May I come with you?"

"No," he replied and helped her to wear her coat.

"Why?" She sharply asked him.

"Because if you come with me, it is certain that I will put another client of mine in prison, like today," he whispered in her ear. However, he didn't miss the opportunity. "You could go to the factory, instead."

"Not a chance, forget that."

"Why?"

"Because the factory reminds me of my dad, and I don't like Emily, that's why."

"Why do you dislike Emily? She is the most obedient person I have ever known, unlike you."

"Very funny, Mr. Kalogerou. Seriously, I don't know. Every time my dad brought the discussion to his secretary, I felt a hand squeezing my heart."

He looked at her in disbelief. "Woman's stupidities, Miss Alexiou. What are you going to do tomorrow?" Kalogerou opened the passenger door of his car to get Alina inside, "Don't tell me shopping, because you're not going anywhere alone."

"Oh, let Stelios come with me, please."

He drive the car out of the parking. At this time of the night, the streets of Athens are empty. He turned to the right and went to the main street of Athens. "Miss Alexiou, you forget very easily. You sent Stelios to the factory every day."

"No, I didn't forget that, smart ash. Let him get me down to the town center after his returning from the factory. Tomorrow is Thursday and the shops are open all day, isn't it?"

"Indeed, Miss Alexiou."

"So, we're all fine. I will have the correspondence from the factory with me in order to bring it in your office. See, I'm such a co-operative person, now I have finished my book, don't you agree?"

Kalogerou was puffing. "Please, Miss Alexiou, give me a break. Tomorrow I decided that I will go to court unprepared. Do I have to go unprepared and the day after tomorrow?" They had reached the house. Kalogerou got off the car and opened the house door for her.

"I thought that you could understand that now I finished my book I deserve a little rest. I always take a break before beginning my next book." She hung her coat next to his in the closet.

"And when are you going to start your next book so we can live our life in peace?" Alina turned on the lights in the kitchen.

"Oh, I don't know. It is too early, yet." She gave him her brightest smile.

"I understand," he said cheerlessly. *From my point of view, I'll probably put in prison many of my clients*, he thought, as he looked her from behind, as long as she served the food. She gave him a bottle of wine to open it.

"Mr. Kalogerou, I want to go out at night." She was biting her food looking him straight into his eyes.

He almost choked on the food. He drank his wine in one sip. "And, may I ask, Miss Alexiou, where do you intend to go?"

"Oh, I don't know. Maybe to a theater or a cinema. Or to a club, perhaps. I don't care. Just to get out of this house and see some people. You see, when I am writing my books is like to live in a monastery. Until I start my new book, I want to get out and meet some people. Is that so bad? Not that I need your permission to do whatever I like, but I don't want to live another reaction of yours like the previous one. That's why I'm inform you for my intentions."

Kalogerou threw a stare at her as he understood what Miss Alexiou was meant 'by going out'. "I understand exactly what do you mean, Miss Alexiou. I wasn't born yesterday," he said roughly.

She gave him her glass to fill it with wine. "What do you mean by that? I don't like the tone of your voice."

"Nothing." He refilled their glasses with wine. "How about a tour of the factory?"

"I want to go out at night," she emphasized each word.

"What about an evening tour then," he winked, "in order to avoid Emily?"

Her eyes darkened and he noticed it. He got up from the stool and approached her. He turned her toward him. "No need to look out of the house to find what you want." His mouth stuck to hers and his kiss wasn't gentle. His tongue swooped into her mouth. He heard her groan as she responded to his kiss. His hand went through her shirt. Her hands embraced his neck.

"I don't understand what you are saying," she said during a small break of his kiss.

His hand unbuttoned her pants and slipped into his panties. She was so warm and wet down there that took his breath away. Alina cried aloud as he put his finger inside her. Her whole body was on fire. She sprang. She felt his mouth on her breasts and groaned in pleasure. She cried out again as he gave her another orgasm with his finger. She stuck on him.

"You want sex, Miss Alexiou, which I can offer it to you, too. So why going to find it somewhere else?" He said as a second finger went deeper making her groaned. Alina hooked on his jacket. He kissed her so violently that her lips became red.

...Oh, what the hell, I want sex and I want him, she thought.

He wanted to take her in the kitchen and she was about to deal with his zip when Kalogerou thought that Alina wasn't any ordinary woman but she was Manos' daughter.

The daughter of his best friend. The daughter who kept secret especially from him. End of discussion. Or better. End of sex. Damn! He got her hand just before reaching his erasing nature. He buckled his pants and his belt. "I have to read for tomorrow court, Miss Alexiou," he said and turned his back to her.

His tone cut her appetite for sex. Kalogerou was so serious while he was telling her about the court. In front of her he was standing a completely different man who managed to dress up in seconds.

Alina got by surprise. She was trying to figure out what had just happened. Now that she had decided to proceed with Kalogerou, now he found the time to back off. His behavior confused her. She stared at him, trying to understand what was that he made him stopped for having sex with her.

She slammed the kitchen door wondering why. *Why did he stop?* She muttered. She went up to her room trying to calm herself down from all the kisses and caresses of Kalogerou.

Dimitris in the kitchen couldn't believe what he had done. "Oh, Manos," he cried and smashed his glass of wine.

Chapter 6

Georgiou listened to Aris who had Kalogerou under surveillance after the visit of Georgiou to Kalogerou's office. But what happened that afternoon was strange even for an experienced policeman like him.

"Mr. Georgiou, I'm telling you, Kalogerou grabbed the girl by the arm and dragged her to his office and then they left the office after several hours in the night – it should be around ten when they both left, sir - in order to go to Alexiou's home. Together, sir."

"Wait for a minute, Aris, I'm trying to understand what you're telling me. So, Kalogerou found a chick on the street, and dragged her up to his office and then instead of going to his home with her they went together to Alexiou's home. Am I correct?"

"Yes, sir. No, sir."

"Yes or no, Aris?"

"Oh, sir, what I mean, is that this girl, perhaps, if I am correct, was not just a chick for him."

"I don't understand what do you mean by that."

"What I mean, sir, is that this girl wasn't some kind of a whore, as from his reaction she definitely means a lot to him."

"To whom?"

"To Kalogerou, sir. The thing that I don't understand, sir, is why they went to Alexiou's villa and not to Kalogerou's home."

"Yea, I understand now what do you mean and that's weird, very weird. Have you seen him with this chick again?"

"No, sir. Every time I followed him he was alone. From Alexiou's home he gets out always alone. He was always going to the factory alone. He was going to the court alone. To his home, he only went once to take some clothes, and then he went to Alexiou's home again. Always alone, sir. It's the first time that I saw him with this woman. Believe me, sir, he was very angry with her."

"Perhaps, he wasn't angry. He was jealous."

Aris thought a little bit before he answered. "No, sir, Mr. Kalogerou looked definitely feared about her being out on the streets, then he was angry for the same reason but jealous, no, sir, I don't think so. However, why should he be jealous? The girl was shopping alone."

Georgiou couldn't make any sense. "Well, you are still following Kalogerou either if he is alone or with her, I don't care." He was very thoughtful.

From where does this girl spring up? And who is she? And why Kalogerou behaved so strange? All these questions flooded his mind like a waterfall. Georgiou was incapable of answering these questions.

IT WAS A WEEK AFTER the incident between Dimitris and Alina in the kitchen. For the next whole week, they had managed to avoid each other successfully. She spent most of her time in her father's office without any particular reason. On the other hand, Kalogerou arrived very late at home in order not to meet with her.

Every morning Alina used to go down after Kalogerou left home and heard the front door closed. When she heard the front door closed, she stepped down the stairs. As soon as Maria saw her, she served her coffee. "Oh, a gift. Maria, for whom is this gift?" she asked cheerless drinking abstract her coffee.

Maria smiled. "Tomorrow is Dimitris' birthday and this is for him."

"Oh, I see, and how old is Mr. Kalogerou going to be? A 200?"

Maria laughed warmly. "Well, someone is cheerful today. Luckily, because Dimitris lately is in a very bad mood. Do you know why? And, for your information, he is going to be forty and he is also the most famous bachelor in whole Athens."

"Yeah, and Athens is such a huge city. And, why should I know that Mr. Kalogerou is in a bad mood? He is always in a bad mood. It isn't something new for him. Perhaps, because he is going to be forty? That's a very good reason, I think," Alina said trying not to show her frustration.

Maria looked at her without understanding what Alina was trying to say. "So, what did you buy for him?"

"Do I have to buy him anything?" Alina answered her back with a question.

Maria looked at her for a moment before putting the pan in the oven. "Yes, you do, young lady. Dimitris is standing by you all this time and besides the fact that he is the partner of your father, he is also his best friend. Do not forget that Missy, okay?"

Alina was drinking her coffee trying to avoid Maria's glare.

An idea passed through Alina's mind making everything looked different. *That's made him stop*, thought Alina. Everything was clear like a crystal. "Maria, thank you very much," she said and she kissed her on the cheek.

"Don't forget the gift," Maria shouted as Alina was leaving the kitchen having a big smile on her face.

"I will give him the best gift ever, don't worry," she cried with joy. She went to her office and stand in front of the small wooden handmade bookcase searching her books one by one. She chose two - three books and sat down on the carpet to think better. "It's difficult to decide," she whispered. "Which one should be the best for him?" Alina murmured.

She spent a long time thinking, wandering around the office, sat down again on the carpet when she came to a conclusion. She wanted one of her best books with hot love scenes in order to give the message to him. When she found it she signed writing a dedication on the first page: "A 'hot' bedtime story just for you", and in the evening, shortly before Kalogerou returned home, she went to his room and left her gift on the nightstand near his bed. *If not tonight, tomorrow morning, he will see it,* she thought as she was leaving his room.

IT WAS FRIDAY MORNING, and Kalogerou had his birthday. Alina waited until hearing the front door closed. Once she heard the door she stepped down the stairs singing. She heard Maria speaking with someone. She swallowed hard.

Why is Kalogerou in the kitchen chatting with Maria? She heard the front door closed. Who got out so early in the morning if it wasn't him? Alina asked herself. For a minute, she hesitated to open the kitchen door. She stayed there and heard Maria speaking with him.

"You have to thank her Dimitris, and take her with you this evening. She needs to get out a bit. She is staying a lot at home. She is a young woman, don't you forget that."

Alina nodded her head outside the kitchen door. Maria was right. After that shopping day, Kalogerou didn't allow her going out of the house. The only option according to Kalogerou was to go to the factory. Alina denied that option so she had to stay at home, without having anything to do and without understanding the reason for staying inside.

Kalogerou didn't tell her why he just asked her in a very menace way not to go out of the house. Everything she wanted she had to buy it from the Internet. That was his exact words. *Where he was supposed to go this evening,* thought Alina as she opened the kitchen door. Kalogerou was sitting on the kitchen couch without looking at her. Alina said good morning to both of them. Only Maria good morning her.

"By the way, Mr. Kalogerou, happy birthday," she wished him with a formal tone in her voice. He said a dry thank to her and left the kitchen.

"What happened to him today? He didn't like my gift?" Alina asked Maria with a surprise.

Maria smiled faintly. "Don't worry. He loved your gift as much as mine ...,"

"Then what?"

"Look, normally on his birthday he used to hang out with friends, but Manos is in the hospital ...,"

"And what? Oh, please tell me, Maria, that Mr. Kalogerou isn't going to celebrate tonight because of my father? What a disaster!"

Maria was picking the dishes. "No, dear, he will celebrate, unfortunately without your father."

"Well, I feel much better ..."

Maria didn't answer to such an ironic comment. "He has arranged something for this evening, and if I'm correct all his friends would be with some company, a female company I mean, and hmm you understand?"

"I'm trying, Maria, but what you're saying isn't very helpful."

Maria looked at her meaningfully.

"What?"

"Think a little harder, sweetie." Something passed through her mind and Maria understood that. "So, can you tell me what did you think?"

Alina looked at her, "you mean that Mr. Kalogerou ran out from chicks?"

Maria raised her hands high. "Oh, please God, help me with these two people. What is wrong with you two?"

"I don't know what you mean. I don't know about Mr. Kalogerou. On the other hand, considering of me I'm fine, just fine, and so much fine, that I was preparing for my whole life for that 'fineness'". Alina cried out with confidence.

"Yeah, now I believe you. Stop murmuring and listen to me. I told Dimitris to take you out on his birthday and guess what he told me."

"No, I cannot guess, but I'm sure that you won't leave me in the dark, don't you?"

Maria passed her irony by making faces. "Well, he told me that you don't want to go out with him ...,"

"That is correct ...,"

"I asked him if he asked you and he said no ...,"

"That is also correct. He didn't."

"Oh, please, stop interrupting me. I know that he didn't ask you to go out with him. You know why?"

"No, but I have a feeling that you are going to enlighten me right away."

"Because he was pretty much sure that you were going to refuse."

Alina smiled. "Well, Maria, for the first time in my life I've to agree with Mr. Kalogerou and you know how much I hate agreeing with him."

"Why? You told me the other day that you want to go out, to go to a cinema, or to a theater. Here's your chance."

Alina looked serious. "Maria, I think that you've lost your mind. I want to go out alone, not with him."

"Why my child? Don't you like Dimitris?"

Alina didn't answer to Maria's last question and went to the office. She liked Dimitris and there is always a 'but', and she didn't know how to manage this.

On the other hand, Maria understood almost everything. There was something between those two, so she decided to call Dimitris on his mobile. Before he could even talk to her she says, "I won't leave the house tonight, unless you ask her to come with you. Do you understand me?"

In hearing that Dimitris growled and hung up his phone without answering.

WHEN KALOGEROU RETURNED home late at the afternoon Maria had made her threat real. She was still at home. *There is no salvation*, thought Dimitris, when he saw Maria waiting for him in the kitchen.

"Where is she?" He asked curtly.

"In the office. From the morning. She didn't even show up to eat for lunch. Is everything all right with you two?"

"Well ...," he puffed, "I will go by myself to ask her, just because of you, but if she says no I'm not going to insist."

Maria took him by his arm with a big smile on her face and they get out of the kitchen together. Outside the office, Dimitris pulled his hand abruptly.

"Maria, I don't think that you would like to be in front of." He glared her.

"I would like to because you see, you are a little wild and clumsy ..."

"Maria ..."

"Well, I'll wait ... there ...," and she pointed a round table in the middle of the house entrance.

"No, you'll wait in the kitchen ...," and he pointed the kitchen with his finger, "... and with the door closed."

From the office, he heard Alina screaming out of happiness. She opened the door and saw them. "Hold on a second. I'll have to ask and I'll tell you ...," He turned to Dimitris. "Mr. Kalogerou, do you know where the Hilton Hotel is?" Kalogerou nodded. "Okay Lucas I'll come to see you, I won't be alone ... and won't sit for long because we have to go to a birthday party. Ah, you don't know how pleased I am. Oh, I love you too, yeah, yeah at half past nine we'll be there." Alina was jumping like a little girl, which made Maria and Dimitris looked at her meaningful.

"Who is this Lucas, Alina?" Maria, who first get over the shock, asked her.

Alina kissed her on the cheek. "A classmate from high school. He is also a writer and, a very good friend. I'm going to get ready to become a goddess," and looking at Kalogerou, "what time do we have to go to your birthday party?"

"At eleven o' clock," he said with clenched teeth.

"Perfect, I said to Lucas around half past nine, and let's say that I need at least an hour to ...oh, Mr. Kalogerou how far is Hilton Hotel from the house?" she asked blissfully.

"Saturday night, is around an hour," he said again with clenched teeth. Maria was holding him by his arm trying to calm him down.

"Good, so at nine o clock, you should be ready." She climbed the stairs so happy.

Dimitris went to the kitchen cursing. He lit a cigarette. "So, are you happy now? Miss Alexiou doesn't need a specific invitation," he took a big puff from his cigarette, "and who the hell is that Lucas? Have you ever heard of him, Maria?" Kalogerou asked Maria looking very suspicious.

"No, today was my first time hearing of him. Could you tell me why she was so happy about Lucas?"

Dimitris glared her as he extinguished his cigarette. "I'm going to get ready ... and I don't have to mention how much I hate your stupid ideas. Oh, and don't you ever speak to me again."

Maria looked at him like he was her son who was preparing for his first date. "Go get dressed, my boy," she patted him on the cheek, "and she won't have eyes for anyone else but you."

"Well, I think that you're nuts. Did you forget what you were telling me when I first saw her?"

Maria stood by her position, "I'm leaving and I didn't forget anything. I'm just saying, that I prefer you from that Lucas. What kind of name is that? Ugh, 'Lucas'. Don't you ever forget that," she took her bag, "and watch out our girl tonight. I'm not going to tell you anything else... at least for tonight."

Alina in her room was getting ready with the music blaring.

I wondering, when am I going to smash the face of this Lucas, thought Dimitris, as he passed out of her room, *as soon as I meet him or afterwards?* He went to his room and closed the door firmly. *As soon as I meet him,* he decided.

He was almost ready when the music stopped. He walked out of his room blaspheming. Alina was standing outside his room. "Oh, Mr. Kalogerou, I see you're ready and on time, that's good."

Dimitris couldn't take his eyes off her. "Miss Alexiou, are you going to get out in this very little black dress?" Alina looked herself in a full-length mirror which was on the wall next to his room door.

"Don't you like it?"

"No," he said severely.

"Why?" she asked honeyed.

"It's very short and has a very wide neckline, that's why."

"Mr. Kalogerou, that's the reason I bought it. Because it is so short and has this very wide neckline. Move it. I want to see Lucas as soon as possible."

With all vexation, Kalogerou descended the stairs, locked the house door and get into the car.

Inside the car, Alina was carving the radio. When she found the song she liked she leaned back in the seat and humming, "Mr. Kalogerou, I think that you are going to like Lucas."

"That's not my intention." *Instead of that, my purpose is to throw him away from the country or better to prohibit his entry into the country from now on. Perhaps Georgiou will be useful for me, somehow,* a malice voice said inside him.

"It's a very good guy, you'll see."

They arrived at the Hilton Hotel on time. Dimitris gave the keys to the valet. Alina went straight to the reception and from there, an employee led them to the restaurant where Lucas waited for them. When she saw him she fell in his arms and kisses him mad. From her voices, all customers of the restaurant were turning and watching them.

He is also a very handsome man and younger than me, admitted Kalogerou, *that's why she is mad at him*. He clenched his fists. As Alina made the recommendations, Dimitris forgot his good manners and he didn't give his hand. *Yeah, right, I won't greet her ex - boyfriend.*

While Alina and Lucas were talking he was boiled in a green jealousy fluid while he was thinking several things concerning Alina and Lucas. *I wonder if they were lovers. If so, how long they were together? Or, why they aren't together anymore? Does she still love him? Does he still love her?* So many questions and no answers and the minutes passed while Dimitris was thinking all these torturing questions. Lucas noticed that Kalogerou was staring at his watch, and he decided to stop discussing with Alina. Their farewell was more quite.

"Well, Mr. Kalogerou, what do you think about Lucas?" Kalogerou didn't speak to her. "Don't tell me that you didn't like him?"

He lit a cigarette. "Don't you miss each other?"

"Oh yes we've missed each other a lot," she looked at him as she opened the radio.

"And you two are just friends?"

"Mr. Kalogerou, we always were friends. Lucas is my best friend."

"Clearly some time ago you two had an affair, Miss Alexiou, I'm not blind. So as you jumped on him ..."

Alina laughed. "Me? With Lucas?" She laughed again, "Mr. Kalogerou, are you serious?"

"Of course, I'm serious."

"Well, Mr. Kalogerou. Let me enlighten you because you are very blind, believe me, if Lucas wanted someone that wouldn't be me, but ... you."

Dimitris tried to continue driving calm.

"Do you know what I mean by that, or do you want me to analyze that to you?"

"I understand what do you mean, I'm not an idiot." His heart went into its place again.

"I'm sure of it."

That was an unexpected development, thought Dimitris. At least, Lucas had never been her boyfriend. That's good. He smiled and looked more cheerful.

She glanced him and stretched her legs, *let see how I can have you on my bed without thinking of my father,* she said to herself and sighed.

He turned and looked at her from top to bottom.

They went to the bar a little late. Apostolou was the only one Alina knew. He hugged her as a father. "Don't worry, sweetheart, your dad is in good hands ... not like my own, but as good as mine," and he kissed her on the cheek.

Dimitris took her from Apostolou's arms. "Hug another girl. That's mine."

Apostolou smiled. "Not yet my friend? Have you lost your mind? You're forty and she took your mind, what are you waiting for?" and he hit him amicably on the back.

Kalogerou couldn't take his eyes off her. So close and not be able to touch her. Not able to make love to her.

Apostolou nudged Dimitris. "Youth," he said pointing to Alina who was dancing for the last two hours without stopping.

"Costas, please, she is Manos' daughter."

Apostolou looked at him. "Oh, now I understand how you accomplished and kept your hands away from her."

Dimitris was just drinking his whiskey.

"And what are you going to do?"

"Honestly, I don't know," Kalogerou shrugged his shoulders, "Perhaps, I'll wait until Manos become well again."

Apostolou sat beside him looking very serious. "And if Manos stayed in that condition for the rest of his life? Or even died?" He nudged him, "Dimitris, what are you talking about? You're crazy about her."

"You think?"

"Don't try to hide that from me. I knew it from the first moment I saw you in the hospital. As your friend and as a doctor I'm telling you that all these thoughts are a pure absurdity. Which is no good for you or for her." Dimitris turned his head to the dance floor where Alina was still dancing. "Also, as a doctor, I recommend you to take her and go home because she is drunk."

Alina was coming toward them. She fell in Dimitris' arms and kissed him on the mouth. "Mr. Kalogerou, would you like to dance with me?"

Apostolou whispered in his friend's ear. "Take her home to sleep if she managed to find her bed or even yours." Apostolou laughed.

Alina turned toward him. "Mr. Apostolou, will you dance with me? Mr. Kalogerou is too old for that."

"I don't like dancing," Apostolou said and pushed Dimitris.

"Come on." He took her by the hand.

"Oh, are we going to dance?" Alina was swaying her body.

"No," he said, "we are going home and put you in bed."

"And have sex or we're going to leave it unfinished like the other day." She was hooked on him and kissed him passionately on the mouth.

Apostolou looked meaningfully to Dimitris. "I cannot recognize you, my friend," said Apostolou chuckling. Dimitris took Alina's things and they went out of the club. Alina was stuck on him kissing him everywhere on his mouth, his neck, his ears. When the valet brought Dimitris' car he helped her to sit in the passenger seat.

"Mr. Kalogerou, we're leaving so early." She pulled him by the tie and kissed him hard.

"It's been five o'clock in the morning, and you're drunk." He removed her from his mouth.

"No, I'm not drunk. I'm fine. Well, where else are we going to celebrate your birthday?" Her mouth found his mouth and kissed him again.

His lips rocked. "We are going straight to home." He fastened her with the car belt in order to avoid further 'attacks' from her. All the way home Alina was singing.

When they arrived home, Alina gets out alone from the car and she would fall down if Dimitris didn't catch her on time. She hugged his neck. "Mr. Kalogerou, this is the second time you saved me. I'm so much grateful to you, I'll have to kiss you."

"You don't have to," he said, but Alina didn't listen to anything. She pressed her lips to his. Dimitris didn't respond. "Miss Alexiou, you're drunk," he said for the second time. He took her in his arms and take her to her room. When she put her on the bed, Alina pulled him close to her. "Miss Alexiou," he said, trying to avoid her kiss, "I have a rule."

Alina looked at him with cloudy eyes. "I like rules."

"I do not have sex with drunk women," she removed his jacket. Dimitris put it on again.

Alina took off her dress and stayed in her underwear. "Well, Mr. Kalogerou, let me tell you that I don't like your rule, it's a very stupid one." Her hands solved his tie and threw it on the floor. Her fingers unbuttoned his shirt.

His body hardened. "No, no, no Miss Alexiou, it isn't a stupid rule, and do you know why?"

"Please, Mr. Kalogerou, inform me."

"Because I want you to understand everything I'm going to do to you," he told her bellowing her hands. His body wanted to stay, but his mind ordered him to leave her room.

Alina pulled him closer to her by the belt of his trousers. "Don't worry, I'll understand everything," and her kiss challenged him more. She felt that his body hardened more after her last kiss.

He realized that his body wanted her bad. Alina was ready for him. He felt his erection through his pants. Instead of taking her in his arms, he got up, "Miss Alexiou, I said no," and he put her under the bedcovers, covering her body only with her underwear as it was. Hot, very hot. He headed for the door.

"Mr. Kalogerou, you lose," she said throwing her bra to him. Dimitris caught it in the air and left it on a chair near him. By the time he closed the door behind him, he heard her breathing rhythmically. *It was about time*, he murmured and went to his room.

He fell with his clothes on the bed. He was exhausted not only by her love attacks but also from the wrath which had not made love to her. He got up and went to the bathroom. He threw a lot of cold water in his face. He put only his pajamas bottoms and lie down on the bed. He couldn't sleep. His mind was stuck to her body.

He turned on the TV, nothing caught his attention. He looked at his watch he had left on the bedside table, to see what time it was. Alina's book was there waiting for him. He took it and began to read it. He sighed. *Oh, my God*, he murmured.

WHEN KALOGEROU WOKE up was Saturday noon. He opened her room door and looked at her. She was sleeping. *Almost naked*, his male voice reminded him, as Alina wore only her underwear. He closed the door.

He went down to the kitchen and made himself a coffee. A strong coffee to wake him up. He sat on the kitchen sofa, trying to read for Monday's court. It was impossible to concentrate due to Alina's book. His eyes fell on the book he had started reading last night. "Even asleep this woman tortures me with great success," he said. He closed the file in front of him and started reading the book. If he didn't finish it, he couldn't relax.

Chapter 7

Alina woke up on Sunday early in the morning long before Kalogerou. She stepped down ready for work. She made coffee and went in the office. Although she remembered nothing of the Friday's night out with Kalogerou, a voice inside her advised her not talk to him, not see him, or better not meet with him.

She stared abstractly the garden outside. It was early March and the winter was still here. The garden was covered by snow and her father had shown no sign of improvement for so long. That was her only concern, although Apostolou and other doctors find always something encouraging to say to her.

That's going to be my life from now on, Alina murmured, *my father lying in a bed helpless, without anything I can do for him, and I'll stick here with him.* Murmuring his name an aura of warmth surrounded her. *Mr. Kalogerou, there is always him, who cannot get out of my mind even for a single moment,* Alina thought. *Please God, I want my dad back. I don't like being here in Greece with Mr. Kalogerou, alone. I want to go back to my home, away from Dimitris.*

She took a look at her watch. Without dealing with something specific she had thickened so many hours locked in the office. She wanted to go to the kitchen. She was sure that Kalogerou should work there. The last thing she wanted was to see him. She tried to remember what happened on Friday night. It was impossible.

The only thing that I'm sure, Alina thought, *is that we didn't have any sex. Again. So, I can go to the kitchen and fill my cup with coffee.* Her coffee was over a long time ago and she was also hungry. *If I don't go now, I will go in an hour, or two at most,* she murmured.

In the kitchen, Kalogerou was sitting on the couch reading his files. He doesn't pay any attention to her. Alina took a look at the refrigerator, without finding something to eat. She decided to make a toast and sat on the kitchen bench to eat it.

Silently, she watched Kalogerou who read all these papers in front of him. He was engrossed. He seemed to be very focused on his reading and his writing, as he didn't say anything to her. The truth was that as soon as Alina entered the kitchen Kalogerou lost his focusing, although his eyes were down to his papers all time long.

Alina left the toast half-eaten on the bench, she went to the office to get a book and returned to the kitchen. She sat on a stool at the kitchen bench reading her book and continue eating her toast. Kalogerou was reading and reading without talking to her trying to gain his focus again, without great success.

After a while, Alina took the book in her hands and began pacing up and down. Dimitris thought that she would stop soon after two or three rounds. He was mistaken. That was beyond his strength. At the end, she had managed to distract him.

On purpose, he thought.

His gaze followed her curves wherever she paced before him. It was impossible for him to work like that. He threw his pen on the table screaming at her at the same time. "Miss Alexiou, why don't you go to your office and pacing over there? Here is 'my office', if you don't mind."

Alina startled by the power of his voice. "Mr. Kalogerou, I'm working, too." She stammered.

"You're kidding me." He got up and took a small bottle of water from the refrigerator. He drank it all in one gulp. Then he crumpled and threw it into the dustbin. He approached her.

"And how do you work when walking all over the kitchen stumbled everywhere?"

"I think ..."

"And what do you think if you allow me to ask?" He had cornered her on the kitchen bench.

"My new novel." She swallowed hard.

"Yes, as the one you gifted to me?" He doesn't let her answer as he closed her mouth with his finger, "and it's weird, Miss Alexiou, how do you manage to write such intense and hot love scenes ... just walking up and down. What kind of method is that?"

She was looking at him straight in the eye. "I didn't say that I write my hot love scenes just walking as you think, and besides that, now I'm thinking to write something different and I have to walk in order to think. I always do that. Is the only way to stay focus on. That's all. Why is that so wrong? Did you like my novel?"

"No, Miss Alexiou."

"Why?"

"I prefer having sex than writing or reading about it." His hands were tangled in her hair. "By the way, Miss Alexiou, which publisher represents you in Greece?"

Alina was trying to remember, but Kalogerou was so close to her that it was impossible to think the name of her publisher in Greece.

"A well-known one," she faltered, "whose name escapes me at the moment."

Kalogerou was bent over her, having buried all over his face in her hair. "At least, could you remember the name of the lawyer that represents you in Greece?"

"I know that. Your father," she said overjoyed.

Kalogerou remained speechless for a while. "My father has been dead for twelve years. Who represented you all these years?"

"I guess ... you, Mr. Kalogerou," she said reluctantly.

"Miss Alexiou, I don't think so, I don't recall any writer being represented by me for the last twelve years," he was playing with the curls of her hair, "and I had my peace, all this time if you understand me."

Alina grimace. "No, I don't understand you. The only thing I can tell you is that I found my contracts at home, I signed them and then I gave it to my dad."

"There is Manos again. How can I forget him?" He blasphemed. Kalogerou removed from her a little. He took his cell phone from his pocket in order to call Christina, who oddly replied his call quickly, although it was Sunday noon.

"Don't tell me that you want me at the office on such a beautiful and cold and snowing day? Do you know that is Sunday?" Christina answers her phone as polite as always.

"I am glad that you're having such a good time, Christina. Could you please tell me if the name 'Alina Johnson' sounds familiar to you?"

"It's one of your clients, you silly. Oh, don't tell me that you didn't have sex with the new chick? Oh, I cannot believe you Dimitris and I have to say that I'm impressed. Oh, you are in love with her, that's why you didn't have sex with her, yet. Am I right?"

I don't know why I still keep Christina as my secretary? He asked himself. "What we know about her?" he asked her as he was staring Alina. *Unless, the fact that she is very beautiful and I like her a lot and she drives me crazy all the time, and, I'm in love with her, everybody knows that*, he kept all these thoughts for himself.

"Her publisher in Greece is Stamatiou. You know the publishing house at the corner of your office. Basically, Mr. Manos knew her very well," Christina paused, "You need sex, Dimitris."

"Christina, concentrate please," he said through clenched teeth. "What kind of relationship had Manos with her?"

"If you ask for my opinion I think that he might have an affair with her."

"And why you say that?"

"I don't know, just a hunch. Have you read any book of her? She is good. For your information, I have read all her books, and I saw all the movies based on her books and I didn't lose any scene if you know what

I mean." Christina stopped as she heard a curse on the other side of the phone.

"Could you please tell me why I haven't seen a single contract of her all these years?" Kalogerou asked Christina while looking Alina, who shrugged her shoulders.

"Oh, cousin, I think that you need sex desperately."

"Christina, could you please answer my question?" *Yeah, I remember now why I do not fire her*, thought Dimitris.

"I always did that by myself according to your father's instructions."

"I must remind you that my father is dead for at least twelve years now ... and don't push your luck because I think that you are going to look for another job from Monday morning."

"Don't worry Mr. I always renew it with all legal charges, then I gave the contract to Mr. Manos who after a week brought it back to me signed by Alina Johnson. I sent a copy to the publisher and I keep another copy for us. I think I'm the best secretary you ever had, don't you agree? And besides that, I thought that you were aware of your father's clientele when you took over the office."

Kalogerou got angry, due to the fact that Christina was right, mainly on the issue regarding the sex, as the abstinence from sex had started striking him at his nervous system. At that particular time, he didn't want to have sex with any woman. He wanted to have sex with the only woman who turned to be Manos' daughter.

He retained his nerves. "Okay, Christina, thank you very much, you were very enlightened. Do me a favor and leave the last contract of this author in my office to have a look on Monday morning, because it seems everyone knows her, apart from me."

"Do you want to lend you also one of her books?" She said with a sweet voice, "I will bring one of my own. She is very hot."

"You don't have to do that, Christina, just the contract, thank you."

"As you wish, but you'll find them very educational, in case you have forgotten how to do sex."

Dimitris hung up the phone turning to Alina.

"Well?" she asked him.

"Miss Alexiou, you're right. I represent you. When is your new book going to release?"

"Oh, don't worry we have plenty of time. As I told you before, I'm just thinking of writing something different and ...."

"Miss Alexiou, concentrate please, I mean the book you sent into your agent just a few weeks ago."

"Oh, that book. It comes at the end of April, I think."

Dimitris beats his cup of coffee on the kitchen bench with all his force. All the coffee had spilled out. She remained calm.

"Oh, great, Miss Alexiou. Thank you very much for your help. Having the factory is not enough, being a lawyer and having my courts is not enough, now I have to deal with you as a writer. Thank you very much for your support. Again." He had cornered her for good.

She congratulated herself that she was remaining cool and smiling although Kalogerou was shouting at her. "Mr. Kalogerou, may I ask you something?"

"No," he said curtly. His fingers came down from her hair and followed the shape of her face. Then they moved to her neck and went to her blouse stroking the curve of her breasts. Her whole body has awakened looking for him. Kalogerou realized her reaction and continued his tortures.

She didn't pay any attention to his answer and asked. "Do you have any idea of your father's clientele?"

That was enough. He bent and kissed her forcefully and she reciprocated the kiss in an even more challenging way. The power of her tongue made him groaned. She took off his sweater he was wearing and her mouth hot and humid started her own love journey. She bit slightly his ear and her tongue licked in his neck. She continued down to his muscular chest and from there on his flat belly.

"I like men with a flat belly."

"Oh, may I ask why?" he said after he felt her lips on his belly and groaned.

"Because … I can … find … my target easy." Her hand gripped his irritated nature over Kalogerou's athletic pants. She heard him sighed and enjoyed it.

His hands had entered through her blouse and caressed her hardened breasts. His whole body was on fire. He put her on the kitchen bench without taking his lips from hers. He took off her blouse and took her breast in his mouth. "You drive me crazy, I cannot stay away from you anymore. I want you right now." His voice was heard heavy with lust.

"And I want you," Alina stammered and stuck even more on him.

"You know that's not going to happen, do you?" He whispered in her ear.

"Oh, yes, it is going to happen, because I want you so much. Why can't you understand that?" Alina asked him.

He took her other breast in his mouth. Her hand entered into his athletic trouser. He groaned.

"You're Manos' daughter," he said breathlessly.

"And why is that a problem?" She tried to undress him.

"I think that just be Manos' daughter is enough, don't you?" he threw her bra on the floor.

"Well, for your information, I have no problem with your dad."

He didn't let her undressed him. "How could you have a problem with my dad? My dad is dead. Doesn't bother anyone." He lowered her jeans.

"Neither my own dad bothers anyone." She succeeded to remove his athletic trouser. *Damn, he put it back on*, she thought.

His lips kissed her mouth and then licked her breasts. "When your dad wakes up, believe me, he will be very annoying if he knows about us."

Alina sighed. His lips had reached her abdomen and Kalogerou took off her underwear.

"Well, we don't have to tell him anything." She felt his lips in her wet nature. Her body leaped across.

"I hadn't thought about that. You're right. We can do that." His fingers replaced his lips down there. She screamed from the pleasure he offered her.

"Oh, please, stop the discussion and take off your trouser at last," she said before screaming as his fingers gave her another orgasm. Alina was melting in his hands. She was determined to finish what they had started this time in the kitchen. Better now than ever.

Kalogerou was also determined. Nothing was going to stop him this time. Okay, she may be Manos' daughter and Manos is his best friend, on the other hand, Apostolou was right. From his birthday night, he was very thoughtful of what Apostolou had told him.

Besides that, Alina was an adult woman. So what Manos could do? Vanish all men from Alina's life? That was impossible. Well, not that Manos wasn't capable of doing something like that. But, after all, he was Dimitris Kalogerou. Not an ordinary man.

"Do you hear something?" He asked her while he was putting his fingers a little deeper into her.

"Bells?" And she screamed once more.

Kalogerou smiled. "In addition to bells, you don't hear something like ..."

"... phone ..." they both said at the same time.

"Which phone is ringing?" Asked Alina with closed eyes and keeping Dimitris' hand inside her.

"The one of the house and my mobile. Get up!" Alina got up reluctantly and exhausted answered the phone of the house while Dimitris answered his mobile.

"Costas, I don't understand. What are you talking about?" Kalogerou tried to meet himself. Alina came closer to Dimitris without saying a word. Dimitris listened to what Apostolou was saying to him. "No, we're coming to the hospital right away."

Within minutes, Alina had dressed. "What happened?" She was pale from fear.

"This time Manos' condition had nothing to do with any infection. This time is something more dangerous. He told me something about a hematoma, but it wasn't possible for me to understand because of..."

Alina couldn't speak. Her father was in the hospital for almost three months, and the truth was that infections tormenting him quite often. Apostolou wouldn't bother them for an infection. *What happened to her father?* She thought and she looked at Dimitris.

"Don't worry," Dimitris said, "whatever it is, we'll deal with it together. Manos is strong." He kissed her on the mouth.

ENTERING THE HOSPITAL Alina didn't wait for him to park the car. She jumped out of it and ran straight to the stairs. Dimitris found her after a few minutes out of the Intensive Care Unit pacing up and down with anxiety. After a minute Apostolou met them. He approached both of them.

He *didn't humor as he was accustomed*, Alina noticed, *oh, my God, things must be pretty bad.*

"What happened to you two?" Apostolou said when he glanced at them. It was much of a rhetoric question as he went straight to the point. "Manos created a hematoma on his head, which we must remove it."

"So, Mr. Apostolou, remove it. What do you expect?" Alina buzzed around the doctor.

"Costas, when did this happen?" Kalogerou intervened, "You didn't mention anything about a hematoma when we talked this morning."

"Two hours ago Manos began to raise pressure and it was a miracle how we managed to revive him. After that, we went for a magnetic tomography and we saw it. It is created in a very difficult point. A neurosurgeon, a friend of mine, saw the tomography and he decided to surge him, but he cannot do it alone."

Alina was sitting on hot coals. "Mr. Apostolou, we are wasting our time. I have told you that is not a question of money," she looked very angry, "how much money this neurosurgeon wants to come and operate my dad ?" She clenched her fists.

Apostolou took a deep breath. *Yes, surely this young lady is Manos' daughter, no doubt about that,* he thought. "Our problem is that we try to communicate with that doctor in America. Unfortunately, all our efforts didn't succeed," he said haggard, "we left at least ten messages in the hospital, in the mobile phone ...," Alina stopped him with a gesture of her hand, obviously troubled.

"Oh, Mr. Apostolou, who is that damn surgeon?"

"Miss Alexiou, it's a woman. Panagiotis, the neurosurgeon who can surge your father," Alina waited anxiously, "said that this woman is unique and the only one who can manage such a difficult operation. She is the only one that Panagiotis trusted."

"Mr. Apostolou, I need a name, please give me a name," she said irritated.

"Jenifer Johnson," Apostolou said.

Alina whispered to him, "Mr. Apostolou, can we go to your office?" Apostolou looked at her without being able to explain her rage. "Please," she said pleadingly. Apostolou led them to his office, where Alina asked Dimitris for his mobile phone.

On the other side of the Atlantic, a gentle female voice answered the phone. "Jennifer Johnson speaking."

"Mom, dad isn't good and he needs you. Hold on I would like to speak with his doctor, Mr. Apostolou." Alina gave the phone to Apostolou saying, "Mr. Apostolou, you're talking to Jenifer Johnson in person ... and she speaks Greek fluently." Dimitris and Costas looked at each other.

Apostolou took the phone. "Mrs. Jennifer Johnson?"

"Yes, Mr. Apostolou, what can I do for you?"

"Mrs. Johnson, besides Manos we have also another mutual acquaintance, Mr. Panagiotis Eleftheriadis recommends you."

"Mr. Apostolou, as I remember, Panagiotis is the best surgeon I know and I'm sure that he can fully handle any problem. He is the best ..."

"He doesn't take the responsibility to undertake this surgery alone without you."

Jennifer Johnson interrupted Apostolou. "Mr. Apostolou, as I said, Panagiotis is entirely appropriate and capable for such a surgery. He had undertaken much harder surgeries here in America."

Alina was about to explode. His father's life was in dangerous and her mother made all this even harder? Not a chance. She plunged into Apostolou's phone annoyed. "Mom, tonight, at ten, you would be at the airport in order Peter brings you in Greece. And, if anything happens to dad because you don't want to surge him, I won't come back to America. Ever!" In her green eyes, large tears twinkled ready to burst.

Defeated by her daughter Jennifer Johnson, on the other side of the line, said, "Alina, sweetheart give me please Mr. Apostolou." Alina gave the phone to Apostolou.

"Mr. Apostolou, tell Panagiotis to prepare Manos for the surgery and send me as soon as possible an e-mail with every tests you have done to Manos in order to study them," she said and hung up the phone without saying anything else.

Apostolou was standing in the middle of his office speechless. Alina looked at him straight in the eyes. "She will come," he said, "don't worry! She'll surge your father with Panayiotis. I'm going to tell him, and we have so many things to do until tomorrow. If you'll excuse me."

Alina nodded and Apostolou went out of his office. Alina collapsed on the couch.

Dimitris looked at her. How many things he didn't know about Manos who supposed to be his best friend. He didn't know that he had a daughter and he didn't know that he was once married to a famous neurosurgeon.

Alina started to cry with sobs. He embraced her and she rammed more in his arms. He couldn't see her crying. He prefers her smiling or even being angry with him. But not crying. Crying was something beyond him. She snuggled more in his arms.

"Why are you crying? You did it and your mom is going to surge your dad." He told her without leaving her from his arms.

"I don't know. Believe it or not, my mother didn't want to come and surge him. I don't understand that woman. She is so annoyed some times."

"On the other hand, I can understand your mother. Coming to Greece after all these years and see your father in that condition it's not the easiest thing in the world. Think about it, Alina. Also, she must be as cold as an iceberg to surge him, without having any emotion about your dad, which is over her powers. Perhaps you cannot understand it but that's a lot of pressure for her."

He caught her face with both of his hands. "Alina, you must understand her. Your parents divorced years ago for some reason and now your mother must surge your father and keep him alive. Could you, please, get in her shoes?"

Alina wiped her eyes with her hands. "You know that she is a very good doctor and a very twisted woman."

He smiled. "Yeah, she reminds me of someone," he said and kissed her on the mouth.

"And I'm sure that she still loves my father. She didn't remarry since she left him and she had plenty of opportunities. She is still a very beautiful woman."

"I believe you."

"And now that she has the opportunity to come to see him my dad is..." Alina couldn't complete her sentence. Dimitris wiped her tears.

"If Manos was well perhaps it will be also difficult, but now under these circumstances, it's much more difficult for her and she is also taking such a big responsibility by surging him. If something goes wrong, you know very well that she is going to blame herself for the rest of her life. You are also going to put the blame on her. Believe me, no one can live with such a load in his soul for the rest of his life. I think your mom is a very brave woman and a very responsible doctor." Alina after hearing these words she felt calm and she slipped deeper into his arms.

Apostolou opened the door and entered the office in a very good mood. Alina escaped from Dimitris' arms as soon as she saw him.

"Costas, what happened this time and you're so happy?" Dimitris asked.

"When I told Panagiotis that he'll surge Manos with Johnson, he wanted to kiss me. Ugh! I didn't let him." Apostolou looked a little bit disgusted thinking that Panagiotis could possibly kiss him. Alina smiled with his grimace.

"You, surgeons, I cannot understand you," Dimitris said shaking his head.

"What are you talking about? Such a surgery it doesn't happen every day, you know. This is the talk of the town in the medical community."

"We're leaving," said Dimitris, "see you tomorrow." Apostolou didn't give him any importance. He was in his marvelous medical world.

Chapter 8

On the other side of the Earth, the most famous neurosurgeon was sitting on her chair trembling. *Life is a great mystery*, Jennifer Johnson thought. After so many years she's going to see Manos Alexiou again.

Her one and only love. The only man she ever loved with all her soul. The man who married her and wounded her more than anyone else. And now, she was holding his life in her hands. One tiny mistake and Manos will die. In her hands. By her hands.

Why did I accept? She murmured. She thought of Alina. How could they confront again if something goes wrong during the surgery? She will destroy Alina's life for the second time, and this time the destruction will be permanent. There would be no turning back for anyone of them.

Her hands sweated. How she could surge Manos with such sweated hands? What a disaster? Why Manos? Why not a stranger one? A complete stranger. She never had a problem to surge a stranger. It's easier to surge a stranger.

She got up from her chair. If Manos died? Her Manos. Alina's father. If he dies during the surgery? Or after it? How would she ever live the rest of her life with that? She looked out of the window and tears flooded her eyes.

She couldn't stand her life if Manos died by her hands. She couldn't withstand such a heavy load. She could bear anything, but not this. She had withstood too much when she had taken the decision to leave him and get back to America. It was a difficult decision.

If Manos died because of her, due to her wrong decisions, at her hands one thing was sure for Jennifer Johnson. Life, her life, her daughter's life wouldn't be the same again.

In her mind, came the day she left Manos and taking their daughter with her. Manos didn't do anything to keep her with him. That was something she could never understand it. He didn't say a word to her. He didn't do anything keeping her with him. Nothing. He didn't even try to change her mind. He didn't even argue with her. In the course of the time, she realized that his ego was to blame for his behavior. Always his ego.

Greek men have a very large ego, she thought, *and Manos wasn't an exception. My ego was also large*, she murmured. She wanted to be the best neurosurgeon in the world but Manos didn't want to discuss such a thing.

Manos was the most traditional Greek man. How he possible could change because of her? Jennifer understood that so she decided to leave him. It was a tough decision. Her parents had warned her many times but she wasn't listening. And she did it. She left Manos and became the best and the most famous neurosurgeon in the world. The most successful neurosurgeon and the loneliest person in the whole world.

After Alina met her father in Greece Manos entered her life again. She waited Alina from Greece to know everything about him. Her heart beat quicker every time Alina referred to her father. She had loved Manos with all her heart and leaving him and taking his precious daughter was a very bad act. That's why she never accepted his invitation for meeting him.

Why? She asked herself once more. A question which was impossible for her to answer it. She never knew. It was obvious that she was still in love with him. She never stopped loving him. She never stopped thinking of him. Alina always told her that her father waited for her. Every time. Anytime she wanted.

She let Alina travel to Greece in order to meet her father as she wished. Jennifer allowed that only because she had no right to deprive Manos of Alina's life. Beyond that, her relationship with Manos was her problem, as Jennifer had said once to her daughter. After that Alina never discussed this issue with her mother again.

But Alina wasn't stupid. She had understood that not only her mother but also her father was still in love with her mother. In his gaze, she could see only love for her mother.

Manos had a bright look when he was talking about Jennifer. His whole face enlightened and his gaze became brighter. His eyes gleamed every time he invited her mother to Greece.

Alina saw them destroying their lives because of their selfishness. They both were so selfish, that sometimes the only thing Alina wanted to do was screaming. To both of them. No matter how many times she tried to change her mother's mind, all her efforts fell on deaf ears. Her mother remained adamant.

Jennifer turned to her desk and sat down on the chair. "Why did I accept? Why?" she said aloud speaking to herself. "Panagiotis is a very capable neurosurgeon. He could manage anything."

Her eyes were turned to infinity. *Panagiotis was the one who requested for her, and ... that was strange,* she thought. Panagiotis had managed to bring out more difficult surgeries when he was in America. She entered her e-mail inbox. Nothing yet.

Why Panagiotis hesitated to surge Manos? That was a very good question, which she couldn't answer yet. After a while, her computer makes a noise and she realized that a new e-mail was waiting for her. *Let's see why Panagiotis cannot take this surgery by his own?* She questioned herself.

With trembling hands, she turned on the e-mail inbox and she was astonished. In front of her was Manos brain in a very bad condition. In an absolute bad condition. That's why Panagiotis wouldn't take the risk. She read the comments that Panagiotis had written about the hematoma in Manos' head and the treatment that Apostolou gave to Manos in order to keep him in repression. Looking again at the hematoma on Manos' brain, she concluded that this couldn't be an easy surgery.

There were a lot of moments when she regretted being a neurosurgeon and this was one of them. *I am not God and I had no intention playing God. I am only a human being, I am just a doctor with a more complex specialty. Nothing more. Why couldn't people understand that?* She burst into tears.

Looking again at the e-mail she realized once more that even if she manage to remove that hematoma and clean the surrounding nerves, it was doubtful whether Manos will manage to live. Whatever she was about to do, Manos couldn't fully recover. Even if he survived the surgery, he will never regain his powers, his strength, he will never awaken from the coma.

This was her medical opinion. She had never mistaken. Although this conclusion was so cruel, it was the truth. The surgery will give him just a few months of sleep without feeling any pain. Nothing more.

She remembered the first time she met Manos. His smile, his eyes, his kisses. The way he made love to her. After learning that she was pregnant Manos loved her even more. They married in a small chapel near his village. It was just the two of them and a friend from the University. When Alina was born their world became more beautiful, until...

Her father interrupted her thoughts. Once he saw her, he realized that his daughter was crying. He embraced her. Jennifer explained him the situation bursting into tears. Her father understood and when he spoke his voice was calm.

"Jennifer, look at me for a while," she lifted her eyes and looked at her father. "If I remember correctly neurosurgery is your big love," she nodded, "I also remember very well that Manos was and still is your other great love, judging by the fact that you were given up many opportunities to marry again. I think that panic is not good for you either as a neurosurgeon or as a woman. Do not subject yourself to the torture of what will happen if Manos' surgery goes wrong. Because, usually, when we surge one person, who is very close to us, the intensity is incomparably greater than in any other occasion. And, as you know very well, in such surgeries sentimentalism never fits in. Don't forget that, my dear." She wiped her eyes.

"So, my advice is to go to Greece and do the surgery as if Manos isn't the patient, but a complete stranger to you. And, please, think of something else. If you don't surge him and someone else do it, instead of you, and the operation doesn't go well," her father paused and looked Jennifer in the eyes, "then, believe me, my child, you would prefer to have done the surgery by yourself and take the full responsibility of it instead of having remorse for the rest of your life," his voice faltered a little, "just like me with your mother."

Jennifer understood what her father meant. "Dad, don't blame yourself for not surging mom. No one could save her. You know that. Cancer had spread to all over her body. It was a miracle that she lived for such a long time. Whoever made the surgery, mom would have the same fate."

Her father shook his head and then looked at her straight in the eyes, "You, however, have the chance to surge Manos and make him well, because I am sure that these magic hands," he said as he caught her hands and kissed them, "would do their miracle once more. On the other hand, if something goes wrong, then don't put the blame on you. Remember what I'm always telling you. We are just doctors, not God." Jennifer hugged him. She loved her father a lot. He always managed to calm her heart and her spirit.

"When do you leave for Greece?" He asked her before he left the room.

"I'm flying at 10:00 p.m. with Peter."

"So, have a nice flight my dear and good luck. Have faith in yourself," he said smiling and closed the door behind him.

Jennifer stared at him, as he left the room. The death of her mother had scathed him, mainly because he considered himself responsible for her death. Because he agreed to surge her mother another doctor although he was as good as him. Jennifer knew very well, as she had entered the surgery room during her mother's surgery, that whoever do the surgery there was no way to save her. The cancer was metastatic and the damages were irreversible.

This time, her father was right. Although Panagiotis is a very good surgeon, something could always go wrong. She took a deep breath. She was going to surge Manos and take full responsibility for his surgery, without thinking anything else. She would go to Greece surging him and as soon as Manos' condition stabilized she will leave Greece and Manos never knew the truth. Ever.

Thinking of Manos' brain she prepared her suitcase. She crossed her fingers. If everything goes well, as she wished to, she could stay in Greece until Manos gets out of the artificial coma and then she would return to Manhattan. Happy.

All the way to the airport her heart was about to break. Looking outside the window she felt a joy in her heart as she was going to see her daughter again. When she thought of seeing Manos in such a bad condition, her face hardened as she realized that she wasn't going on vacation. She flew to Greece in order to save the life of the only man she ever loved to.

She saw a photo of Manos with Alina taking last summer. She could admit that Manos was a handsome man with some gray hair in his temples making him even more irresistible. When the car arrived in front of the staircase of the private jet Jennifer went on resolutely. Peter waited for her at the top of the stairs. She greeted him. Jennifer sat in a seat and set her lap – top in order to see once more Manos' magnetic tomography.

IN ATHENS, MANOS' SITUATION progressed badly, so Apostolou had to find the best doctors from every specialty. All night he was preparing the surgery staff. The morning found him sleeping on the couch of his office. This was the most difficult night in Manos' life as he came very close to death. Doctors manage to stabilize his condition and Manos was out of danger. For how long? He didn't know.

Apostolou decided to give him heavier drugs for keeping him in deeper sedation. It was the only way to preserve Manos' vital organs so his body could rest and endure the long surgery. Panagiotis Eleftheriadis arrived at the hospital early in the morning.

Alina and Dimitris stayed all night long by Manos' side. During the evening Alina was in Dimitris' arms, in the uncomfortable couches outside the Intensive Care Unit. Dimitris looked Alina sleeping in his arms and enjoyed it.

Before Manos' accident, everything ran smoothly in my single life. I had my job, I didn't like commitments, and I had in my bed any woman I wanted at any time. Manos' accident messed up my whole life. Manos had managed once more to mess my life, Kalogerou thought, *and the thing is that I like this mess,* he saw Alina asleep in his arms. Apostolou approached him.

"Costas, how are things going?" Kalogerou asked, keeping his voice down, in order not to wake her up.

"Well, Manos had a difficult night, but having such an experiencing staff, I'm not afraid."

Panagiotis Eleftheriadis saw them talking. "Mr. Kalogerou, I would like to ask you when is Mrs. Johnson about to arrive?"

"She has landed. The car is waiting at the airport to bring Mrs. Johnson straight to the hospital." Panagiotis was ecstatic. "Mr. Eleftheriadis, how did you meet Mrs. Johnson?" Kalogerou asked.

"We made the same specialty in America. She is an astounding doctor. Mr. Kalogerou, if you meet her you will understand what I am talking about. She is the best doctor in the whole world. She is also a very sensitive human being. I remember once that she decided to surge a four – year – old child after having a surgery for hours and, although, she was exhausted she didn't hesitate to stay for another ten hours in the hospital. She never complained about it and she didn't take any money from the child's parents. The next day, she was the first one who went to see her patients. When you'll see her, you will understand what I'm talking about. Please, trust me. Only Mrs. Johnson could surge your friend with success. Only her," said Panagiotis and left them alone. Alina was still sleeping in Kalogerou's arms.

"Costas, what chances do we have?"

"If everything goes just as we planned, there is a very strong chance our friend become well and all this would be a very bad dream."

"If something goes wrong," Dimitris' voice broke.

Apostolou understood the anxiety of his friend and tried to give Dimitris a little more courage. "Dimitris, I'm going to tell you the truth. Manos' health is in a very critical condition. I'm not going to hide you that the night before I would almost lose him, that's why I gave him heavier drugs and immersing him in a heavier repression. But you know me. I like to be an optimistic person. Manos is a very healthy man despite his age. On the other hand, his age is a serious problem for his condition and for the surgery. Yes, he has a strong heart, and he can withstand the surgery although there are going to be many obstacles, for which we are also prepared. So, I think that, if he withstands the brain surgery, we could have hope." Dimitris listened thoughtfully.

Apostolou pitied him and said to him in order to ease his friend's mood. "Despite this, I believe that the surgery will go very well, and Manos will be healthy again. It will take some time of rehab, and then, my friend, I would like to see you how you're going to persuade him that you are the perfect guy for his precious daughter," said Apostolou showing Alina.

"Costas, I don't intend to persuade him. Manos knows me. I'm not perfect. Nobody is perfect. Even Manos."

"Are you going to tell him that?"

"Tell him what?"

"That he isn't perfect."

"No, are you crazy? The only thing that I'm going to tell him is that I love his daughter and I'm going to marry her. That's all." He clenched Alina in his arms as the tone of his voice sounded very serious.

"Well, that's love, my friend. Manos knows what is love and he isn't going to cause you any trouble. Yes," Apostolou murmured, "I think that he is aware of what love is, don't worry. Apart from that you're right, he knows you really well and that's good for you, isn't it?"

Dimitris didn't speak. He said everything with his gaze.

"I would like to ask you something, Dimitris. If Manos said no to you, and brings every single objection and obstacle he could imagine and doesn't let you be with his daughter, what are you going to do then?" Apostolou asked him in a serious tone.

Kalogerou hadn't thought about this possibility. He was sure that Manos wouldn't have any objection whatsoever. He didn't have the chance to answer him because Georgiou was in front of them pissed off.

"Mr. Kalogerou, I'm calling you to your cell phone all night yesterday. It is off, as usual." Dimitris pulled his cell phone out from his pocket and saw that he had no battery. Georgiou continued, "And from your office, they informed me that I would find you in the hospital. Is it something wrong with Mr. Alexiou?"

"Mr. Georgiou, everything is going pretty well. Soon Mr. Alexiou will be as good as new," said Apostolou with a wide smile as he was leaving.

Georgiou looked at Apostolou curiously. "Why are you so happy, doctor? Oh, please tell me that I can speak with Mr. Alexiou? I would like to ask him a few questions. It won't take long."

Dimitris was looking at him with a stare. Georgiou noticed the beautiful woman who was asleep in his arms. He understood that this woman was the same woman that Aris had seen on the street with Kalogerou. *His friend is between life and death and Kalogerou doesn't go anywhere without his chicks*, thought Georgiou. Kalogerou noticed that Georgiou looked Alina all the time.

Instead, Apostolou said with excitement. "Oh, Mr. Georgiou, I'm happy because in a few hours we will open Mr. Alexiou's head. Isn't it excited? " said Apostolou as he was leaving. Georgiou couldn't understand Apostolou. Opening a head is not something exciting from his point of view. Kalogerou noticed Georgiou reaction to Apostolou's words.

"So, your questions will have to wait," added Kalogerou in an ironic way. Georgiou wasn't affected, "and why were you looking for me?" Kalogerou asked him.

"Oh, yeah, right. I just wanted to inform you that we put all your employees of your factories under research. Well, everybody turned to be so clear as crystal. That's bad, very bad for our case. You understand it, don't you?" Kalogerou wasn't follow Georgiou. "As you can understand we don't have any suspect. But we don't give up," said Georgiou without trying to hide his impatience.

Kalogerou smiled at him. *Perfect, another crazy guy*, Kalogerou thought, seeing Georgiou full of happiness. "Mr. Georgiou, is good to hear that."

Georgiou was about to leave. "Mr. Kalogerou, I have one last question."

"I'm hearing," he answered while he was clutching Alina in his arms.

"Mr. Kalogerou, we all hope that this kind of surgery will save Mr. Alexiou's life. But could you, please, enlighten me on a subject?"

"What's that subject Mr. Georgiou?" Dimitris suspected the clarifications that Georgiou was asking for but he remained calm.

"If Mr. Alexiou dies, who is going to be the president of the factory?" The fact that Kalogerou didn't punch him was due to the fact that Alina was still sleeping in his arms.

"Not me, I will be the Vice President of the factory, even if Manos dies, if that is what you want to know," Kalogerou answered with an even more ironic style.

"Mr. Kalogerou, I know that I'm bothering you. And I won't apologize as you have to understand me. I'm only asking because you've told to me once that Mr. Alexiou has no children and I was wondering ..."

"Mr. Georgiou, stop wondering and find the person who did that to Manos. That is your job, I presume."

"You're right, but you didn't answer my question clearly ... yet."

"Mr. Georgiou, I didn't answer your question because I don't know the answer. As soon as I read the regulation of the factory, then I will inform you, don't worry."

The police officer wasn't pleased. He understood that Kalogerou wasn't in a mood of any discussion at that moment and he was sure that the beautiful woman in his arms was the reason.

"I wish everything goes well with Mr. Alexiou. Who is going to surge him?"

"A neurosurgeon from U.S.A." Kalogerou declined to give him any more details and hopefully get rid of the police officer. Georgiou decided to leave.

Sometimes this man is very annoying, thought Kalogerou.

Alina woke up and when she saw that she was sleeping in Kalogerou arms she stood up without saying anything to him. Dimitris informed her that her mother will arrive at any minute.

After Georgiou's leaving, Kalogerou noticed a young man wearing a jean and a black jacket sitting on the couch across them. The first time he saw him, Dimitris had the strange feeling that this man was there for them. But he wasn't sure if this man was there for keeping Alina alive or for killing her. That last thought made him shivering. After a while, Alina's mother entered the waiting room accompanied by Stelios. Alina fell into her arms.

"Oh, mom, how nice seeing you," she whispered and kissed her. Her mother kissed her, too. "Mom, I'd like to introduce you to Mr. Kalogerou, the Vice-President and Legal Counsel of the factory." Jennifer gave her hand to Kalogerou.

"Also I would like to introduce you to Mr. Apostolou," Alina said pointing to Apostolou who, at that time, was passing in front of them.

Alina's mother tended her hand on Costas Apostolou. "Mr. Apostolou, nice to meet you."

"Mrs. Johnson, the pleasure is all mine. I'm impressed because you speak Greek fluently and Manos is awaiting for you in the surgery room, like the rest of our staff."

Manos is waiting for her, not in the way he used to some years ago, thought Jennifer and a faint smile appeared on her face, "Mr. Apostolou, I'm ready to begin," she added with confidence.

Apostolou didn't need to hear that twice. They went to the surgery room informing her at the same time about Manos' difficult night in the Intensive Care.

Alina fell back heavily on the couch. Dimitris sat beside her. The strange man was still sitting opposite them reading a newspaper without paying any attention to them. *Perhaps, I was wrong,* thought Dimitris.

In the surgery room, Johnson was more than ready to keep Manos alive. She started the skull opening process. She avoided seeing Manos' face. That was her plan from the beginning. *Don't see his handsome face, his shapely mouth,* a voice was saying inside her. She detected the hematoma and made the incision in the scalp. She knew Manos very well. He was athletic and a very strong man. She also was aware that this surgery wasn't easy and it will last long. She knew that it was a great risk as Manos' body was weak enough.

She was requesting information on Manos' vital organs almost every few minutes. The Greek doctor team and the nursing staff that Apostolou had assembled were excellent. Their organizational skills and their cooperation were exemplary. Besides that, she realized that Manos had very good friends, like Apostolou and Kalogerou and that made her smile.

During the surgery, thousands of thoughts were passing in her mind. Jennifer remembered the day she met Manos. She was in Greece for a European medical conference. A day before the end of the conference, she decided to take a walk in Athens. Although it was late December the weather was sunny. She provided herself with a city map before she started her small adventure.

The hotel was in the center of Athens and from there she went by train to an area, just below the Acropolis, called "Monastiraki", where she found an open market with many beautiful things. It was the most magical part of the city. People from all over the world filled the streets.

Jennifer entered a group with a tour guide who seemed to know many things about ancient Athens. She followed them to the Museum of Acropolis learning a lot of things about ancient Greeks. She had the opportunity to admire the statutes and the other exhibits. She was amazed from the Parthenon's pediments. Then she followed them to Acropolis and she learned how ancient Greeks managed to build this magnificent monument.

After hours, Jennifer was tired and sat on a large rock. The sun warmed her skin. Enchanted by the beauty of Acropolis, she didn't realize that the time was passed until a guard informed her that the archeological area was about to close in a few minutes.

The evening breeze was pleasant. The city lights gave another glow in Athens disguising in a different city. She decided to return to the hotel on foot. Loitering everything around her she didn't notice the car and from one moment to another she was found herself lying on the street. She stood up and then she saw him.

A man was out of the car shouting and gesturing in that strange Greek way. She noticed that he was the most handsome man she had ever seen in her life. She couldn't understand Greek language so she was just looking at him all the time. She smiled at him several times without saying a word.

He was taller than her and his dark green eyes with those long black lashes made him look like a Greek god. His hair was black and thick and his mouth, although he yelled at her all the time without taking any breath, having the color of a cherry was made her wanting to kiss him.

When the man stopped shouting at her, she stammered an apology in English. The man held her by her arm observing her better. She was tall, tawny and blue-eyed. He realized that she wasn't Greek and started speaking in English. Jennifer still remembers their dialogue as if it was yesterday.

"I guess you didn't understand a word, didn't you?" The man smiled at her and his smile made him even more irresistible. The next thing she remembered was this man sitting on a chair next to a hospital bed.

He smiled again. "You fainted and I brought you to the hospital," he said as he was bent over her. She stared at him without being able to speak. He was so close to her. She could smell his perfume, she could see all the shades of green in his eyes. Instead of anything else she stammered once more an apology.

Then he introduced himself, "My name is Manos Alexiou. Can you tell me your name without apologizing again?" Jennifer smiled. She gave him her hand and said her name. That was it. She fell in love with this Greek man.

They stayed at the hospital talking all night long. In the morning, the doctor informed her that she could go home. Manos suggested to escort her to her hotel, instead of going to the hotel, they went to his home making love all day and all night for the next few days.

The conference ended and Jennifer stayed in Greece because of Manos although her parent's different opinion. Manos was studying economics. Jennifer had finished Medicine School and had taken her specialty. The only thing left was to find a job in a hospital. She decided to postpone that step for a while. Perhaps she was nuts but she was in love with Manos.

Manos was different from the other men she knew. Manos didn't know and didn't care if her father was the manager in the greatest hospital in Manhattan. The way he spoke, he moved, he made love to her made Jennifer deciding to stay with him.

It had a positive reaction for Manos who for three whole years in Economic School he never sat down for the semester exams, until he met Jennifer. The day he graduated she announced him that she was pregnant. He was the happiest man in the whole world. Manos proposed her to get marry and she accepted without thinking. They got married in a small chapel just outside his village.

They didn't face any financial problem as Mano's father was a wealthy man. He also had started a small dairy factory near the area they lived. It was an innovative factory for that time. So, they decided to return to his family village and lived there.

When Alina was born their happiness was taken off. At the same time, Manos' work in the factory was also succeeded. As long as Manos' father lived, Jennifer had the opportunity to live a happy life with her husband and her little daughter.

His father's death changed Manos. He was leaving early in the morning and returned home late at night exhausted. Jennifer was involved with the baby all the time. She fell alone in Manos' huge house. She was alone in that huge house.

She didn't know what to do, had nowhere to go and no friends. Mornings in the house were endless and when Manos came back from work he was always tired. Even to speak to her. She didn't want that kind of life. She was a neurosurgeon and she was stuck in a Greek mountain village with no future.

She tried to speak to Manos and every time Manos was aloof or aggressive. She stood that situation up for almost a year. When Alina was one-year-old she decided to go back to America. To her parents.

One evening, she tried to tell Manos about her decision. He didn't say anything to her. He didn't even argue with her. He just went to their bedroom and fell asleep. In the morning, he drunk his coffee and left the house by giving her a cold kiss. His behavior broke her heart as she realized that she would never see him again.

JENNIFER MADE THE INCISION in Manos' scalp by slow and constant movements. She proceeded carefully in order to remove the bone. The hematoma loomed before her eyes. As soon as Jennifer and Panagiotis saw it, they wondered how Manos had survived with this on his head.

Jennifer progressed methodically by removing it little by little and cleaning the surrounding area at the same time. One wrong movement and Manos would be dead. She couldn't bear the responsibility of his death. No, she came to Greece with a single purpose in her mind. Saving Manos' life, so Alina could have the opportunity to rejoice her father.

She remembered the day that Alina told her that she wanted to meet with her father. Jennifer didn't oppose to her decision. At first, she thought to inform him by phone. She changed her opinion when she remembered Manos' deep and warm voice. So, she decided to write a letter to him. She liked this idea. In that way, she could control her feelings.

Then she found out that writing a letter wasn't something easy. She threw the first one because her crying made it illegible. No one could read it. Even her.

The second one was too professional and cold. No way Manos will accept her proposal and see Alina. The third one was very emotional. She just threw away the fourth one without remembering why. She just didn't like it.

She got into her hands a photograph of Alina since she was a baby, then a toddler, then in elementary school, then in high school and, at the end, a photograph with Alina at the age of sixteen. Having all these photos in front of her eyes she wrote that his daughter wanted to know him and if he would accept her that could be great.

She also informed him that she had told Alina everything about her father from the first moment and if he agrees then Alina could come during the summer vacation when schools are closed. Also, she wrote that Alina could stay in Greece as long as she wanted.

On the other hand, she could understand his denial. She put all these photos in an envelope and sent it to Manos, who responded by letter to Alina, not to her. In his letter, Manos wrote that Alina could come to Greece whenever she wanted and she could stay as long as she wanted.

Jennifer was in Greece in order to surge Manos. When everything ends and the surgery goes well, as she was thinking, she would leave for America again, without Manos finds out the person who surged him. Apostolou and Kalogerou assured her that they would tell him that only Panagiotis Eleftheriadis surged him.

That was her only condition for coming and surging him.

Jennifer asked Panagiotis for help. From now on, their movements should be fully coordinated. As if they were one person.

Panagiotis took a deep breath. *If this guy lived after such a surgery,* he thought, *then Mr. Alexiou owed to both of them a lot and that had nothing to do with money.*

Chapter 9

The hours passed irritatingly slow in the waiting room. Agony was about to drive Alina crazy. She was staring her watch as if time will run faster. It had passed six hours from the time that her mom left her in order to surge her father. Six whole hours!

Okay, they wouldn't begin immediately and her mother had to be prepared for the surgery, but how long my God, sighed Alina. She had confidence in her mother, however, someone could come upstairs and inform her about something, anything. Alina stood up and paced up and down the hall. She couldn't bear in the waiting room for another minute. She needed to get some fresh air.

"Where are you going, Miss ...?" Kalogerou didn't finish his question, as he realized that the man, who was still sitting on the couch all this time, stood up when Alina rose.

"I'm going outside. If I sit here for another minute, I'm going to lose my mind," Alina answered with a squeaky voice and walked away with rapid steps.

"Wait. I'm coming with you." Kalogerou ran behind her.

As the cold air hit Alina in the face, she felt chilly. Dimitris was behind her. She rammed in his arms and burst into tears. Dimitris hugged her and trying to calm her. "Don't worry, I have a feeling that everything is going fine down there."

The suspicious man came down the stairs without noticing them speaking on his cell phone. Dimitris and Alina went to the cafeteria and ordered coffee. They drank their coffee in complete silence. Sitting in the cafeteria a woman approached Kalogerou.

"Mrs. Stefanidi, what are you doing here? Is everything all right at the factory?" Dimitris asked her with a worry in his voice.

"Mr. Kalogerou, don't worry. Everything is all right. How is Mr. Alexiou doing?"

"Doctors are still operating him. You could call me on the phone if you wanted to ask something like that. Is something that concerns you?"

Mrs. Stefanidi nodded her head and took Kalogerou a little farther away from his chick. She was aware that Kalogerou always has beautiful women on his side, but now she wanted to tell him about some factory issues and she didn't want this chick hears them.

"Mr. Kalogerou, I don't know how they found out that Mr. Alexiou undergoes a serious surgery on his head and from the morning the reporters phone us from several TV stations and newspapers asking about his condition, the name of the surgeon and all that stuff," Stefanidi faltered, "you wouldn't believe it, Mr. Fotiadis also called."

A blaze of anger hit Kalogerou. "What did you say to him?" asked her while he was looking Alina.

"Nothing. My answer to everybody was that it will be an official announcement by Factory's Press Office." Kalogerou lit a cigarette looking very skeptical.

"Mr. Kalogerou, may I suggest something?" Kalogerou nodded. "In my opinion, we should prepare an official announcement which will be released to the press as soon as possible. In this way, we could control every single information and, at the same time, we will reassure the investors, the employees and the consumers that everything is under control. That our factory is still working although its President is in a very serious condition. If we don't do this, then rumors will spread all over and I think that something like that it won't be in the interest of neither of Mr. Alexiou nor of the factory."

Dimitris thought that Stefanidi was right. Rumors are always a bad thing concerning the phone call from Fotiadis. "I agree with you. Prepare the announcement for the Press, I trust you," and without telling anything else he went to Alina. Mrs. Stefanidi looked at him and thought that this man would never change. Always he would run after a woman.

"How are you? Did you calm down a little?" Kalogerou hugged and kissed her on the mouth.

"I'm fine. Who was she?"

"The lady you saw is the Communication Manager of the factory Mrs. Stefanidi."

"Is everything alright at the factory?"

"Something came up, but everything is under control. Don't worry."

In the surgery room, things went well. Jennifer and Panagiotis made a determined effort to remove the hematoma and cleaned the area. Both they were happy and agreed that the last residues didn't cause any problem in brain function. Besides that, medicines will absorb it during the rehabilitation.

Jennifer was happy because Manos was doing well during this long surgery. His heart didn't create the slightest problem. Jennifer closed the dura and then she added the part of the bone that she had removed. Finally, she sewed the incision of Manos' skull. Manos was ready. Her hopes revived.

The next few days would be critical. She would stay in Greece in order to watch the progress of the patient after the surgery. As soon as Manos showed the first signs of improvement she would go back to America. Apostolou and Panagiotis promised that Manos will never find out who surged him.

This was the best for both of us, Jennifer thought, as she got out of the surgery room. She went with Apostolou to the waiting area to inform Alina and Dimitris. When Alina saw her mother she ran into her arms.

Her mother reassured her, "Everything went according to our plan. All his measurements are normal," she told them and Alina smiled. "We won't wake him. We'll have to wait ... this is the best for him ... you understand that, aren't you?" Alina nodded.

Apostolou looked at Kalogerou, "Mrs. Johnson did a fantastic job," and turning to Jennifer he said, "You must go to sleep. Manos is in good hands." Jennifer argued a little, but Apostolou didn't listen to her. "Dimitris, I think that the ladies must go and have a good sleep. Manos is much better."

Apostolou turned to Jennifer telling her, "If you want, you can come tomorrow morning, doing the morning shift in order to Panagiotis get a rest."

Jennifer agreed. "Okay Mr. Apostolou, till tomorrow then. Please, inform me of any change of his condition, would you?" Apostolou smiled as he understood that the best surgeon in the whole world had still strong feelings for his best friend.

"Mom, Mr. Apostolou is right. You need some rest, take a bath, eat something and get some sleep, please, you're almost 24 hours awake," Alina told her.

"You're right. I have booked a room in a nearby hotel so if something goes wrong I will be here in a minute."

Alina looked at her with anger. "You won't stay in a hotel. You will stay at dad's home. With me," she added.

Jennifer tried to resist, but Alina's fatigue was stronger and to berate Alina won't lead anywhere. So, Alina and Mrs. Johnson went to the villa with Stelios and Kalogerou followed them with his own car.

It was then when Kalogerou noticed that a motorbike followed Stelios's car and another one, ridden by the man who was sitting all this time in the hospital's waiting room, followed his car. Kalogerou startled. *How many assassins would be after us?* Kalogerou murmured with irony.

At the villa, Maria waited for all of them. Alina went with her mom to show her room, as long as Stelios was unloading Jennifer's suitcases. Alina settled her mother to sleep in her father's bedroom.

Chapter 10

Aris was informing Mr. Georgiou quite often about the strange reactions of the chick. "She was more anxious than Mr. Kalogerou and I don't understand why."

Neither Georgiou couldn't understand why Kalogerou's chick was so anxious about the health of Alexiou. Why? He had drawn a big question mark on a piece of paper in front of him. What could be the reason? Asked once more to himself.

"Mr. Georgiou, I think," Aris continued, "that maybe Alexiou had this chick in a first place, sir."

The chief police officer was thinking of all possibilities. "Why do you say that?"

"Only this explains her reaction, sir."

"Maybe. The thing is that, after Alexiou's accident, this chick is with Kalogerou because when I went to the hospital to speak with him she was sleeping in his arms all the time and Kalogerou seemed to enjoy it, which means that their relationship isn't platonic. However, that doesn't answer why she is so much worried about Manos Alexiou. Aris, something is missing here and I don't know what it is. Let me ask you something else?"

"Yes sir," Aris replied.

"If this chick is with Kalogerou, who is also, at least, twenty years younger than Alexiou, why is she worried about Alexiou so much? It doesn't make any sense."

"I don't understand your reasoning, sir?"

"What I want to say is that if this chick is with Kalogerou, I guess she prefers Alexiou dead, in order to stay with Kalogerou."

"So, sir, you mean that Kalogerou and this chick are responsibly for Alexiou's accident?" Aris replied scratching his head.

"Perhaps." Mr. Georgiou said although it wasn't sure enough about this thought of his.

"So, what do you want me to do, sir?"

"Watch them both closely," Georgiou said to Aris.

THE NEXT MORNING, WHEN Dimitris opened his eyes, the sun had begun to rise. He walked into the bathroom and took a shower. He shaved and dressed up. He looked at his watch as he went down the stairs. *Strange*, he thought, *Maria doesn't come so early in the morning.*

Someone was in the kitchen. Perhaps Alina and a huge smile showed up to his mouth. When he opened the kitchen door he saw Jennifer Johnson, who smiled warmly at him.

"Mr. Kalogerou, good morning. I have made coffee, orange juice, and the croissants would be ready in just three minutes. You want some coffee, don't you?" Dimitris accepted the offer and she put a cup of coffee in front of him. When he drank the first sip, Jennifer starts speaking. "From what I see, you prefer to get up early in the morning, unlike my daughter."

He nodded and drunk another sip of his coffee. "Did you speak with Apostolou? How is Manos?"

Jennifer noticed the anxiety in his voice. "Mr. Kalogerou, I would like to inform you that I did what was humanly possible during this surgery which was the most difficult one in my whole career. I'm a doctor, not a God. Manos will be in a heavy repression for several days, perhaps weeks in order to his body could enable the necessary time to recover. I thank God that Manos is still alive after such an accident and such a surgery."

"So, you cannot make any prediction?"

"What do you mean by that?"

"I mean, if there is a chance for Manos to recover, if Manos could ever recover and, after his recovering, if he could ever have the normal life he used to, that's what I mean."

Jennifer smiled. "Oh, Mr. Kalogerou, you go too far. It's too early to even think something like that. The only thing that matters is Manos couldn't feel anything. His injuries are still too heavy. The pain is unbearable. Indeed, his injuries and pain are so unbearable that they can cause irreversible shock to his body if you understand what I mean." Dimitris understood her very well. Jennifer continued in that cruel way. "Don't expect him to recover soon. Manos will be heavily sedated for a long time and I will be very happy if there would be no complications."

Doctors are always speaking about complications. "What kind of complications?" he asked.

"There are many kinds of complications to be aware of," Jennifer continued without showing any mercy to him. "So, if there are no complications after a very long time and, when his wounds are healed, we could pull him out of the artificial heavy repression very slowly. Only when Manos wake up and regain his strength, we will be able to assess more accurately how extensive the brain damage could be." Alina's mother didn't pity him while she informed him about Manos' recovering.

"What do you mean by that?"

"I mean that although there is always the possibility of Manos to recover fully, even if he manages to overcome his heavy injury, there is also a very strong possibility of becoming disabled. There is also the chance to stay in a coma, and die without ever wake up again." Kalogerou's eyes darkened. Jennifer realized that Kalogerou was anxious about this conversation and decided to calm him down. "Mr. Kalogerou, as I told you before, it's too early for all that. One step at a time. That's my advice."

FROM THAT DAY, ALINA'S mother always returned home at dawn and went straight to bed. Manos' health didn't show any development. Jennifer considered that as a good sign. Despite the fact that Manos was in bed sleeping, he hadn't lost his handsomeness and his 'qualifications' as the night – shift nurse informed her, making her job more difficult than it was. She was always prepared for the possibility that Manos perhaps had an affair, but no woman showed up during these days. She couldn't resist and not caressing his hand. A tear showed up in her eyes. This touch brings to her a lot of memories. She adored his long fingers, his masculine hands. His body was in a very good condition.

Jennifer reminded herself that she was there as Manos' doctor and nothing more and pulled her hand from his. Panayiotis came for his shift and saved her from the torment of her memories.

If she was staying next to Manos a little longer seeing his shapely lips and caressing his hand, she could give him a gentle kiss on his mouth. She was dying to feel the taste of his lips and that was unprofessional. When Panayiotis say a good morning to her, Jennifer ran away without speaking to him.

GEORGIOU USED TO GET up early on Sundays to enjoy his coffee. He would like to enjoy also the quietness of the house since the children had grown up and had their own families. About twelve o' clock his wife brought him a snack with a glass of ouzo, sitting next to him drinking her own cup of coffee sand making company to him.

"How is Alexiou going?" asked Mrs. Georgiou her husband with genuine interest. From the first moment, she was watching all the reports and developments on Alexiou's injury through the newspapers and TV news.

Georgiou drank a sip of his ouzo. "I don't like the fact that Alexiou isn't going to recover fast. Also, there is another thing that worries me." His wife looked at him curiously. Never before her husband had worried about something in a case. He knew Mr. Georgiou very well and he always knew who the guilty was from the very beginning.

"So, I presume that the lawyer isn't a suspect anymore?"

Georgiou nodded negatively. "No, the lawyer is no longer a suspect and searching a list of his employers I couldn't find anything. Only two or three of them have some unpaid traffic police calls. That's all. Nothing serious. Only for one person, I cannot find anything."

Mrs. Georgiou looked back at him curious. "Is that so? I find it hard to believe that."

Mr. Georgiou didn't notice the irony in his wife's words and continued. "There is a woman, aged 26-28, who appeared with Kalogerou, and all this time was in the hospital worries about Alexiou's surgery. As a matter of fact, Aris ..."

"Oh, how is Aris?" Mrs. Georgiou asked him. Mr. Georgiou glared at his wife and continued as if nothing or nobody had interrupted him.

"Aris told me that this lady was so anxious with Alexiou's bad condition that she was crying all the time. She was expecting the neurosurgeon with impatience. Also, the other one that Aris and Themis told me was ...," Mrs. Georgiou was about to interrupt him asking how was Themis, although, Mr. Georgiou's glare stopped her, "that this chick is Kalogerou's chick."

"So, I don't see where your problem is?"

"My problem is that according to her reactions Aris and Themis thought that this chick was Alexiou's chick first and after the accident, Kalogerou offered to console her, but this doesn't explain the fact that her reactions were too excessive for a chick."

"I'm sorry. I'm not following you."

Mr. Georgiou cursed a bit and tried to explain to his wife his thought. "What I'm trying to say is that if this woman was Alexiou's chick in a first place and now is Kalogerou's, why she is so much worried about Alexiou, as she could prefer to stay with Kalogerou. How can I explain that to you further?"

"In your own words ..." Mrs. Georgiou said.

"If I was a woman like her I would prefer to stay with Kalogerou, as he is as rich as Alexiou but much younger."

"... and more handsome," added his wife while drinking her coffee, "according to the magazines."

Georgiou looked reproachful his wife, who didn't say a word. "Also another dark sign. If she was Alexiou's chick it would be fine to stay at Alexiou's home. On the other hand, if she is Kalogerou's chick it will be fine to stay at Kalogerou's home. But they are staying both at Alexiou's home. How could you explain that?"

"So, you're saying that Kalogerou and his chick are staying at Alexiou's home?" Mrs. Georgiou looked at him trying to think a reason.

Mr. Georgiou shook his head condescendingly. "Isn't it weird? And another question is why this beautiful girl was in the first place with Alexiou. Alexiou is close to sixty."

Mrs. Georgiou shook her head. "These chicks don't go with young men if you understand what I mean!" She winked. "What's bothering me is that when Kalogerou has a new chick there is always a photo of him in a magazine, in every single magazine. I haven't seen a photo of him with or without a woman for almost three months."

"Alexiou is in the hospital for almost three months when this woman showed up." Mr. Georgiou told to his wife about the incident when Kalogerou dragged her from the shops into his office.

"What do you think about Kalogerou's reaction?" he asked his wife.

"As if Kalogerou feared of something, I suppose," she said reluctantly.

"According to police, this movement of Kalogerou was interpreted as a protective, rather than anything else. But why? Why Kalogerou wants to protect Alexiou's ex-chick?"

"I suppose that only Kalogerou knows the reason," Mrs. Georgiou added, "and he didn't tell you for some other reason you don't know and that annoys you, isn't it?"

That it was something very annoying for Mr. Georgiou as making his research more difficult than it was and Mrs. Georgiou knew that. Mrs. Georgiou continued shrugging her shoulders, "Somehow I know that this girl is very important to Alexiou. Do you have any photo of this woman?" Mrs. Georgiou asked his husband.

Mr. Georgiou pulled out his cell phone from his pocket and found the photo that Aris had sent him a few days ago. "Here it is!"

Mrs. Georgiou glanced at the screen of the mobile phone and she grinned as the girl in the picture looked like Alexiou. Last summer a reporter had interviewed him and the magazine had some photos of him in his factory in Athens. Since then she had imprinted in her mind that Alexiou was a very handsome man despite his age and a single one. What she remembered most was his eyes. His big green eyes with long black lashes. Such green eyes she hadn't seen in her life before. Just like the eyes of the young lady in the photo.

Mrs. Georgiou gave the mobile phone back to her husband. "Well," she said, "I don't know if this girl is Kalogerou's chick, but she is Alexiou's daughter. Look at her eyes. She has her father's eyes. I am a hundredth percent sure that she is Alexiou's daughter."

Mr. Georgiou looked dumbfounded. "I don't think so because you see, Kalogerou said that Alexiou is not married. Never was married. How he could have a child?"

Mrs. Georgiou smothered a giggle. "Through the regular and most common way, I presume. In our days, it isn't obliged to someone to get married in order to have children, although according to her age, Alexiou had to get married to this girl's mother."

Georgiou couldn't recover from the surprise. "But I asked Kalogerou several times and he told me that Alexiou has no children. He refused it all the time made himself very believable."

"So you know that great lawyers say great lies, in a very believable way, big deal," she said picking up the things from the table.

Mr. Georgiou stood up pissed off and walked out of the house. On his way to the Police Headquarters, he called Themis in order to meet him. He was about to send him to Alexiou's hometown. It was something there that need to be searched. In his office, Georgiou brought to his mind the reports of his men about Kalogerou's movements understanding very well that Kalogerou was protected Alexiou's daughter.

He also brought to his mind the safety of Alexiou's home. The security of the villa was beyond imagination. Now everything was in its place.

Another question came up to Georgiou's mind. Why Kalogerou didn't tell him anything about the daughter. *Because he didn't trust me, that's why*, he murmured. Georgiou got up from his desk pacing up and down to his bureau.

No, it cannot be that. Kalogerou didn't say anything to anybody in order to protect her from the killer. The puzzle was completed, although the case became even more complicated. Because till when could Kalogerou keep secret the identity of Alexiou's daughter?

Georgiou called Aris, who was at the hospital. "Aris, Georgiou is speaking, how are things going there?"

"Everything is under control, sir. They are sitting in the waiting room. Kalogerou is sitting near to his chick all the time. Also, the chauffeur is here. He is so huge, sir. They both give me the impression that these men are guarding the chick."

"From today, Aris, you are going to guard the chick, too."

"Is something wrong with the chick, sir?"

"Everything is wrong with her, Aris, and for your information, this chick is the daughter of Alexiou!" Aris didn't say a word and Georgiou continued. "So, Aris, you must be careful. Themis will be absent for a couple of days, which means that you're on your own. You go where she goes. Do you understand me?"

"Yes, sir."

"Did you learn where does the surgeon stay?"

"Yes, sir. At Alexiou's house."

"No way," Mr. Georgiou exclaimed. Then an idea, a crazy one, passed his mind. All he needed to confirm his thought was a photograph of the neurosurgeon. "Aris, take a picture of the neurosurgeon and send it to my mobile phone."

"I have a photo of her, sir. I'll send it to you right away, sir."

Georgiou left his phone on his desk. In two minutes he heard a sound. When Georgiou saw the picture he realized that the surgeon except the fact that she was a famous surgeon she also must be the mother of Alexiou's daughter. If his instinct was right, Themis would find soon enough the marriage certificate of Mr. Alexiou.

Georgiou was anxious. He ought to meet with Kalogerou the sooner the better, and ask him how many people knew about Alexiou's daughter. This time, he won't accept any lies. He wanted the truth. The whole truth. One thing was certain. The empire of Alexiou could easily be continued due to his daughter. His job was to find the person who killed Alexiou. Georgiou called Kalogerou from his mobile phone.

"Hello, Mr. Georgiou. How are you? Do we have any news?"

The tone of Georgiou's voice was calm. "Mr. Kalogerou, nice hearing you. Yes, something came up and I would like to discuss it with you. Now. Where and when can we meet?"

"In half an hour I'll be at Alexiou's house. We can talk there if you don't mind."

That was perfect. Georgiou thought as he could meet Alexiou's daughter. "Very well, Mr. Kalogerou, I'm on my way," and he hung up the phone.

From the first time after the accident, Georgiou had checked Alexiou's past. He found out that Alexiou had started with a small milk-unit somewhere in his hometown, not far away from Ioannina and now had three huge factories throughout Greece. Alexiou's factories also had a lot of exportations.

He had found out that Alexiou was the most loyalist industrialist of Greece. All his financial movements during the last thirty years have been according to Greek law and comply with all Greek labor laws. According to Tax Office Alexiou had no debts. He also paid his employees on time as his suppliers, too. Alexiou was the perfect boss. Also, his company was awarded twice during the last three years as the best company in Europe. It was awarded for the best working environment for its employees.

Georgiou had also found out that many years ago there was a scandal involving Alexiou and Fotiadis. Some plans about new dairy products were found in Fotiadis's office and although everyone would expect that Alexiou will turn against Fotiadis, Alexiou didn't do anything, thanks to the lawyers.

From that day, there is a large hostility between them. He even thought to arrest Fotiadis, the other 'milk – guy', but thanks to lawyers like Kalogerou, Fotiadis will be out of prison before he could even interrogate him. That's why he doesn't like lawyers, in general. Especially, lawyers like Kalogerou. For Georgiou, all lawyers are always annoying.

Chapter 11

Georgiou arrived at Alexiou's house in thirty minutes. Kalogerou was there waiting for him. Outside the house, Georgiou saw Aris sitting on his bike. However, he didn't see the chauffeur. *The security of the house was excessive, just to guard any chick,* Georgiou noticed. His wife was right. The girl that Aris saw the other day was the daughter of Alexiou. As he entered the house, he looked everywhere in order to find her. He saw her in the kitchen.

"Mr. Kalogerou, your girlfriend is a very beautiful woman," Georgiou said pointing the woman sitting on the kitchen bench.

Kalogerou agreed. "Mr. Georgiou, how are you? Yes, she is very beautiful and she isn't my girlfriend. So, is something you want to tell me?" Georgiou realized the grief of Kalogerou as he saw the woman in the kitchen. "And please come to the office so we can talk in private." They came into the office and Georgiou sat on the couch. Kalogerou sat on the chair behind the desk.

"What's her name?"

"Mr. Georgiou, I don't think that you came all the way to Kifissia just to ask me about her name? She is just a chick. Who cares?" He pulled his cigarettes out from his pocket and lit one.

"Well, Mr. Kalogerou, that's weird because you see the young lady in the kitchen is my news as I found out that she is Alexiou's secret daughter. Or am I wrong?" Georgiou's eyes were darker. He sounded dead serious.

Kalogerou didn't lose his temper. "How did you find out about her?" His voice was icy.

"I'm a police officer. I have my sources," Georgiou continued without any politeness. "Do you realize that you put her life at a great risk? The killer is still out there. Free."

"Mr. Georgiou, I think that you make a very big mistake. I'm acutely aware of the difficulties we face, so I have taken every measure in order not to endanger her life, both by increasing the security of the villa and to be near to her either me or Stelios, you know, our chauffeur. If you add your own men," Georgiou smiled, "Miss Alexiou is the most protected person, from my point of view." Kalogerou completed his phrase.

"I see that you take notice of my men. That's good but Mr. Kalogerou you must admit that we are dealing with a killer here who won't hesitate to hurt Alexiou's daughter. Could you tell me how many people know about her?"

"Only the chauffeur and Maria, the housekeeper. They know Alina from her teenage and they never talk or speak about her to anyone. They are working for Manos for over thirty years. They are like family not only to Alina but to me, too. I even remember them when I was a child. They kept her existence secret even from me all these years. Mr. Georgiou, I suggest that you should look at in another place to find Mano's murderer."

"What about the employees at the factory? Did anybody somehow know about her?"

"No one."

"Not even Mr. Alexiou's executive secretary?"

"Not even Emily. Manos wasn't that kind of man sleeping with his secretary or telling to his associates that he had a daughter in America."

"So, how many people know about her?"

"I told you, no one. Besides that, Miss Alexiou refuses to go to the factory. She is a writer, you know. Stelios goes to the factory every day and brings me all the papers. I handled all the paperwork by the fax behind me, just not to make a mistake and someone discovered her. You see, that was the only condition by her mother, who didn't want to see her daughter's photo in all over the gossip magazines and newspapers. Mr. Alexiou accepted that condition and kept it that way all these years. As you see, we are all working for them to keep their secret." Kalogerou extinguished his cigarette.

At that moment Alina entered the office holding some papers in her hands when she noticed that Kalogerou was not alone.

"Oh, Mr. Kalogerou, I'm sorry, I didn't know that you had an appointment. Stelios brought these papers for you."

Dimitris took the papers from her hands and introduced her to Mr. Georgiou. "Miss Alexiou, how do you do?"

Alina looked at Kalogerou with bulging eyes. Georgiou noticed her reaction. "Miss Alexiou, you have nothing to afraid of me."

"Whom do I have to afraid of?" Alina asked Georgiou, looking at Kalogerou at the same time.

Georgiou looked Kalogerou, who adversely nodded his head in a negative way meaning that he didn't say anything to Alina about the murder attempt against her father. Georgiou took the responsibility to explain everything to Miss Alexiou. When the police officer finished his narration, she turned to Kalogerou.

"Mr. Kalogerou, did you know about this?" Alina asked Kalogerou almost breathless.

Kalogerou was standing before the desk. "From the very first moment, Miss Alexiou."

Her eyes opened wide. "And why you didn't say anything to me?" Dimitris didn't speak. Her eyes gouged sparks by lust. Alina stepped closer to Dimitris and kissed him on the mouth in a way that she had never kissed any man before.

AFTER LEAVING ALEXIOU'S house, Georgiou went straight to the Police Headquarters. Themis' fax confirmed his thoughts. Alexiou was married to an American woman, whose traces were lost for almost thirty years now. So, the whole family is united in Greece.

That's a very strange coincidence and, as a police officer, he hated coincidences. Georgiou was happy with the developments, although the existence of the daughter created an additional stress to him.

Chapter 12

Several weeks have passed after the surgery without a dramatic improvement of Alexiou's health. Kalogerou was spoken to Apostolou to the phone many times during the day. In his last calls, Apostolou sounded worried. It wasn't the first time that Manos hassled of an infection. Infections were normal in his condition and every time doctors could exceed them.

Only this time Apostolou's voice was somewhat different. "Dimitris, I would like to inform you that Mrs. Johnson is going to stay at the hospital all night long. You don't have to worry about anything. I will be also with her."

Dimitris stood up from his chair, looking outside the office window. "Costas, do you think that it would be better for us to come over there in case of..."

"No, Dimitris, at this time we need to be focused on Manos only. There is no need to put Alina's life in danger. Please, stay home and I will keep you informed of everything."

As expected, the body of Manos after four months in a coma and after several very serious infections and the major brain surgery was tired enough. Manos Alexiou died a few days later.

ALINA COULDN'T BELIEVE that her father had died, even when they put him in the grave. She was a wreck. Seeing her in this mess Kalogerou was sinking in grief, too.

The death of Manos was tough for everybody, even for Dimitris. It was as if he lost his father for the second time. It was not only Manos' death who had to overcome with. After Manos' funeral, all media refers to the only daughter and sole heir of Manos Alexiou: Alina Alexiou. This was something beyond his strength. Kalogerou won't bear the fact that the woman of his life was in such great danger.

Apart from the killer Kalogerou had to concentrate also to Alina who was locked in her room crying all the time. Maria tried to make her eat, Alina refused to eat anything. Maria fed her a few bites in the mouth and that's all. Kalogerou also tried to persuade her to eat, but Alina was lost in her memories. After her father's funeral, she was always holding an album full of photos and every time she saw her father smiling she was crying.

For how long? Kalogerou thought. *Then what? What can he do to protect her? Because he was sure that Manos' killer will chase Alina. And what about the factory? After the funeral, he just couldn't go to the factory. Everything there was full of his best friend's presence. As for Alina? Who could dare to tell her to go to the factory? In such bad psychological condition? No way,* he thought. *And Jennifer Johnson vanished after Manos' funeral. She left for America the same night. She couldn't stay another moment in Greece. The whole family fell apart after Manos' death.*

"Why? Why? Why?" monolog Dimitris, as he sat on the chair behind Manos' desk without noticing that Alina was sitting on the couch silent, lost in her world. As soon as he saw her his heart deeply sighed. He got up and went closer to her.

"Miss Alexiou, I'm sorry, I didn't see you came in. How are you?" Dimitris kneeled before her. Alina awakened as if she was in a dream. In a bad dream. Her eyes were red from crying. She was crying for so many days that the green of her eyes had been lost.

Alina looked at him deep in his eyes. "Mr. Kalogerou," she stops talking and looked at him. How much she hated the fact that

Kalogerou was right from the very first moment in the plane. Ten thousand families depended on her. She couldn't be thrown out all these families leaving them without a job. Her father couldn't ever forgive her if something like that would happen. Kalogerou was holding her hands, "...how are things in the factory?"

Dimitris looked astonished when he heard her. "Miss Alexiou, I don't think that the factory must be your concern at the moment. Your father is dead and you aren't in a very good condition. So please forget the factory for the time being."

Alina stopped him by putting her hand to his lips. Kalogerou sensed her smooth warm fingers to his lips and his heart had broken into pieces. Manos was dead and his beautiful daughter was still in great danger.

"Mr. Kalogerou," she said, "I would like to go to the factory tomorrow otherwise if I sit another day in the house doing nothing I will be crazy."

"Miss Alexiou, you know very well that if you want to get out of the house we should inform Mr. Georgiou first."

"So, inform him." Her voice sounded a bit more decisive.

Dimitris wasn't ready to give it up. He didn't want to put her in danger. He tried to persuade her. "You know that your father's killer hasn't been arrested yet, right?"

Alina nodded it. "Yes, I know that, but if I stay here in the house another day," she cried, "and I have to admit that you were right..."

"What are you talking about?"

"About the factory. That ten thousand families working at the factory, they cannot be thrown away. You made it so clear to me from the first moment of our meeting in my plane. Do you remember?"

He remembered everything since the day she invaded in his well-organized single life. "I remember, but now the conditions have changed. I agree with Georgiou. It's too dangerous for you to go to the factory. I'm sorry I can't do that ... to you or to me. You can ask me anything else you want but not this."

Alina got up from the couch. Her eyes became alive. So did her voice. "Mr. Kalogerou, perhaps I wasn't clear enough."

Yes, her voice was steadier now than it was a few moments ago.

"Please, contact with Mr. Georgiou or anyone else you need to. I don't care. The only thing I want is to go to the factory tomorrow morning. I won't tolerate any further delay." Alina stood beside Kalogerou with clenched fists.

He turned and looked at her. Kalogerou got up from his chair and grabbed her by the arms. "You know that there is a man out there who killed your father and, perhaps, he wants to kill you, too?" He said through clenched teeth. She felt his breath hot in her ear. His eyes were dark blue like the sky during a heavy storm.

Alina didn't scare. With a steady voice, she announced her decision once more. "Tomorrow morning I will go to the factory with or without you. That's my final decision."

Kalogerou pushed her away from him. He turned his back and said with a cold voice. "I'm not sure for tomorrow. I have to contact with Georgiou first."

"That's fine with me. And remove Emily from her position. I don't like her ... she would remind me of my father. Also, prepare all the necessary paperwork in order to function the factory without problems. You are the Legal Counsel of the factory I cannot remember everything," she cried and left the room without saying another word.

Even though he desired this woman so much she will never stop to unnerve him. Never! And he couldn't let Alina go to the factory just like that. She knows how to drive him crazy. He called Georgiou, who after listening to the requirements of Miss Alexiou he beat his hand on his desk. "Mr. Kalogerou, I'm on my way," he said in madness and forcefully hung up the telephone.

GEORGIOU WAS PACING up and down in his office after hearing that Alina wanted to go to the factory. When he went to the villa he was muttering all the time. "Women, women, women. You must always do whatever they want, no matter how crazy it is." After two days Georgiou gave his permission to her in order to go to the factory. That morning the whole house was filled with policemen.

The first day of Alina in the factory created great anxiety not only to Kalogerou but also to Georgiou. Apart from that, Kalogerou had to face Maria's stress.

"Dimitris, be careful," said Maria that morning, "be careful of our girl, because, otherwise, don't even think to come back home. It is already difficult to me to realize that Manos is dead, I couldn't bear that Alina could also ... she's like my daughter, do you understand me?" Her voice was squeaky.

"Yes, I understand," he answered her back with nerves in bright style and he left the kitchen like he was chased.

Alina got furious when she saw all these people waiting for her. She went down the stairs and when she saw Kalogerou coming out of the kitchen she screamed, "Mr. Kalogerou, in my office, now." Dimitris followed her to the office. "Could you please tell me what all these people are doing in my house?" she said as she entered the office. Her eyes gouged flames.

She is so beautiful wearing these black silk trousers and the same jacket with a small top inside it, Dimitris thought. *Oh, concentrate* Dimitris said to himself and tried to calm down. Maria had unnerved him as if he wanted to put his future wife's life in danger.

"Georgiou asked for it and I agree with him. If you want to go to the factory, this is the only way to go," he said curtly.

Alina didn't believe him. "I want to speak with Georgiou. Find him."

Not needed. The door office was open and Georgiou was there. He walked into the office proudly. "Miss Alexiou, is there any problem?"

"What do you think?" She said pointing her arm around the house where policemen walking up and down.

Georgiou wasn't shocked by the hostility of her voice. It wasn't the first time that he faced such a situation. He was used to such bad reactions. Georgiou approached her. "Miss Alexiou, I'm going to tell you that once and for all. If you want to go to the factory or anywhere else outside your home this is the only way. Take it or leave it! Unless you want to abut dead like your father. That's fine with me."

Alina looked at him and realized that she would hate that police officer a lot. No one had ever spoken to her like that in her life. "Very well gentlemen," Alina said straightening her jacket. "Since you two have decided to make my life more difficult than it is that's fine. We are leaving in ten minutes." She left the office and headed for the kitchen.

Georgiou looked at Kalogerou with a smug smile. This young lady wouldn't be the slightest problem for them. He hit Kalogerou at his shoulder friendly. "My friend, be careful, you are so in love with her. That's a very bad thing my friend, very bad and for God's sake, you are such a famous lawyer."

Kalogerou looked at him, "I think you are right," he said after some minutes. Then he prepared his briefcase and they all left.

AT THE FACTORY, EVERYONE has expected Mr. Alexiou's daughter with impatience. Although Manos knew all employees by their first names, no one at the factory seemed to know that their boss was married once and had a daughter. Everyone talked about this and how they could cooperate with a spoiled daughter.

Once their car entered the factory accompanied by a police motorbike and a police car, most employees had gathered at the windows trying to see their new boss. Everyone knew that Mr. Alexiou was murdered, so no one was surprised with the great security which surrounded the only daughter of the 'great' Manos Alexiou. Also, the fact that their new boss is a woman was something new to them. Some of them didn't find that a good idea.

Alina Alexiou with Dimitris Kalogerou went straight to Manos' office. Before exiting the elevator that led to her father's office, her heart tightened. He turned to Kalogerou. "I hope that you put Emily to another position." Dimitris didn't have the chance to reply as the elevator doors opened and all the departments' managers were at the lobby in order to meet her.

Kalogerou accompanied Alina straight to her father's office. When they get to the office she was furious. "Can you tell me which one of them is Emily?" She asked with a trembling voice.

Dimitris raised his eyes from the papers on the desk and looked at her. "Well, I can't understand you." Kalogerou stood in front of her trying to calm her down. "You're asking me to putt Emily to another position when you don't even know who she is or how she looks like. I think that you are crazy."

She didn't like the tone of his voice. "I don't care for your opinion. I just don't like her. That's all. I don't want her near me. Ok?"

Kalogerou decided to follow Georgiou's advice. He caught her by her waist and pulled her close to him. Alina didn't resist to that movement. They were so close and she made no move to escape from him, as she used to do. "Emily stays! There is no reason to be afraid of her or of anyone else at the factory. Mr. Georgiou made a thoroughly research for everyone in the factory." He kissed her.

Alina didn't make any move to elude him. Instead of that, Kalogerou felt that she waited for his lips. He also had the impression that she responded to his kiss a little. He felt his heart pounding. A flame flared inside him. A smoldering flame that, all this time, was hidden. Neither the place nor the time was right for such thoughts or such acts. He moved away from her. He needed fresh air.

"Let's go. I want to recommend you to the company's executives, and then I'll make you a tour of the factory." Alina nodded. She also needed fresh air after his kiss.

After the necessary recommendations with everyone of the staff, they came out. Kalogerou showed her all of the factory areas. Alina watched him talking to the employees by greeting everyone in person. He knew them all by their first names. After an hour, Alina caught her head. Dimitris turned and looked at her worried, "Are you ok?"

"I don't think so. I hear children's voices instead of the machines."

Dimitris smiled, "Come with me, I want to show you something," he said and grabbed her hand. His hand was much bigger than hers and warmer. Her hand was cold. So cold.

"Are you cold?" He asked her as he clenched her hand into his. Before she could answer, Alina was standing in front of the most beautiful view. A nursery school. Alina stopped walking. Dimitris stood beside her. "This kindergarten almost exists for ten years now," he told her and pulled her into the building.

Inside, the kindergarten was even more beautiful. All the walls were painted in bright colors showing small children playing and having fun. Kids were running everywhere yelling and screaming. The manager of the kindergarten went out of her office, as soon as she saw Kalogerou. She understood that the woman next to him must be Mr. Alexiou's daughter. Kalogerou made all the necessary recommendations while Alina was looking around amazed. For the first time, after her father's funeral, Alina smiled. She looked at him speechless.

"Miss Alexiou, could you please follow me." The manager showed Alina around the kindergarten. They opened a door and a smell of baby powder hit their noses. A woman was holding a baby in her arms. The babies were so small and so cute. One of the women there gave to Alina a baby to hold it. At the beginning, Alina looked scared, but when the little baby smiled at her, Alina smiled, too. She saw their small beds, their changing tables, and their baths. The most important thing was that she saw love in those women's eyes.

After the nursery room, they went into another room. Alina heard children's voices singing. Once the door opened all the boys ran over to Dimitris. That was something new for her. She thought that Mr. Kalogerou didn't like children. It was the first time that Alina saw the unbearable Mr. Kalogerou surrounded by kids and enjoying it. *What a surprise,* thought Alina.

A little boy came close to Alina, "You're very beautiful. Do you want to marry me?" Dimitris cleared his throat and the boy just disappeared.

Alina laughed a lot. "Mr. Kalogerou, as I see, you are the best example for all the boys here," she said to him.

Kalogerou shrugged his shoulders. "Miss Alexiou, I'm trying to do my best."

Leaving from kindergarten, Alina's mood was much better. *At least, she forgot Emily,* thought Dimitris.

Back to the office, Alina gave him the last paper signed. "Mr. Kalogerou, I also want to see the other factories. As soon as possible."

Kalogerou looked at her grimly. "Do you know that one of the factories is in Ioannina, where your father began his empire and the other one is in Thessaloniki? I think that Mr. Georgiou won't agree with that, and you are well aware of the reason."

Alina got up from her chair and approached him. "Well, Mr. Kalogerou, I have a proposition for you. Contact with Mr. Georgiou and persuade him that I must visit the other two factories, or, at that moment, I sign the dismissal of Emily," hitting her heel on the floor.

His eyes darkened. "I don't understand you. What's your problem with that woman? You don't even know how she looks like. She is harmless. She is the assistant of your father for thirty years and never causes a problem. Never! Unlike you."

"So, from my point of view it's time for her to retire, don't you think?" she said and her voice was so cold, full of malice.

Dimitris approached her even more, "When will you understand that Emily isn't going to harm you or anybody else?" He embraced her. She felt his hands warm around her waist. His face was close to hers. He felt her warmed breasts on his chest. He listened to his heart beating in a crazy rhythm. He wanted her so bad right there at the office, but Miss Alexiou landed him to the reality.

"Mr. Kalogerou, I expect an answer from you."

The only answer he wanted to give her was to throw her on the couch and make love to her, instead of that he asked her, "If we leave on Friday for visiting the other factories, are you going to forget that 'Emily – thing'?"

Alina smiled enigmatically, "No, I'll just postpone her dismissal till the first mistake she makes." Her voice sounded even colder than before.

He was still holding her very close to him, "You will find me opposed to such a movement." His mouth had approached hers. How he wanted to kiss her. Her lips were so inviting, yet so challenging.

"It won't be the first time, so you must get used to it, and, let me go." Kalogerou didn't detach from her. He pulled out of his pocket his mobile phone and called Georgiou. Alina heard Georgiou furious as Kalogerou informed him about her visit plans to the other factories.

"Mr. Georgiou wants to talk to you," he gave her his phone.

Alina was determined to insist on her decision. "Mr. Georgiou, I will depart on Friday morning with Mr. Kalogerou for Ioannina and on Saturday for Thessaloniki. Stop yelling at me. Do your job and let me do mine."

She gave the phone back to Kalogerou smiling victoriously at him, "I suppose that there is no need to repeat what I've told to Mr. Georgiou, do I?" Kalogerou left her without kissing her.

Chapter 13

Georgiou postponed Alina's trip to the other factories for the next weekend. Aris will escort her. Kalogerou and Alina agreed with that decision. When the private plane landed at Ioannina airport a company car waited for them. In the factory, Alina realized once more that Kalogerou was beloved among the employees.

"Mr. Kalogerou, I wonder, how could you remember everyone by their first names?"

Kalogerou looked at her with a dark look, "Thanks to your daddy."

Alina realized the irony in his voice, "Are you imply something?"

"Miss Alexiou, I'm not implying anything. I'm telling you straightaway. Whenever you decided to come and see your daddy, I had to travel to all over Greece. As a soldier, I had fewer transportations than being a Legal Counsel of this factory."

Alina chose to smile ironically at him and not telling anything because it was certain that if she answered him back they will end up arguing again. During the previous week, when she started going to the factory every day, Kalogerou was opposed to her in every single thing. It was a nightmare working with him, and – on the other hand - he never missed the opportunity of making her life difficult by getting very close to her and giving her small kisses on her neck or her ears or her mouth.

Their visit to the factory in Ioannina, although, went very well, and that surprised both of them. When they left the factory it was late at the noon.

"Are you hungry?" Dimitris asked her. She nodded. "Good, because I know a terrific tavern by the sea, not very far from here."

"Mr. Kalogerou, you're surprising me."

"What do you mean?"

"Never mind."

They boarded the car. Alina was distraught and Kalogerou noticed it. "What is now? Is something wrong?"

"Everything is wrong with you. The most annoying thing is the fact that you know everyone by their first name. I find difficult to remember the names of the directors in the Athens factory and you remember everyone in Athens and in here and I'm sure that you know everyone in Thessaloniki factory. Am I correct?"

He smiled and his smile made him irresistible. "What can I say, Miss Alexiou, I'm a natural talent. That's all."

"Oh, please, give me a break."

THE TAVERN WAS AT A very good location. Behind it, there was a lush forest and in front of it the Lake of Ioannina. They sat at a table near the window in order to enjoy the view. Dimitris ordered fresh fish and a bottle of white wine. When the waiter left them, Alina wasted no time.

"Mr. Kalogerou, may I ask you something?"

"Whatever you want."

Alina took a deep breath. She wanted to ask something, in fact, an idea that crossed her mind and couldn't forget it. "Did it become aware of you that there was something between my dad and this Emily?" The tone of her voice was pejorative when mentioned the name 'Emily'.

Dimitris lit a cigarette in order to gain some time before answered this weird question. "How does this stupid idea ever crossed your mind?"

"I was just thinking ..."

"Miss Alexiou, let me hear what you were thinking? I'm very curious, indeed." The waiter brought the salad and the bottle of wine. Kalogerou was smiling at her.

"I was thinking ... why not ... my dad with Emily, regardless the fact that every time I saw her I want to throw up, she is a beautiful woman despite her age," she looked him straight into his dark blue eyes, "So, I was thinking why not. My father was alone all these years, she is alone, as far as I know," Alina left her sentence unfinished.

"Yes, but ... you know she is older than your dad," Kalogerou cleared his throat and continued, "Manos didn't like older women. He preferred younger ones." He told these last words to her when his mouth was stuff, in order not to be heard awkward, "not so much younger, if you know what I mean," The waiter brought them the rest of their order.

"Of course, I understand. I'm not stupid." She paused for a moment. "How my dad ... you know?"

"Know what?" He asked her as he was eating his fish with a great appetite.

Alina had stopped eating long ago, "You know what I mean," she said with an evil voice.

"No, I don't. You must be a little more specific."

Alina found it difficult to be more specific. "Mr. Kalogerou, don't play games with me. You know what I mean." Dimitris shook his head in a negative way. "Very well, since you're such an innocent boy, I will be more specific as you put it. Had my dad ever have any chick? And be careful what your answer would be because if my father hadn't any I will ask you another specific question," she had cornered him for good and Kalogerou didn't enjoy it.

He put down the cutlery and drank a solid sip of the white wine he had in his glass. "How could I know something so personal?"

Alina had noticed that whenever Kalogerou would like to speak calmly he made a question in order to earn some more time to think.

Such a lawful trick. "Leave this kind of speaking to me. I'm pretty sure that you are very well aware of such personal things of my dad. So, I'm waiting for a straight answer."

Dimitris left his glass on the table and sighed. Alina was a tough woman. "All I know is that occasionally your father had some 'affairs', don't imagine anything serious. I think that you understand that he couldn't wait for your mother all these years."

"I'm trying to understand men's nature, with no success. Could you please tell me where did my father found those 'affairs'?"

"Mainly, from our business circle. The last woman I can remember was the Executive Advertising Manager of our last campaign. A very beautiful one and much younger than Manos. At least one or two years older than you." Dimitris giggled. Alina noticed it and felt a tweak in her heart.

"Mr. Kalogerou, could you please explain me why are you laughing?"

"Oh, no nothing."

Alina looked at him pissed off. "Please, don't be shy and tell me. I would like to laugh, too."

Dimitris gathered. "Oh, nay, it isn't something important."

Alina's curiosity had skyrocketed, so she kicked him under the table. Dimitris sprang out of his chair from the pain.

"What's wrong with you?"

"Nothing is wrong with me. If you want to get back to Athens in one piece tell me everything about this woman. Every single detail." She nailed him with her big green eyes. Dimitris stayed silent. "Mr. Kalogerou, I'm waiting, and my patience is running out as time passes." Her leg under the table was moving up and down.

"Well, since you want it so much I'm going to tell you. When Manos saw this advertising executive he almost fell in love with her. She was a very beautiful woman."

Alina cleared her throat. "You are wasting my time."

Dimitris filled their glasses with wine and drank a big sip from his own. "I wasn't present during their first appointment. Manos had seen her by himself. After a few days, when I went to the factory, Manos was talking about her all the time, not about their meeting and the arrangements for the advertising." Alina watched him without talking.

"Manos told me that she will come back in a few days and then I would have the opportunity to see her. I agreed because it was the first time that Manos was so passionate with a woman and I liked that. After two or three days, I was in the factory signing some papers and saw her. It was late in the afternoon, so as your father has the opportunity to go out with her... you know, I presume."

Alina nodded it. She knew and why her father would be an exception. All men in all ages and in all countries all over the world are the same and that is something that never would change. Men's fantasy is always below zero. "Mr. Kalogerou, please continue," she said politely and Dimitris continued his narration.

"To make the long story short, I saw her while I was going to the meeting room but I never attend that meeting."

"May I ask why?" she drunk the rest of her wine.

Dimitris faltered. "Because I didn't want to spoil Manos' romance, that's why."

"Why you would ruin my father's romance? I'm sorry, I'm not following you." She ate the last piece of her fish, and she got the whole bowl with the salad in front of her. "It's very simple, Miss Alexiou, please try to think harder for once."

"Oh, Mr. Kalogerou, give me a break and tell me before I kick you again, harder this time," she smiled with mannerism.

"Miss Alexiou, sometimes you are very sluggish." Alina kicked him again under the table. "Ok, I'm going to tell you, stop kicking me all right? As I was going to the meeting room I saw Mrs. Stefanidi, you know our Executive Communication Manager, talking with this lady in the corridor, and I recognized her. Then I saw her entering Manos' office."

"Proceed, Mr. Kalogerou. I can imagine why she entered my dad's office. Big deal, I've done it myself."

Kalogerou had got brutal. This last thing he heard didn't like it a lot, "The next day I learned was that the meeting was delayed half an hour."

"You are talking all this time and I cannot understand 'how you could spoil my father's romance'?"

"I'm starting to think that you aren't so much clever as I thought. What did you expect me to do? To go to the meeting room and pretending that I didn't know her. I couldn't do that to Manos. Because you see a few months ago I have met with her for several times and we weren't just going out if you understand me or do I need to explain that?" His blue eyes looked straight at hers as he drank a sip of wine.

"Oh, no, please, I don't need so many details from you," she said grimly. "You've just taken me by surprise."

"Why?"

"This masculine solidarity between men is something I have to investigate. What did you do?"

"I called Manos and told him that one of my clients was in prison. He believed me."

"Tell me something, we still have this Advertising Executive?"

"No, when Manos broke up with her, Mrs. Stefanidi found another advertising agency. Now we have a man. Well, Miss Alexiou, did I answer all your questions?"

"No. I have another one."

Dimitris opened his hands begging God in order to end this peculiar questioning. "What else do you want to know?"

"When there were no such – let's say - 'opportunities', in order to put it politely, what did my father do?"

"I guess that he did what other men used to do on these occasions, and, this time, think harder because I'm not going to explain to you anything."

Alina grimaced.

"I am pretty sure that there was no such issue between Emily and your father, otherwise, I will know about it."

"How could you possibly know something like that?"

"We are men, Miss Alexiou. Believe me, Manos didn't have many opportunities for having sex. If he had sex he couldn't hide it from me. Besides work issues, we used to discuss other things, like women used to do. Don't tell me that you don't discuss such matters with your best friend ... or even with Lucas?"

Alina shook her head, "Mr. Kalogerou, I'm going to say one thing to you. Although you are a man you gossip too much."

Dimitris got angry and after paying the bill they left.

THE BAD LACK OF KALOGEROU continued to pester him. In the hotel, his wrath launched its zenith.

"What do you mean that you have booked only one room?" He asked the receptionist girl.

She looked back on the computer that was before her. "Mr. Kalogerou, I'm sorry, we have booked one room for you, sir. However, you don't have to worry, sir, as it has two beds if that helps." The receptionist said that professionally, looking him through her glasses.

"Good, will keep this room for me, and book another one for Miss Alexiou," he said impatiently.

"I'm sorry, sir, we don't have another room. There is a commercial exhibition this weekend and all the hotels are booked," and turning to Alina she said with a business smile, "if Miss Alexiou doesn't have any problem, she can share the room with you, sir."

Alina went in front of her. "I, personally, have no problem," and confirmed her word by stressing one by one all the syllables.

"Well, I have ..." Dimitris growled looking to Alina.

"Oh, Mr. Kalogerou, please," and bowing to his ear she whispered, "Don't worry. I'm not going to rape you." Addressing to the receptionist she told her, "Give us the damn key. I'm not going to discuss it further."

Taking the key in her hands Alina went straight to the room. As she opened the door and saw the beds she smiled. She got into the room first and then Kalogerou followed her.

"They must be kidding me," Kalogerou said looking the two beds, which had been turned into one double bed.

Alina looked indignant, "Oh, you are behaving like a baby. Do you know that?" He glared at her without saying anything. "I'm going to the bathroom first," she said without waiting for an answer.

Dimitris looked at the beds suspiciously. He tried to remove each other, but it proved impossible. *They had stuck them together*, he thought as he was scraping his head.

"Could you, please, tell me what are you doing?" Alina came out of the bathroom, wearing a bathrobe and wiping her hair with a towel.

"Nothing!"

"Yeah right, just trying to separate the beds. Without success as I see. Well, Mr. Kalogerou, we are going to sleep together tonight, that's for sure."

Dimitris puffed. "It's my turn for the bathroom," he said as Alina was still standing on the bathroom door, not letting him get inside.

"I would suggest you take a very cold shower," she said smiling slyly.

Kalogerou didn't say a word, just banged the bathroom door behind him. After a few minutes, he came out angrier. "Miss Alexiou, you didn't leave me any hot water, you know that?"

"That's because I care so much about you," she said without taking her eyes off the TV. Kalogerou growled and get to the bathroom again.

AT LEAST, SHE IS DECENTLY dressed, he thought Dimitris as he threw a look at her body when he got out of the bathroom. Dimitris sat on the other side of the sofa holding some papers in his hands in order to read them. Alina was changing channels at lightning speed ignoring him.

After a few seconds, Dimitris looked at her frowning. "Will you stop playing with the remote control at last?" She ignored him once more and continued to play with the remote control.

"Miss Alexiou!"

"What?"

"Stop torturing the television."

"And may I ask who can I torture?"

"No one. Don't you have something to do? Let's say writing a new book?"

Alina threw him a glance. "No, today I'm not in the mood for doing anything. So the only thing I can do is torturing the TV since you're working with such verve and not talking to me."

She continues to change channels until she found an interesting movie. She left the remote control on the table in front of her. Kalogerou thanked God. Alina was watching a thriller movie and every now and then she gouged screams and went nearer and nearer to him. At the same time, Kalogerou tried to move away from her until finding the end of the sofa. Alina was stuck on him. Her breasts touched his arm.

"Miss Alexiou, why don't you change the channel?" He asked her trying to control himself.

"Why would I do that? It's a very interesting movie," she said seeing a horror cry. "Yes, but this movie scares you." He looked on the film playing the TV. He had seen this movie and was one of the toughest thrillers. He bent to pick up the remote control when she grabbed his arm and rammed from below. He remained motionless.

"Finished?"

"It depends on how you define the word 'finished'."

"Did she kill her or not?"

"He did and after that, he chops her and this point has not yet begun."

Alina was all over him. "I don't want so many details ... tell me when this point is over."

Kalogerou sighed. "There is a comedy on the other channel. Why don't you watch this?"

"Oh, I can't do that," Alina whispered as she was buried in his arms and closed her eyes again, "If I begin to see a movie, I can't leave it in the middle. I don't like to leave things in the middle," she said to him and this intimation made him sighed.

"Yes, but from this particular movie you've managed to see only three seconds, the rest of the time you have your eyes closed."

"Still not finished that scene?"

"No, he is still cutting her ... actual he cuts her right hand at the moment...."

"Oh, stop, I told you I don't want details, it would be impossible for me to sleep at night ..." she rammed more in his arms, "when he finished tell me ... with no details, if you please."

Kalogerou left the papers at the table since there was no chance to be able to read them, as Alina was climbed over him. Kalogerou decided to watch the film.

"How can you see such horrible things?" she asked him with closed eyes.

"Miss Alexiou, these are all fake. I hope you know that."

"I know, but they make it looks like being very real and it's very scary ... does he finish?"

"No." His hand caressed her hair.

"Oh, it becomes tiring, how much time does he need to cut her in pieces?"

"He wants to do a good job, so it will take a little bit longer," he said half smiled, "Miss Alexiou, I'm asking you again, perhaps it's better for you to see the comedy on the other channel, in order to be able to finish my work, because as you climbed over me I can neither read nor delight the movie."

"How can you delight that kind of film?"

"I like that kind of movies, what can I say, well, be patience he has only a foot of her." Alina clenched her arms around his neck.

"I said I don't want details … what do you not understand?"

Although she was afraid her voice stroked his neck like a caress. All her body was in his arms. Her long silk nightgown had lifted revealing her toned leg. His fingers caressed her naked back. With his other hand, he pulled the curls from her face. His lips touched her neck. He felt her sticking more on him. She turned her face to his.

"Did he finish?" she asked him.

"No," he replied, although the disputed scene was over several minutes now.

His lips were very close to hers. He kissed her and she responded. His second kiss wasn't so smooth. It was more demanding, more conquest, fierier. She responded to his second kiss, too. Her body leaped as Dimitris got the one strap of the nightgown down. He kissed her shoulder and heard her sighed. She passed her other leg on the other side of his body. The nightgown rose more, revealing the other leg till the thigh.

Kalogerou sighed. "Now he finished," he said as he got the other strap down kissing her left shoulder. Alina felt his lips burning her skin. "Aren't you going to watch the movie until its end? It's not long," he told her as revealing her breasts. Alina groaned.

"I found more interesting things to do," she told him and undid the top button of his pajamas. Her breasts touched his chest. His deep sigh pleased her enough. She enjoyed it more when she felt his hands caressing her back. And even more, when she felt his hand in her nature. She moaned.

His caress was magnificent, as he gave her an orgasm. "Mm, I like it there," she whispered in his ear. Her body was moving slowly, following the movements of his hand. His mouth sought hers. His kiss was brutal. He wanted to possess her on the couch. He wanted her as it was all over him. He wanted to get inside her as fast as possible. He couldn't bear another moment. His body was blazing of passion for hers.

Alina was ready, too. She was hot and wet, ready to receive him when he heard a soft knock on their room door. They heard it both. "Don't you even think to open the door," she said and kissed him firmly on his mouth. This time, she was determined not to leave anything in the middle. After a while, the hit on the door was a little bit stronger.

"Maybe we should open the door," Kalogerou said, "It may be something important." He tried to get up, but Alina kissed him more passionate.

"And what we're doing here is also very important," she said pushing her nightgown down. The sight of her naked body took his breath away.

"Your arguments are very convincing." He laid her on the couch. His lips began kissing her from her neck going down to her breasts. He took one of them in his mouth. His hand was crazy her down there. A cry escapes from her mouth. A loud one.

"Mr. Kalogerou," it was Aris outside their room door, "Mr. Georgiou wants to talk to you on the phone, sir ... yours is out of battery ... sir ... again," he paused, "and it's urgent," and after a while, "Are you all right, sir?"

Kalogerou growled. "Yes, everything is fine," he muttered, trying to detach himself from Alina's hands. He stood up, giving her nightgown to wear. Dimitris wore on his pajamas before he opened the door. Aris startled as he saw him, understanding what was happening in the room.

Dimitris closed the door behind him and went out into the corridor. Aris gave him his cell phone.

"Mr. Georgiou, what can I do for you?" said Kalogerou cheerless, "well that is something that I cannot remember. I should see my files at the office," he stared at Aris frowning, "I let you know and I will charge my phone, don't worry, goodnight," he growled and gave the phone to Aris.

"Mr. Kalogerou, I'm very sorry about that," Aris said trying to keep his most formal style. Kalogerou glared at him and entered the room. Alina had worn her nightgown and waited for him at the bedroom door looking very angry.

"Well, you are going to sleep on the couch ...," she threw him a pillow and she closed the bedroom door with force. Kalogerou kicked the pillow and left the room, hitting the door behind him. Then he knocked Aris' door. "What happened again?" Aris asked.

"She kicked me out," Kalogerou said. Aris looked at him compassionately, "how many beds has your room?"

"Two," Aris replied. Kalogerou went inside. "So bad?" he asked and Kalogerou shook his head.

"I don't understand. It's as if Georgiou had a camera in our room."

Aris laughed.

Chapter 14

The next morning Alina was still pissed off with Kalogerou. When she realized that Kalogerou slept in Aris's room, and not on the couch, her anger was extended on Aris, too. When she saw them at breakfast, the two men realized that traveling to Thessaloniki wouldn't be easy.

"Don't talk to me both of you," she told them with clenched teeth and sat at a different table.

The two men sat at the next table and after a while, they began to relax and laugh with some incidents that Aris narrated in Kalogerou about Georgiou. Alina was boiled in her broth.

She had been stayed all night up, flushed, as Kalogerou left her in the middle but he was behaving as if nothing had happened. And he must have slept like a baby because he was so fresh. *Oh, how I hated him,* she thought. From now on, I'm going to make his life miserable. The job in Ioannina was over and in two hours they will fly to Thessaloniki. *That's the perfect place for my revenge,* thought Alina.

During the flight to Thessaloniki Alina didn't even speak to neither of them. When they landed at the airport of Thessaloniki Alina entered the car first. Aris with Kalogerou descended the stairs of the plane. "Mr. Kalogerou, don't worry," Aris said, "I will make sure not to happen again."

Kalogerou just shook his head. "If the TV has a thriller tonight, I hopefully get lucky." They both laughed out loud. Entering the car and seeing Alina they both get serious.

The factory in Thessaloniki was also as impressive as the other two. As always, Kalogerou knew everyone there, and that irritated Alina even more. In the Administration's office, Alina after signing some papers she stood up tossing her pen on the desk.

"Where are you going?" Kalogerou asked her trying to keep his voice down.

"For shopping," she glared at him, "with or without your permission 'your majesty'." "Miss Alexiou, we are not finished, yet," Kalogerou stressed the words one by one.

"Well, Mr. Kalogerou, I'm going for shopping without any further discussion." She took her bag and left. Aris followed her.

"We will meet at the hotel," Kalogerou said to him who nodded and ran behind her.

Once Alina was boarding the car Aris got inside. When she saw Aris she flashed and banged. "Perfect, are you coming with me? I don't want you with me," she said furiously.

"Miss Alexiou, I will always be with you," Aris said and sat in the front seat, next to the driver.

Alina leaned toward him, "You interrupted us last night and I hate being interrupted," she said to him kicking his back seat. Aris didn't react to her nerves, he just tied his belt.

When they reached the Mall in Thessaloniki Alina went to every single shop without felt tiring for one second. Instead of Aris who was fed up.

This is the way that women took their revenge, he thought as they entered the hotel five hours later.

When Kalogerou arrived in the hotel it was after ten o'clock. Alina was in her room. Before he goes to Alina he first visited Aris, who was lying on his bed exhausted. Once he saw him Kalogerou understood that Alina bought everything for every single store at the Mall and Kalogerou pitied him. "Are you still alive?" Kalogerou asked him.

Aris just shook his head and recited the scene in the car. "As for me, Mr. Kalogerou, you are free to do whatever you want tonight. Even if the chief of police called I don't even have the courage to lift my phone from the nightstand."

Kalogerou smiled and goodnight him. He knocked Alina's door. She opened looking deadly serious. Dimitris glanced the room and saw the chaos of the bags that were discarded everywhere. "Well, as I can see, you will find something to put on in order to get out tonight with some acquaintances of mine," he said and without waiting for her answer, "in an hour I will come and pick you up."

"And how are you so sure that I'll go out with you?"

He leaned over her kissing her on the mouth, "you got an hour," he said and went to his room.

In Thessaloniki, Kalogerou had his own room, although he liked the idea of sharing the same room with Alina again. After an hour Kalogerou knocked her door. She appeared before him wearing a loose blue dress, which left her entire back out. He helped her to wear her coat. "You will catch a cold in a dress like this."

She smiled. "Mr. Kalogerou, don't worry, I will find someone to warm me, and make sure that he won't leave anything in the middle."

Kalogerou glared her, "In three hours from now you will yell my name behind this door," he whispered in her ear, showing the door of his room.

She grimaced, "It would be a very interesting and exciting development," she said and they boarded into the company car.

"Where are we going?" Alina asked casually.

"We are going to meet some classmates of mine from the university," he replied. His gaze fell on her leg sighing deeply.

"I didn't know that you studied in Thessaloniki?"

"I didn't study in Thessaloniki. They studied in Athens."

"I see, and they are all singles like you?"

He looked at her trying to understand her intentions. "No, Miss Alexiou, unlike me they're all married and have children." He had cornered her to her side of the car. "Therefore, I expect you to behave decently, not like the other night, on my birthday." He kissed her neck, but she remained imperturbable. He looked into her eyes.

"What are you expecting? You are going to leave it in the middle like always." Kalogerou blasphemed and sat in his side.

THE PLACE WHERE HIS classmates had gathered was a quiet bar - restaurant near the White Tower in Thessaloniki. The view was indescribable. The White Tower was illuminated giving a magical sense in the whole area. The sea spreading before her was so stormy, as her heart. Dimitris recommended her to everyone and everyone shared the pain of her father's loss.

"What do you want to drink?" Kalogerou asked Alina, as he got up to go to the bar.

"Hemlock with plenty of ice," she answered sulkily.

Dimitris didn't pay attention to her mood and went alone in the bar. He returned with two drinks. "This is yours," he said leaving the glass in front of her.

Alina drank a sip "Ugh, what is this?" she grimaced with disgust.

Dimitris who spoke with a classmate of him he heard what she said and he whispered meaningfully to her ear. "There is no alcohol in your drink because I don't want you to get drunk tonight."

She drank a sip of his drink. "Ugh, your drink is also awful and as I can see you are going to be drunk," she left the glass on the table. "I doubt if you can understand what you will do tonight and you'll leave it in the middle, what a surprise."

He took a deep breath. "Don't worry sweety, I'm not getting drunk. Go with the other ladies over there and leave me alone, if you want to have a splendid night tonight with me." He said pointing the women sitting on another couch of the restaurant.

Alina got up and instead of going to the women she headed to the bar. She sat down and ordered a whiskey. Kalogerou admiring her back, and as he knew the bartender he nodded him of not giving her any alcohol. The bartender nodded.

"Show me your identity?" said the bartender and Alina looked at him who seemed to be serious enough.

"What? I'm over 18. Give me my drink."

"Perhaps, but to me, you look like 17 years old, and if you don't show me your identity the only drink I can get you is an orange juice."

Alina returned to Kalogerou who was engrossed in discussion with his classmates. Then she looked imploringly the bartender. "Oh, come on, give me my drink." She gave him her sweetest smile and leaned forward to him leaving her breasts in full view.

The bartender was uncompromising. "Your identity, Miss."

Alina searched her clutch, but she didn't find her identity. "I changed bags and left my identity at home ... in Athens," she said to him with clenched teeth.

The bartender laughed and brought her an orange juice. "Well, Miss, this is the first time that I hear such a stupid excuse. Yeah right, in Athens."

All this time, Kalogerou watched her from the sofa. When he saw the orange juice a wide smile showed to his face. His gaze traveled to her back, which was all out. He felt chills all over his body. Most likely when he realized that she wasn't wearing any bra. He wanted to take her out of there and make love to her as soon as possible.

A young man approached Alina at the bar. The bartender sent him away before he could sit next to her. Kalogerou seemed to have an interesting evening with his classmates as they remembered the time they had as university students and didn't leave any girl not only at the Law School but even at the other schools of the university. They remembered a story from their senior year and their laughter came to the bar.

Alina turned and looked at them. The thing that Kalogerou was having fun and she was bored to death, pissed her off even more. She didn't drink the orange juice and sat on the couch next to Kalogerou. "Give me your mobile phone?"

Kalogerou turned his head. "Why?"

"I want to call my mother. I'm trying to communicate with her since my dad died, and she isn't answering either her cell phone or at home or in the hospital. I can't reach also my grandfather and I'm a little bit worry. And when am I going to have my mobile phone for Greece?" Kalogerou gave her his cell phone.

Alina tried to call her mother without success. She sent her a message as she had done several days ago but nothing happened again. No one answered or sent her any message. She gave Kalogerou his phone back puffing.

"What happened again?"

She shrugged her shoulders. "Oh, I'm getting so bored here. When are we going to leave?" she murmured, a little louder than she should be, as several heads turned and looked at her. She tried to drink a sip from Kalogerou's drink, but he took it from her hand. "This is mine," he said severely.

Alina nervously waved her leg and her dress opened up more. Several men had the opportunity to admire her beautiful legs. Kalogerou tried to focus on the discussion with his colleague. It was impossible.

He stood up saying, "Andrew, you have my card so anytime you come to Athens, please don't hesitate to call me," and turning to Alina he told her, "We are leaving." He greeted the others and went out. He held her by the arm. "Next time try not to think aloud," he said, waiting for the car company to come and get them. She ignored him. "Did you find your mom?"

"No, and I'm worried ... maybe I should go to America for a few days."

Kalogerou looked severe at her, as they boarding the car. "Don't you even think something like that, I need you at the factory." His tone was cold.

"I'm worrying. I'll be back in a few days, just to make sure that she is all right. Please."

"No, end of discussion. Your mom is a big woman. She can surpass Manos' death by herself." Kalogerou looked outside, without bothering about how her mother could feel after her father's death. He was such a heartless jerk. She threw him her bag. Kalogerou gave her bag back. She did it again. He came close to her.

"Next time you'll do that I'm kicking you out of my car," he said and kissed her on the mouth. They arrived at the hotel. Alina stepped out of the car furious by slumping the car door. Dimitris followed her and walked with her to the elevator. There he caught her and pulled her close to him. "I don't like slumping my car's door, so don't do that again," his lips sealed hers with accumulated passion.

She tried to resist, but his tongue knocked her last resistance down. As his one hand was busy with her breasts, he opened the room door with the other hand. Without letting her lips they entered the room.

"I promised you something," he said before he removed her dress and getting her breast in his mouth.

She sighed. "I'm not impressed so easily anymore," she groaned as Dimitris took the other breast in his mouth. "You're going to leave it in the middle as always," she said resolving his tie.

"Not this time." He sought her lips.

Alina felt his lips hot crushing her own. She undid the buttons of his shirt. His fingers lit bonfires all over her body. "You're not going to need this," clutching her underwear in his hand.

"No, unless you leave me in the middle," she kissed him on his chest.

"There is no way ..." he said panting.

"We will see." She threw his shirt to the floor and pulled him closer to her by grabbing the belt of his trousers. She groaned as his hand slid between her thighs. She hooked on him.

Her hands solved the belt of his trousers and lowered the zipper. Dimitris couldn't stand much longer. He wanted to get inside her, to feel her in all over his body. "No more discussion, get ready to shout my name," he said as getting inside her fast and demanding.

Alina cried as Dimitris lure her in a passionate love which she enjoyed. His love was frenetic and possessive. Alina closed her eyes. Her warm breath caressed his neck. Her body was burning from the heat of their passion.

"Oh, Dimitris," she cried his name as laminated passion waves deluged her.

"What I expected to hear for so long." His eyes were blurred by the pleasure her body gave him. Alina's body stretched from another orgasm. His movements weren't soft. He had oppressed his passion for so long. She liked the way he made love to her. She wrapped her legs around his waist. She wanted him deeper inside her and he did it. He sank deeper inside her, making her cry his name once more.

"If you continue to yell so much Aris will invade into the room and then you'll put the blame on me," he said and closed her mouth with a kiss. Alina moved toward him making him finished inside her. His moan was stronger.

She kissed him on the mouth by holding him inside her body. "You are the one who is screaming."

"Aris is guarding you, not me," he said trying to find his breath as he was supporting his head on her shoulder. He listened to her heart beating and kissed her on the line between her breasts.

She smiled and her hands stroked his hair, "finally," she said and he laughed. He took her in his arms and went to the bed, where he laid her down in a smooth and beloved way and fell beside her exhausted.

Alina caressed her hand to his chest. His hand tangled her hair. Alina turned into his lap and whispering in his ear, "I want more," biting him slightly at the base of his neck. Dimitris looked at her smiling. "Don't tell me you're ready for a second round?" Alina didn't answer.

"Alina, tomorrow we fly to Athens, don't you think that," he left his sentence in the middle, as he felt her hand caressing his erection, and before he could continue, he felt her lips on his manhood.

"Mm, well I think that you're completely ready." Her face appeared cheerful from the blanket.

"You cheated." Alina heard him groaning and she appeared again from the blanket saying "Do you want me to stop?" She said with an innocent tone. Alina heard him growled again. "I'll take that as a 'yes,'" and she slipped under the rug.

It was hard for him to hold his passion as Alina sent to him one wave of pleasure after another using her lips. He detained by the headrest of the bed in order not to cry, because then surely Aris will enter the room without any hesitation. She managed to make him want her again in a short time. Alina understood that and went over him.

Dimitris slipped inside her without any delay. He kissed her mouth so passionate that her lips became red. Alina was moving over him with rhythmic movements that drove him crazy. In every move Alina made, he was entering in the most extinguish paradise he ever knew. In an unprecedented paradise. Although he had a great experience in that area, making love to Alina was like feeling paradise for the first time. He wanted this paradise for the rest of his life. When Dimitris came in culmination Alina cried out loud and fell on his chest with satisfaction.

"You make too much noise, you know that?" he told her biting her lips. Alina didn't speak, just rammed deeper into his arms trying to feel him till the last cell of his body.

Dimitris watched her sinking into a deep and peaceful sleep as her body have had enough of his love, enough of his passion, enough of his body. It was the sweetest sleep she had ever had. All night long in his strong arms.

In the morning, Alina sought her hand to find Dimitris, his side was empty. She sat up in the bed and saw him coming out of the bathroom with a towel wrapped around his waist. He went towards her. She stood up wrapping the sheet all over her body.

He took her in his arms and kissed her. "I ordered coffee," he said before his mouth gave her another fiery kiss. She didn't let him go. "I don't want coffee, I want you," and her hands moved to the towel.

He smiled and kissed her again. "Let's get dressed. I want to show you the sights of Thessaloniki. Thessaloniki is a marvelous city, you know." Alina left the sheet rolling on the floor. Her body left him breathless.

"Putting that way, I think that I follow you in bed," he said throwing her to bed "Sights could wait," he said as he fell over her. "I also changed the departure time," his hand caressed her breasts with circular movements.

She was left in his caress closing her eyes. "What time do we fly?" He kissed her breasts and then her belly.

"At nine o'clock in the evening." His tongue was on her breasts making Alina sighed.

"I think that we have enough time to ..." she stopped talking as his tongue went down to her belly, made a circle around her navel, and then went down first in one thigh and then the other.

He came over her, "What's on your mind?" He asked, as he sucked one of her breasts and then followed the same path, only this time he invaded to the area between her legs. Her body bends from pleasure. Alina didn't say a word. Dimitris drove her crazy down there. "I'm sorry, I can't hear you." Alina groaned, "Yes, I agree with that," he told her and made her groaned again. He put his finger into her making her cried. "I suppose that you like it?" And pushed his finger a little more.

Alina lost the world, as he travelled her in another dimension she never was before and never wanted to leave.

He kissed her on the mouth with passion and slipped inside her. She was held by his arms and left her body moved according to his movements, which were soft at the beginning and becoming more and more intense. She lifted her pelvis and moved with him. She heard him shouted with pleasure and as Dimitris intensifying his rhythm Alina responded with the same intensity. "I feel so good," she heard him saying, "I wanted you from the first time I saw you."

"I know that," she said as she was moving her pelvis a little bit faster, "but your way was unbearable, you are well aware of it."

"I am, but you weren't also a very good person, you are also well aware of it."

"Are you talking back to me?"

"Yes, I am, get used to it, my love."

"Oh, now I am your love..."

"My one and only love for the rest of my life. You're driving me crazy, I can't stand another minute," he said and finished inside her casting her into the sky.

Their simultaneous climax left both of them breathless. Dimitris collapsed onto her body and she like hypnotized caressed his back, his hair, his arms. A faint smile etched on her face and her lips kissed his shoulder. She liked that he was inside her and his weight on her was so sweet that wouldn't let him get up.

DURING THE TRIP FROM Thessaloniki to Athens, Dimitris was reading some documents when he felt Alina's leg stroking him under the table. He raised his eyes to look at her. Alina seemed to focus on her computer. He didn't pay any attention to her, thinking that it was something random, so he continued his own work.

After a while, he felt her leg fondling him more than he could bear. Looking at her he saw her eyes full of lust. He changed seat in order to be able to concentrate. Alina continued caressing him.

Dimitris left the papers on the table and approached her. "Stop doing this. In Athens, we have to be careful and not do things like this," he kissed her on her mouth.

She approached her face to his. "Mr. Kalogerou, when do we arrive?"

Dimitris looked at his watch. "At a half an hour, we've just taken off, why you ask?"

Alina puffed. "And what am I going to do all this time?" she gently bit his ear as an answer to her rhetoric question.

"We can't do anything because the journey to Athens doesn't last long," he kissed her on the mouth, "if you were a good girl you could have me when we were coming from America, then we had too many hours at our disposal and we were alone without Aris watching us." Alina made a grimace, "so, be patient until we get home."

She winked. Dimitris looked very serious and put down the papers he was holding. "You know that we are going to have a big problem, don't you?"

"What problem?"

He went and sat down next to her to avoid her leg. "Just think of Maria and Stelios and all these police officers."

"Well, all these people go home after dark. Isn't it just perfect?" her finger dragged onto his shirt, playing a bit with his tie.

He laughed. "Yes, but they all gathered very early in the morning. What do you think about that?" his finger followed the line of her face, came down her neck followed her neckline until he touched her breasts.

Alina came closer to him, "... true, but they don't come upstairs where the bedrooms are, so ...," her fingers played with the belt of his trousers.

He took her hand and kissed it. Alina continued playing with his belt with the other hand. "Well, Mr. Kalogerou, considering the circumstances, I don't think that we face any particular problem," she said trying to undo his tie. Dimitris was about to give in, when the signal to tie their belts sounded, suggesting that they would land soon enough.

Thank God, he whispered.

"Did you say anything?"

"No, nothing, sweetie."

Stelios awaited them at the stairs of the airplane, as always. Alina went down first, giving him a big kiss on the cheek and boarded overjoyed to the car. Stelios noticed the changing in her behavior and when Kalogerou arrived before him he couldn't resist and asked him "Mr. Kalogerou, what happened to Miss Alexiou?"

Kalogerou looked at him bluntly. "How the hell should I know why Miss Alexiou is like that? Why don't you ask her?"

Aris who was coming just behind Kalogerou he also declared ignorance by lifting his shoulders. Aris sat next to Stelios. Dimitris sat back just opposite to Alina, who wanted to torture him a little more before they reached home. All the way home, her leg caressed Dimitris, who threw her his most fiery glances.

As soon as they arrived home, Stelios and Aris left them alone. Dimitris waited until they get out from the house yard. He found Alina in the kitchen. She stared him indifferently. He came towards her, "You're a very naughty girl."

She passed her hands around his neck. "Yes, and I like it a lot." Her fingertips wandered around his neck, his chest, and his belly.

He put her on the kitchen bench lifting her dress. "I think that we've left something unfinished here," he fondled over her tights which put Alina on fire. He took them out without being in a hurry, kissing all over her leg. She shivered and pulled him closer.

She took off his jacket, his tie and undid one by one the buttons of his shirt. With her fingers touched gently every muscle of his sternum, every muscle of his flat belly, every point of his body. His lips sought hers. From his kiss, she understood that he would take her over there. And she wanted him so desperate. She solved his belt and her hand went through his pants. She got his erection. Dimitris left a deep sigh.

"You like to drive me crazy, don't you?"

She stroked him with more intensity. "This is the only thing that I like most." She undid his pants. Her lips kissed his mouth without her hand stop caressing him. Her tongue fought with his tongue, stimulating them both.

Her tongue tortured his whole body. In every move she made she listened him groaning. When her tongue reached under his belly she replaced her hand with her mouth. His crying echoed throughout the house. She had him in her mouth and she was pleased heard him moaning. He put her on the kitchen bench again. Her panties were on the floor, like her dress.

"I want you so much," he said hurriedly. Alina hooked on him as she felt his erection inside her. Their movements made them both groan out of pleasure.

"How much I like it when we don't leave anything in the middle." He held her in his arms. Her soft and deep voice stroked his neck before reached his ear. "I guess that you agree with me." Once again he tasted her lips full of passion even if they had just completed their love. "We can't sleep together tonight."

Alina got by surprise. "You aren't serious?" She said as her hand ran all over his chest.

"I'm very serious, as from now on you'll be the most decent girl." He got her down from the kitchen bench and Alina gathered her clothes.

"And if I disagree what will you do about that?" she approached him defiantly.

"You won't disagree until I could think of something." He kissed her on the base of her neck and then in her breasts.

"Mr. Kalogerou, you'll better think something fast because I don't know for how long I can stand without kissing you." She turned and her lips stuck to his. They went upstairs together. He cornered her in the door of her room kissing her until he heard her sigh.

"I don't have any problem if you want to come to my room," she said playfully.

Kalogerou laughed. "Tomorrow morning I'm going to have a big problem and the name of that problem will be 'Maria'. Sounds familiar to you?" Her hands passed through his open shirt. Her lips kissed his earlobe and got down on his neck.

"Think of it once again and come to my room," she said, biting his other ear. Kalogerou stuck on her and if he didn't go away from her soon, they will end up in the same bed making love all night long. Instead of that, he gave her a hot kiss telling her "Goodnight and have sweet dreams with me."

He went to his room and headed for the bathroom. He urgently needed a shower in order to stand the night without Alina beside him or under him or over him. After showering, he put on his pajamas bottoms. Before he lied down in bed he went to her room, opening her door trying not to make any noise. He saw her covering with the rug. He shouted her name. Alina didn't respond. *She is probably sleeping,* thought Dimitris, and he closed the door.

He went to his room and got some papers from his briefcase to read lying in bed. He began to read it when he realized a gentle hand caressing his abdomen. He felt the hand coming up and then going down and down. He realized that it would enter into his pajamas pants.

"Alina?" he cried and lifted the covers.

"What? Did you expect another woman?" Alina was over him. "Answer me," as her hands set him on fire.

"No, you know very well that you are the one and only woman for me from the first moment I saw you on my plane."

"First of all, that's my plane, you seem to forget that all the time but I forgive you, and, as you gave the right answer, I'm going to be very good with you."

"I presume that you won't leave me alone, don't you?"

"You are quite correct."

Dimitris left himself in her caresses and kisses. When he couldn't stand any more he put her underneath him. Kalogerou was holding her in his arms, looking her beautiful face with those big eyes, and that watering cherry mouth. He couldn't believe that such a beautiful woman wanted him and only him.

He had known many beautiful women in his life, but all these women wanted him only for his power and his money. Alina was different. Alina didn't care about his money as she had her own. She wanted just him and that was something new for him. He would do everything to find that man who murders her father and then he will marry her and live with her all his life. He wants to have children with her. "I think that I'm going to fall in love with you," he said holding her in his arms, "and that's something new for me, you know".

"Well, Mr. Kalogerou, I don't know what to say? I'm impressed."

"Perhaps, that you are going to fall in love with me, too? That could be nice."

"Hmm, Mr. Kalogerou, I'm not sure about that."

Kalogerou gets serious. "I'm sorry, I thought that you had some feelings for me."

"That's true but I'm not going to fall in love with you because you see I've already loved you, you idiot."

His smile came back in his face. "I love you so much..."

"Could you please stop talking and..."

Kalogerou kissed her on her mouth, his hands caressing her face, her neck, her breasts, "oh, I love you so much," he said while he was kissing her abdomen, "and I want you so much," Alina murmured his name, and without further delay he was sliding inside her while Alina received him with a deep sigh.

His rhythm was slow and romantic. Kalogerou made a romantic love to her and it was his first time doing something like that. Her body was hot from his love. He breathed her name and Alina continued to move according to his moves but faster. She cried his name in his ear, she cried that he loved him with all her heart and her soul and that no one could ever apart them. Not even death. Her words took him off, as he finished inside her. He put his head on her breasts exhausted. His heavy breath caressed her breasts making her sigh. Her fingers wandered across his back, which was huge and all muscles.

"I couldn't let you sleep alone," she whispered in his ear.

Dimitris muffled a giggle. "I know. I don't want to sleep alone anymore, so you can sleep here, I haven't any problem. When Maria finds you in my room and started shouting that I seduced you, you're a big girl and you're on your own." He relied on his shoulders and looked at her.

"Don't worry," she said and kissed him on the mouth, "I will assure her that you were a gentleman and I seduced you."

He laid on his back and took her in his arms. He was thoughtful. "However, we have to think something on this issue, because I can't stay long away from you." She sprang from his lap and came over it.

"Really?"

"Really, now sleep and I'll think of something, I don't know what that could be ..."

"If we just say to Maria, that it would be good for her, too."

Dimitris looked puzzled. "Could you, please, explain to me how sleeping together would be a benefit to Maria?"

"Oh, don't you understand? She won't have to make two beds and tidy up two bedrooms every morning, but only one. What do you think of that?" Alina's serious tone made him burst out in laughing.

"Yes, she'll definitely appreciate the help that we would offer her, you can count on that," he kissed her on the mouth. He pulled her hair from her face and kissed her once more.

Once again she couldn't get enough of him. If they didn't have to wake up early next morning he would continue to make love to her all night long. He loved Alina deeply and whoever couldn't understand that, including Maria and Stelios, it was their problem, not his.

His own problem was to find the person who killed Manos and not jeopardized Alina's life ever again. He clenched her in his arms promising to himself that he didn't allow to anyone to put Alina's life in danger.

In the morning they managed to get up early and go down to the kitchen. *It is very quiet here. Something is wrong with these two, but I don't know what that is,* thought Maria, once she saw them drinking their coffee in the kitchen without fighting.

Kalogerou was sitting at the table gathering his papers together. Alina was also there, drinking her coffee without paying attention to anyone. They got up both at the same time as soon as they saw Maria.

"Where you two going so early?" She asked them. They answered different things, and Maria understood much more than they were trying to hide in. Alina went straight to the office. After a while, Kalogerou came out from the kitchen, went up to his room, and then got back to the kitchen to get some papers. Then he went to the office.

Alina looked out the window at the garden, where everything was perfect, thanks to the gardener and not to his father. That thought depressed her enough. Kalogerou saw her depression. He approached and hugged her, kissing her on the mouth.

Aris and Stelios just entered the house. Maria went to the office to inform Dimitris that the two men were in the house. She opened the door without anyone could notice her. She saw Dimitris and Alina kissing each other and she smiled. That was the most wonderful thing. Alina is perfect for him and Dimitris is a very good person.

She knew him from the time he was a young boy, a naughty one, but she knew that his heart was made out of kindness. "Oh, these two are together and that jerk didn't tell me anything," Maria murmured.

"Good morning, Mrs. Maria," Aris told her.

Maria threw him a glance. "Would you like a cup of coffee?"

"Yes," Aris replied with hesitation because Maria always seemed to be very cautious with the policemen.

"Well, come into the kitchen. I will serve you a cup of coffee if you tell me everything. And don't try to hide anything from me."

"About what?" He followed her to the kitchen looking hazard.

"Oh, please, don't try to fool me, I'm not Georgiou." Something occurred from Aris's mind and one thing was sure; Maria wasn't Georgiou. In less than a minute, Aris had told her everything, which made Maria happy. "Mrs. Maria, please, you didn't learn that from me, ok?"

Maria assured him by winking her eye conspiratorially to him.

Aris knocked the office door before entering inside. "Mr. Kalogerou, we are ready, sir."

Kalogerou gave a kiss at Alina. "Okay, we are coming. Give me a few seconds to get my cell phone from the kitchen."

Dimitris went to the kitchen to get his cell phone and Maria was humming. "Well, Maria, I see that you are very happy this morning. May I asked why?" He drank another sip of his coffee in a hurry.

"After so many years Alina made her bed by herself," she replied with seriousness. Kalogerou cleared his throat trying to read the file he had in front of him.

Maria came toward him. "You know how long it took me to teach her how to make her bed, don't you?" She looked at him straight in his eyes.

Alina met Dimitris in the kitchen. When she saw Dimitris with the soiled shirt she frizzed. "Maria, don't put the blame on me. I didn't throw him anything today." Maria stared first at her and then at Kalogerou.

"Oh, don't worry, I'm not going to blame you. You see, my sweet girl, Mr. Kalogerou, is happy because I told him that something magnificent happened this morning to me." Maria was smiling at both of them.

"Oh, that's good Maria. Could you also tell me, or it's something between you two?" Asked Alina supposedly indifferent.

"I can tell you. It isn't secret. You see, I'm very happy as you learned how to make your bed." Maria blasted Alina with her look. Alina tried to keep calm although she was ready to faint. She murmured something like "it wasn't Dimitris' fault."

Maria stopped her. "What upsets me more is that you two tried to hide that beautiful love from me," and she hugged Alina with the whole of her affection and love.

Kalogerou recovered from the shock. "So, Maria, is everything all right with you?" he said with faded voice.

Maria approached him and stood before him, "In other words, Mr. Kalogerou, if - for any reason – you're going to hurt Alina then you'll have to deal with me. So simple."

Dimitris puffed relieved. "Maria, this is not going to happen, believe me. Never!"

"So, everything is all right then," said Maria and kissed him on his cheek.

Apart from the fact that Manos' killer is still unknown and not arrested yet, he murmured when he got upstairs to change his shirt.

"It's time for you two to go to the factory, and don't play such tricks with me." Maria farewell both of them to the front door. Stelios awaited there and saw that Maria was happy.

"Maria, what happened to you? Did you see another romantic movie in DVD player last night?"

Maria blasted him with a flick of her hand. "Oh, give me a break, smart-ash," and she winked to Dimitris.

Chapter 15

They had been three months since Manos was dead. Alina was writing her new book and she was working with Dimitris at the factory. They were both adjusted to their new lifestyle. Dimitris wasn't left her alone not even for a second.

Apart from that day, which Dimitris will never forget.

On the other hand, Georgiou and his superiors were in confuse. It has been so long after Alexiou's death and the murderer was disappeared. He didn't even make an attempt against Alina Alexiou during this time. Georgiou's superiors in the Police Headquarters asked him to withdraw his men as presuming that the killer wanted only Manos Alexiou dead and not his daughter.

Georgiou opposed to that, although his research had led to nowhere. He had only a hunch and nothing more. Just a hunch. But he couldn't say such a thing to his superiors. After a three – hour meeting, he only managed to have Alina Alexiou under surveillance for another week.

"THESE PAPERS ARE SIGNED, too," Alina gave the signed papers to Kalogerou. Dimitris couldn't take his eyes off her. *Lately, Alina is getting beautiful and beautiful,* he murmured. His heart jumped in his chest. He kissed her on her mouth and he will make love to her there, in the office, if it wasn't his damn cell phone. He took the phone out from his pocket and looked at the screen.

"Kalogerou speaking." Alina watched him as he was pronounced his name. She caressed his hair with her hand while Dimitris was talking on the phone. "Don't worry, in an hour, I'll be there. No, you aren't going to stay in prison. I said don't worry." His voice was angry. "I told you, in an hour I'll be with you. I'm on my way."

He turned off his phone and enjoyed Alina's caress for a while when he remembered the phone and stood up. "I have to go," he said and kissed her on her mouth. "The police arrested one of my clients for a financial fraud and I should go. Will you be okay on your own?" He asked her, as Alina grabbed her head. This headache was awful and was getting worse hour by hour.

"I'll be fine, don't worry about me. What time will you be back?" Dimitris looked at his watch. He may take him all night long to get his client out of the jail. He took her in his arms and kissed her with all his passion. "Don't wait for me here. Go home with Stelios and I'll meet you there as soon as possible," he said and kissed her again.

"You'd better do that, Mr. Kalogerou because I have plans for you tonight." Alina winked. Dimitris smiled and went out of the office.

Alina stayed at the office with the taste of his kiss on her mouth. When her headache was extremely terrible she decided going back home. Stelios waited outside her office. Emily had left a few minutes later after Kalogerou's leaving.

Stelios escorted Alina to the car. In the courtyard, Aris wore his helmet in order to follow them. The route was a well-known one. They had done this hundred of times during the last three months. Why would tonight be a different? Like all the previous days so that day nothing was suspicious.

Except for one but most importance difference: Kalogerou was absent.

ALINA WAS SITTING IN the back seat of the car searching her bag to find some painkiller for her headache. The view was marvelous. Summer was here, at last. The trees were flourished. End of June and the sun threw its beams on earth when a shooting interrupted her thoughts.

Shooting? She said to herself. Who was shooting and why? She looked at Stelios. She shouted his name but Stelios didn't react. He was lying dead on the steering wheel. Then she looked back and saw Aris fallen down on the street. Another car was stopped in front of them. She felt a hand pulling her out of her car. She tried to resist when a man slapped her and dragged her out. The man gave her a shove, as he pulled her into the back seats of his car.

She heard another shot, and after that, she heard a burst of fire. Perhaps it has been Aris who reciprocated the shots. She couldn't dare to lift her head to see what was happening. The man, who dragged her out of her car, was the driver and he was badly injured. The other man was lying dead on the street. She looked at him, but she couldn't see his features, as he had his face covered. The car ran away in speed and disappeared to an unknown direction.

KALOGEROU WENT TO HIS office to get some papers in order to set free his client. For an hour, he was trying to contact with Alina due to her bad headache. He called her at the factory phone, and then to her mobile, he couldn't reach her. He called Stelios's cell phone without success.

A shadow passed across his face. And apart from the fact that Alina or Stelios didn't answer their phones, the police officer of the central police department of Athens made his life so difficult, as he refused to release his client although he had all the necessary documents for it.

He puts his phone in his pocket. Kalogerou was pacing up and down outside the office of the police officer. He was trying to put his thoughts in order and set free his client as fast as he could. He wanted to go back home soon and gave Alina the ring he bought for her yesterday. It was about time to propose her. His mobile phone rang. He answered it hoping to hear Alina. It was Georgiou.

Kalogerou couldn't understand what Georgiou was telling to him. Kalogerou was out of control. He was shouting. "Mr. Georgiou, what do you mean that you lost Miss Alexiou? ... What did you say about Stelios? ... And how do you know that they didn't shot Miss Alexiou, too? ... How is Aris?"

The officer in charge came out of his office in order to make him stop shouting. Now he remembered who Kalogerou was. It was the famous lawyer Dimitris Kalogerou, the one who after Manos Alexiou's death began to appear with Manos Alexiou's secret and very beautiful daughter.

"Mr. Kalogerou, is everything all right?"

Kalogerou looked at him without speaking. The police officer gave orders to another policeman to bring to Mr. Kalogerou a glass of water. Kalogerou didn't have the courage nor to keep it, let alone to drink the water. From Kalogerou's mobile phone a voice was heard. He took the phone from his hand. "Danezis speaking, Police Officer on duty. Who is it? Mr. Kalogerou isn't able to talk to you."

Georgiou was taken aback. He had to speak with Danezis for years. They graduated together from Police Academy many years ago. For some time, they had served to the same police station, but that was more than twenty five years ago.

"Danezis? Is that you? Georgiou speaking my old friend."

"I can't believe it. Georgiou, how are you? What is going on with Kalogerou? Do you know him? He doesn't seem very well. Do you know why?"

Georgiou recited to Danezis what happened to Alina Alexiou. This was a shock, even for Danezis, let alone for Kalogerou who was obviously in love with her. The daughter of the dead Manos Alexiou was kidnapped.

He decided to offer his help to Georgiou. He gave the mobile phone back to Kalogerou. "Mr. Kalogerou, Georgiou asked you to wait here, sir. Come into my office, please." Kalogerou followed Danezis unconsciously in his office, where he collapsed on the first chair he found before him.

The most horrible scenario became a reality and he couldn't do anything for the woman he loved. He felt helpless. He was helpless.

Danezis watched him with a little bit of a suspicious look, although Georgiou assured him that Kalogerou wasn't responsible for Miss Alexiou's kidnapping, nor for Manos Alexiou's death. As an experienced police officer, he had to be cautious. He lit a cigarette and offered one to Kalogerou. "However," started Danezis the discussion, "if you ask me, from some things that Georgiou told me, I think that they want her alive. They don't aim to kill her, as they did with her father."

Dimitris stared at him with tears of anguish. "What if they kill her later?"

"With so many shooting, Mr. Kalogerou, I don't think so. They want Miss Alexiou alive. Alive is more useful to them. For the money!" Dimitris didn't speak. Although he was a very experienced lawyer, he couldn't understand this paranoiac logic of the policemen.

If they asked for ransom he will give them. He will give them everything they asked for just to take Alina back. Alive. On the other hand, what prevents these criminals kill her after taking the ransom? This thought made his blood freezing. Kalogerou shuddered. When the door opened Georgiou walked into the office.

As Danezis saw Georgiou he welcomed him very friendly. Kalogerou watched the two police officers sharing information on

Alina's kidnapping. Georgiou was trying to understand why Kalogerou was at the Police Department. Yes, it's seemed very suspicious the fact that the kidnapping took place when Kalogerou wasn't present.

For some reason, the kidnappers didn't want him on their way. Why? No one could know. Perhaps they didn't want to hurt him. They wanted only Alexiou's daughter. Alina Alexiou was the target, not Kalogerou, and his absent gave them the perfect opportunity.

"What a devilish coincidence," Dimitris whispered, "and Alina could be dead."

Maybe not so devilish. They just wait the day. Dimitris couldn't understand who could watch him.

Perhaps someone else from the factory. Who? He asked himself. Perhaps Fotiadis? Kalogerou couldn't understand how Fotiadis could track his phone calls or villa's phone calls. Perhaps with the help of Emily. *Emily has involved in the other story some years ago*, he thought, but from that day Emily never caused a problem. No, not a chance. Emily was a very reliable person and a respectful secretary.

Who else? Dimitris was trying to figure out who wanted Alina dead. The same person that killed Manos, he decided, although he cannot think who that person could be.

Perhaps it was just a coincidence. A simple coincidence. A diabolical one. A frightening one. He grasped his head and took a deep sigh. And he wanted tonight to give her the ring. He was going to propose her. Tonight! He put his hand in his pocket and pulled out a black velvet box.

Georgiou saw it. "Mr. Kalogerou, what's that?" Dimitris, as he was lost in his thoughts, he didn't answer. Georgiou took it from his hands and he opened it. He showed its context to Danezis who shook his head. Georgiou gave it back to Kalogerou. "Mr. Kalogerou, come with me. We must go to Alexiou's home and set up all the equipment in order to track the phone calls." Dimitris followed him without bringing the slightest objection.

Inside the police car, Kalogerou called another lawyer from his office in order to go to the police station he was and set free his client. He didn't say anything about Alina's kidnapping. When they arrived at the house, lots of police cars waited for them outside the house.

Georgiou gave orders and the police officers in the van with the necessary technology were ready to trap all the phones of the house, so they would be able to identify the location where the kidnappers keep Alexiou.

Kalogerou wanted to be alone, so he went straight to the office. He collapsed in his chair. He took the box with the ring out from his pocket and left it on the desk before him. Opened. Then he put a double whiskey. Someone knocked the door. Dimitris didn't answer. Aris went inside. Dimitris threw him a glance.

It was the first time in three months that Kalogerou looked so old. He was unable to do anything for the woman he loved, and the worse thing was that he knew it. Aris also knew very well that he cannot do anything unless the kidnappers called. Only one thing they can do. Wait! Dimitris looked at him as if he awakened from a nightmare. He remembered that Aris was also shot.

"How are you?" He asked him.

"I'm all right, sir, and as I said to Mr. Georgiou I emptied my gun on one of the kidnappers. One was killed and the other one must be seriously wounded. They will surely take him to a hospital, and we have sent police cars to all hospitals. Even to the private ones." Dimitris beckoned positively with his head. Aris didn't leave the office. Dimitris looked at him again. "Mr. Kalogerou, I want to apologize. Although I wasn't surprised, it was impossible to prevent the kidnapping of Miss Alexiou. I'm very sorry. It was impossible. I was alone and they were two of them shooting all the time. Stelios was seriously injured. I gave the car registration and the sketch of the kidnappers, which are distributed to all police cars. They cannot get away, sir. You'll have to believe me. I did my best. Honest." Aris was in despair. He liked both of them. Mr. Kalogerou and Miss Alexiou had nothing to do with the rich people who snubbed everyone else. They were good ones.

"And if they kill her as they did with Manos?" His voice was harsh. His gaze was very dark. This development was beyond him.

Aris looked at him straight in the eye. "Mr. Kalogerou, I think that if they wanted Miss Alexiou dead they had plenty opportunities to do so."

Dimitris shook his head. "Everyone tells me that, but I don't believe you. Anymore."

Georgiou came into the office looking for Kalogerou, who at that time was drinking the third double whiskey. "Mr. Kalogerou, I want you sober. Stop drinking, please."

Kalogerou grimaced. "Mr. Georgiou, I'm very much sober, don't worry about me, sir, it's better to worry about Alina."

Georgiou didn't insist. He can understand Kalogerou very well. Kalogerou had changed a lot after he met Alina. "Come with me please." He took him by the arm.

They went into the living room, where the police had set up their monitors and other equipment in order to be able to trace the phone call when the kidnappers demanded a ransom. Georgiou explained that he should keep them on the phone as much as he could, at least, more than two minutes, he said at the end. Kalogerou shook his head.

"When will they call?"

"Mr. Kalogerou, we don't know that. They can call in at any minute, or at least in twenty - four hours. From my experience, however, I can tell you, that the sooner, the better."

THE FIRST NIGHT OF the kidnapping Dimitris slept on the sofa for an hour. He couldn't to go in his room. He wanted to be near to a telephone in case that kidnappers called him. He was all the time locked up in the office, isolated, without having any contact with anyone. During the rest of the night he was staring at the small velvet box before him and he was filled and refilled his glass with whiskey. The hours were passed, and this damn phone didn't ring during that night.

DURING THE SECOND DAY, Kalogerou was a wreck, suffering a great agony. He was unshaven and insomnia, no one could dare to speak to him. He cursed them all. Even Georgiou and Aris. He broke up in tears in Maria's hug, who sat in the kitchen wiping her eyes.

"All this is Manos' fault. If he didn't crash into his car, I'll have been in America, knowing nothing about her and never fall in love with her like a fool. Do you understand me?" he cried breaking Maria's heart.

It was the first time that Kalogerou was in such a bad condition. "And I wanted to get married to her." He showed to Maria the box he had in his pocket, "... how can I get married to her if she isn't alive. It passed a day and no one had called." He collapsed on the sofa. "Why didn't they kidnap me?" His question shocked Maria. She tried to calm him down, but Dimitris freed from her embrace like a beast.

He came out of the kitchen and ran into Georgiou, whose face wasn't very encouraging. He erupted to him first. "How much we would expect them to call? Until they bring Alina dead to me?"

Aris and Themis restrained him. They both looked at Georgiou.

Then he erupted on Aris, too. "And you? Where have you been? You were the first one I told you that I love her. And you promised me that she was safe. Very safe. It gets dark and Alina is missing since yesterday afternoon and no one has called us. Can you tell me where is she? Why don't you give her photo to the media, at least, find her in a hospital. Dead." Aris and Themis didn't speak. They would feel the same, if that happened to their girlfriends.

Georgiou was worried. He talked with Aris and Themis. They couldn't explain this delay. Something was very wrong with those kidnappers. What was that? And that wrongness had to do with Miss Alexiou, or it was something between them? They couldn't assume something. Anything. If they had already killed her? That's could be a very good reason for not calling them. Always a question without an answer.

Georgiou entered the office where Kalogerou was guarded by a policeman because they were afraid of harming himself. He said something to Themis, who left right away.

"Nothing yet, I presume," Kalogerou said as if he was speaking to himself. Georgiou felt a knot in his throat. He beckoned his head. He couldn't speak. Kalogerou hid his face into his hands. "So we assume that she is dead, isn't she?" His voice was icily.

"Mr. Kalogerou, I'm afraid that we couldn't say such a thing." Georgiou was haggard.

It wasn't the first time that he was in charge in a kidnap case. And if Miss Alexiou was killed, this would be a very bad development. He had felt so awful in the previous kidnapping of a businessman three years ago, as they found him murdered after his wife having delivered the ransom.

Georgiou grabbed his head. In that case, too many things were wrong. This time, he had learned his lesson. So far, nobody had learned about the kidnapping of Alina Alexiou. Nothing had leaked to the Press. Everything was under control.

Or it wasn't? The fact that the kidnappers had not yet called for ransom, meant something. What was missing here? Things showed an agonizing slow progress.

Throughout the villa had spread a silence of death. Kalogerou felt a cold air froze his bones. His whole body shuddered. If Alina was dead, he had taken his decision. He couldn't live without her sweet voice, her smile, teasing him of his age, her caressing. Without Alina, he would lead an aimless life.

He looked at Aris. "Have you ever read Romeo and Juliet?" Aris didn't speak, as he hated literature since he was at school.

Kalogerou continued his own monolog. "I don't remember who dies first? Romeo or Juliet?"

Aris looked at him with his black eyes. "Whatever dies first is irrelevant to me. In our case, nobody is going to die. When we find Miss Alexiou you will burden her for the rest of your life." Kalogerou didn't laugh with Aris's humor.

His mobile phone rang. Aris and Dimitris froze. Dimitris looked at the screen of his mobile. "What does this asshole want?" He didn't reply. His phone stopped ringing for a while. After a few seconds, his mobile rang again. Kalogerou saw the screen again and grimaced.

"I think that you should answer this," Aris said to him.

"Why? It isn't the kidnappers," Kalogerou answered back to him with an arrogant tone of his voice. Aris answered the phone and then gave it to Kalogerou.

Kalogerou swore and was very rude. "What do you want?" Kalogerou growled. For the next few minutes, Kalogerou couldn't even breathe. "And how do I know that your client isn't involved, 'my dear colleague,'" with a voice full of irony.

It was impossible for Aris to understand who was on the phone and what he wanted from Kalogerou. Kalogerou was screaming. Georgiou walked into the office. Kalogerou turned and looked at him. "Mr. Georgiou, is Mr. Fotiadis arrested?" Georgiou beckoned affirmatively with his head.

"Mr. Kalogerou, who's on the phone?"

"The lawyer of Mr. Fotiadis claiming that his client wasn't involved neither in the murder of Manos nor in the kidnapping of Miss Alexiou. Although they have many differences with Manos these differences were only in the level of trade and nothing more. Mr. Fotiadis could never kill Manos or his daughter." Kalogerou was reporting to Georgiou what the lawyer of Fotiadis was telling him on the phone.

"Mr. Kalogerou, that's something that Themis will decide it through the interrogation." Kalogerou gave his phone to Georgiou in order to speak directly to the lawyer of Fotiadis.

From his point of view, he didn't want to hear a word anymore. He didn't want to see anyone. He felt as he was drowning staying in the house. He grabbed the car keys and before Aris could stop him, he boarded to his car. Aris ran behind him with his motorbike.

Kalogerou was driving very fast. *He wanted to kill himself, considering that stupid conversation about Romeo and Juliet. Romeo? Who the hell was that idiot?* Aris thought. Kalogerou could almost kill them both.

Aris requested for assistance and several motorbikes and police cars surrounded Kalogerou's car and led him back to his home with safety. Georgiou couldn't believe what Kalogerou had done. Kalogerou was obviously a man deep in love but trying killing himself was out of question.

Themis, the police officer that interrogated Fotiadis, couldn't figure out anything that lead to the conclusion that Fotiadis was involved in Alina's kidnapping, so he released Fotiadis after a few hours, and having him under close surveillance.

THE THIRD DAY AFTER Alina's kidnapping found Kalogerou sleeping on the couch. The kidnappers hadn't phoned yet. Kalogerou was a wreck. He was pretty sure that the kidnappers weren't going to phone him. Something did go very wrong and Alina was dead. He took the velvet box and threw it in the last drawer of the desk. He wasn't about to use it. *Ever*, he thought and burst into tears.

At noon, Aris came into the living room looking up for Georgiou, who was sitting next to a man in front of a computer. Aris went close to him and whispered something in his ear. Georgiou looked worried. The two men were whispering.

"Are you sure about that?" asked Georgiou once more.

"Yes, sir. The officer who saw the body confirmed that too. He's being executed. But, sir, I shot him in the belly, I'm sure, not in the head, otherwise, he couldn't drive the car." Georgiou glared at him. This last development didn't like him. It was obvious that they were dealing with unscrupulous criminals. At least one of the kidnappers was dangerous as he preferred to kill the injured man rather than sent him to the hospital or to a doctor. *That's not a good sign. Not a good sign*, Georgiou murmured.

"Mr. Georgiou, we are dealing with a rogue," said Aris, "although our informants assured us that no one entangled in such a business during the last few days." Georgiou pacing up and down in the living room. "Also, I checked all hospitals. Nobody appeared with an injured girl like Miss Alexiou."

Georgiou nodded relieved for a moment. "Unless they want to surprise us and let us find her in a trash," he said undertone. Instinctively that thought just flew far away.

Something was wrong with the kidnappers, and somehow deep inside him, he knew that Alexiou was still alive, although no one had phoned all these days. Why? Why didn't the kidnappers call yet? That question troubled his mind day after day. Georgiou was sure that Miss Alexiou was alive. *That hunch again*, he said to himself.

It was about time to adopt a most hostile approach. Georgiou briefed Kalogerou that they are going to become more aggressive in order to force the kidnappers to make a mistake. Kalogerou just shook his head. For him the woman of his life was dead. His gaze was icy while Georgiou was talking to him. If Alina was dead he could never love again another woman. That's for sure.

Georgiou decided that Alexiou's kidnapping must become the focus of media attention. During the following hours, all radio and television stations in the country deal with the kidnapping of Alina Alexiou. They also sent her photograph in all hospitals. *Just in case*, as Georgiou thought.

Once notified by the police that Alexiou was kidnapped Kalogerou's phone never stopped ringing, making his martyrdom even more unbearable. Journalists were gathered outside the villa in Kifissia, setting up several vans for immediate information, making the way to the villa difficult not only for the policemen but also for the personnel.

Chapter 16

A shot made Alina opened her eyes. She was afraid that it was her turn. She terrified. She tried to calm down despite the terror she was living in during the last days. Her head was still aching. She couldn't even move her head. She felt as if someone had beaten her on the head. She put her hand on her head and realized that someone had actually beaten her.

She caught a bump with her hand. Developing her sense of hearing she heard steps coming towards her. She closed her eyes and tried to stay as still as possible. The door opened, someone came close to her and saw that Alina was sleeping. Then someone locked the door. After that, she heard the apartment door opened and closed. Then nothing, just quietness.

Her eyes adapted to the dark. She stood up a little. Her legs were numb and her body was all aches and pains. She rubbed her legs in order to stand up. She couldn't remember how many hours or days was unconscious. She couldn't remember anything. The only thing she could remember was the hand that grabbed her from her car after killing Stelios and pulled her into the other car.

She relied her back on the wall in order to be able to get up. She pressed something and made noise. She stayed motionless, thinking that someone would come back again into the room to check her. She listened carefully. Nothing happened. Silence! Nobody came in. As if she was alone. She was alone. They left her alone after all these days. That was a very good opportunity to escape.

She saw that she had pressed five or six plastic plates with leftovers. She tried to remember, in vain. From the leftovers, she concluded that they gave her breakfast, lunch, and dinner, so it must have been locked up in this filthy room nearly two days, maybe three.

It was impossible to remember. Her head ached terribly, and so her stomach. What kind of garbage fed her all these days? And who were those people? And what they wanted from her? They had killed her father. Why didn't they kill her, too? She remembered Dimitris and her eyes filled with tears. No, she didn't want to die. She wanted to live and she would do anything to live.

Her legs were better and she was able to do a few steps. She walked to a window, or so it seemed. Eventually, it was a window. She tried to open it, but it was stuck. She put all her strength. The window was her salvation and she didn't intend to abandon the effort. She tried once more, although the fear had paralyzed her.

A wave of despair conquered her. She didn't know how much time she had. Luckily the window opened after her third attempt. The sea wind beat her in the face. *I must be somewhere near the sea*, thought Alina, although she couldn't figure out where. She pulled her head out of the window and saw that there was a small balcony.

She jumped out on the balcony. She jumped without thinking. This small balcony was her way to rescue. She jumped to the second balcony, and then to the third. In a few minutes, she would be free. In the fourth balcony, she was lucky. Through the window, she saw an old lady cooking in the kitchen.

She beat on the glass door. At the first place, the old lady didn't appear to pay any attention to her. She beat the window a little stronger. The old lady turned and looked at her in amazement. The warm smile of Aline calmed the old lady who opened the door.

"Do you have a phone, please?" Alina asked reluctantly. The old lady took her by the hand and they went into a small living room. Next to a worn couch was a small table with an old telephone on it. Alina kissed her on the cheek. She picks up the handset, but she couldn't remember any phone number.

Neither the number of the mobile phone of Dimitris or Georgiou or Aris. She thought of Stelios. *Stelios is dead*, she reminded herself. She wiped her eyes from tears. Oh, my God, Stelios is dead. She tried to remember the telephone number of the house. *Oh, concentrate,* she murmured. It was impossible to remember any phone number. She panicked. She didn't want the kidnappers to find her again. She must remember one phone number at least. She was almost free. She had to call Dimitris.

She called the telephone number of the National Phone Numbers Information. She heard the phone rang. The sweet and warm voice of a woman calms her down. "Please, I want the phone number of Manos Alexiou, in Kifissia," she said with a trembling voice. The woman typed the name, and then asked her, "Do you want to connect you, madam?"

"Yes, please," Alina stammered.

The woman thanked her and then she heard the phone of her house ringing.

WHEN THE PHONE RANG at Alexiou's villa everybody alarmed. Dimitris was in the office when he heard the phone in the living room ringing. At first, he didn't pay any attention to. He thought that it was too late for any kind of negotiations. Georgiou rushed into the office and took him to the living room. The phone was still ringing like a possessed.

He picked up the phone and replied with a broken voice. "Kalogerou speaking."

Alina couldn't believe that she heard Dimitris' voice. She only managed to whisper his name before she burst into sobs.

"Alina? Is that you? Where are you, my love? How are you?" Alina couldn't speak. She was listening to Dimitris' warm voice and crying.

Georgiou took the phone from his hand. "Miss Alexiou, Georgiou is speaking, could you please tell us where could you possibly be?"

If I knew where I was, I wouldn't stay here, Alina thought. "Mr. Georgiou, I don't know where I am," she said sobbing. "Please, come and get me, I don't want them to find me again, please."

Dimitris listened on the phone that Alina was crying and begun to lose his patience.

"Miss Alexiou, whatever you do, please do not hang up, I beg you," Georgiou said as throwing a glance to his colleagues on the computer, who tried to trace the phone call. All eyes were on the computer screen. "A few more seconds," an officer said.

"We found her!" Aris cried and he gave to Georgiou a piece of paper with the address on it.

"Alina, we are coming to get you out of there," Dimitris shouted on the phone.

"Themis, talk to her until we get there," Georgiou ordered Themis, who began to speak with Alexiou, trying to calm her down.

The three men boarded on a police car and informed the local police department to send as many police cars as they had to exclude the building, where the call was traced. "Do not let anyone, enter or leave the building. Neither the tenants." Georgiou screamed through the police radio.

In the old lady's apartment, Alina recognized the voice of Themis on the phone.

"Themis, where are they?"

"Don't worry, Miss Alexiou, they just left, please don't hang up the phone."

"I'm somewhere near the sea, Themis. I can smell the sea, but I cannot see it."

"We know that. They need around twenty minutes to come to you. Don't worry. Mr. Georgiou also sent two police cars from the local police station."

The old lady brought her some food. "Come and eat. You're too weak and that is not good in your condition," she told her and left the food in front of her. Alina saw herself in the mirror. Indeed, her condition was miserable.

She couldn't eat, not until Dimitris get her out of there. She smiled at the old lady, but she didn't touch the food. She whispered a thank you to this noble woman and continued pacing with the handset in her hand around the table.

From the north suburb of Athens, Kifissia, to the south suburb Lavrio the distance seemed endless to Dimitris, although the police car was running all the way long.

"Mr. Georgiou, the whole block of apartments is blocked." A voice from the police radio informed them. Georgiou was relieved.

Alina sat on the couch. "Themis, are you still there?"

"I'm here, Miss Alexiou. Don't be afraid."

"They aren't here yet. Why?"

"Miss Alexiou, they will be with you in three or four minutes. Don't worry."

"My head hurts me a lot, and I have a bump. A large one."

"Don't worry about the bump, Miss," Themis said to her.

"Is Dimitris with them?"

"Certainly, Miss Alexiou. Together with Mr. Georgiou and Aris."

Alina was beginning to calm off someway. "And if the kidnappers find me first?" Themis realized that Miss Alexiou was about to panic again.

"I don't think so. The police had blocked the whole building."

His words calmed her a lot. She tried to gather her mind. She couldn't remember many things from the last days. A strange feeling laid on her heart. A voice, a female one, was very familiar to her. She couldn't remember where she had heard this female voice.

Outside the apartment, she heard noises. She sprang upright with fear in her face. She thought that the kidnappers found her. When the door opened, Georgiou and Aris came in first. Then Kalogerou. They didn't expect to face an old lady. Alina ran into his arms.

"Oh, my God, thank you. Are you all right, my love? Tell me that they didn't hurt you? Oh, please, stop crying and tell me. Are you okay?" Dimitris said between the kisses he gave her.

Georgiou went to the phone. "Georgiou speaking, thank you Themis. She is all right."

Dimitris was kissing Alina all the time. When he left her down Alina gave him a punch in the stomach and then she fainted in his arms. The old lady went toward him. "Don't worry, sir. There is nothing wrong with the girl. She is just pregnant!"

Kalogerou looked the old woman with bulging eyes. Georgiou and Aris looked at Kalogerou, who looked them back apologetically.

"Make sure she eats well and sleeps enough and everything will be fine," said the old lady to him and she went again to her kitchen. Dimitris got Alina unconscious by ambulance straight to Apostolou's clinic.

DIMITRIS WENT NEAR her with a look of adoration.

Apostolou entered the room with a broad smile. "Well, my friend, the old lady was right." Kalogerou and Apostolou looked Alina, who had begun to awake. "There is no way to know about it. It's too early," Apostolou said and anticipating the next question of Dimitris he told him, "... and I don't know how the old woman found it out. Go and ask her." He beat him friendly on the shoulder, "Congratulations, my friend."

Alina awakened and watched them. Apostolou looked at her. "Oh, Miss Alexiou, I'm very glad that you woke up and except a small bump in your head everything is perfect. Everything. Oh, congratulations, by the way."

Dimitris murmured.

"Well," said Apostolou "I'm leaving." Apostolou was very happy and Alina was staring at him without understanding anything. *All doctors are strange, but this one is something else,* she thought.

"I was the one who being kidnapped. Is he all right?"

Dimitris smiled. "Doctors. What are you expecting for? They have a very strange sense of humor. Tell me how do you feel? Do you want something to eat? Let me put a pillow on your back."

Alina stared at him curiously. "I'm all right, thank you, and apart from my stomach which still hurts me, I don't want anything, thank you," said Alina.

"Well, my stomach also hurts from the punch you gave me. But you're right to be angry. That's why from now on I won't leave you on your own again. Never! I swear." He bent on her and kissed her on the mouth. "Are you hungry?" He asked her. Alina glared at him without answering his question. "OK, I won't ask you again." And kissed her again in the mouth.

The tingling in her stomach didn't stop. She looked Dimitris, who looked at her with a besotted style. "Now that you mention it, you know what I'm thinking. Maybe my stomach hurts me because I haven't eaten for three days?" She said rubbing her stomach.

"What do you want to eat? Do you want something special?" He asked her, as he was thinking what would be the most appropriate way to inform her about her pregnancy.

"Oh, please tell them to bring me something to eat," she said angrily. Dimitris called Apostolou. In a few minutes, a nurse entered the room with a huge tray.

"Here you are, Miss Alexiou, and eat it all, doctor's orders. And if you want more, please, let me know and I'll bring you right away."

The nurse smiled strangely. In this clinic, everybody behaved strangely. *Perhaps, due to the kidnapping,* she thought and start eating.

Yes, okay this was a hospital food, it was much better from what she ate during the last days.

Dimitris watched her horrified. Alina always used to eat a lot, but it was the first time in his life seeing her eating so quickly. He approached her and stroked her cheek "Are you ok?" He asked her.

"No, I'm still hungry, but the food here isn't so delicious to ask for another round. When I get home I'll tell Maria to cook me," she stopped talking and she smiled. *Oh, Maria could cook her a lot of things much more delicious from the food of the hospital*, she thought.

Dimitris sat in front of her and put his hand on her belly. "What do you want to cook for you?"

She shrugged her shoulders. "Many things, I don't know exactly, but for three days I was only eating hamburgers ugh," she was about to vomit. She got up and ran to the bathroom. Dimitris panicked and phoned to Apostolou. Alina was still in the bathroom trying to recover from the queasiness she had. She went back to her bed.

"Mr. Apostolou, you should change your chef," she said to him angry when she saw him.

"Miss Alexiou, don't put the blame on the chef. You are just pregnant. That's all. Congratulations again. You didn't tell her, yet?" He turned and looked at Dimitris.

"I didn't ...," Dimitris apologized. He looked at her with a sparkling look. "You are pregnant. The old woman told us and Apostolou confirmed it. Isn't it great?" He took her in his arms with the blanket.

"Put me down, please." He left her down and Alina ran again in the bathroom throwing up for the second time. She came out of the bathroom and glanced to Dimitris.

"Well, I think that I'm pregnant." She laid down on the bed again. Dimitris shone with joy. "How that happened?" Alina wondered aloud.

Dimitris hugged her. "I think you know how these things happened?" He stroked her belly.

"Don't be silly, I know how babies are made."

Dimitris pulled out a box from his pocket. "Good. This is for you. I'd give you a few days ago, but due to the kidnappers, I'm giving you now."

Alina opened the box and froze. She gave the box back to him. "No, I don't think I will marry you," she murmured.

That was something he wouldn't expect it. "Why?" he asked her trying to remain calm.

"You want to marry me because of the baby," she said pissed off.

He had heard that pregnant women have nerves. He took a deep breath. "And what are you going to do? You will leave with my baby to America as your mother did?"

Alina growled from anger.

He took a deep breath. "Forget it. We are going to get married. If Manos learned that I have a relationship with his daughter who, I have to mention that I love her a lot, don't forget that ever, and you are also pregnant, yes, you were a naughty girl, but it's ok, I haven't any problem with that as you know..."

Alina began to flare up. "You should be ashamed of you and why you mention my father. My father is dead. He isn't going to ask you anything from where he is. My answer is no, no, no and no." Alina was beaten across the bed like a little child whose mother put her to sleep early.

"Oh, no my little girl. I'm not so far away. Yet. What is going on, sweetie?" Manos' voice obsess her as it was heard from this world.

Dimitris gets aside and Alina saw her father in the door with crutches accompanied by her mom. She couldn't speak. She looked once at her parents and once at Dimitris.

"How that happened? I saw you in the hospital and you weren't breathing, and doctors confirmed so ... mom ... I don't understand. What is going on?"

"Miss Alexiou, you will understand everything." Georgiou entered the room. "First of all, I assume that everything is all right with the baby?"

Alina looked at Dimitris pissed off.

Manos looked at Dimitris pissed off.

Only her mom kissed her.

Georgiou continued, "I'm very glad that you are both very well."

Dimitris muttered something through his teeth. Georgiou looked at him without understanding what was happening. "Forgive me that I put you at a risk. It was the only way to end this story once and for all."

"Mr. Georgiou, I'm sorry, I don't understand," Alina said looking confused. "So wasn't my father injured?"

Georgiou smiled. "Miss Alexiou, your father was seriously injured. But it was your mother who gave me a marvelous idea.

Alina looked angry at her mother. "What idea?"

"She told me that after all these infections if Manos had the slightest chance to be healthy again that would be only if he changed the hospital environment. So with the help of Mr. Kalogerou and your mother, Mr. Alexiou was transferred to another clinic in a very bad condition, believe me, but I expand this idea a little bit, just a little bit."

"May I ask how did you accomplish that?"

"To die your father, what else? And then put my plan into action." Georgiou was proud of his whole plan. Alina looked at him without believing why Georgiou was so happy about. "Mr. Apostolou found a rehabilitation clinic, which kept secret the fact that Mr. Alexiou was there by giving them a serious amount of money," Georgiou glanced to Kalogerou and Alina understood that Dimitris had paid that serious amount of money, "so your dad had been transferred there a day before his funeral accompanied by your mother as his doctor."

Turning to Mr. Alexiou, Georgiou asked him "Mr. Alexiou, tell me how did you find your funeral? I found it extremely marvelous, sir. Everybody was there. Everybody."

Manos Alexiou smiled.

"Dimitris, why didn't you tell me that my dad was alive?" Alina meanwhile was sitting in bed with Dimitris beside her, who caressed her belly.

Instead of Dimitris, Georgiou answered her question. "Mr. Kalogerou was following orders. My orders. If you knew that your father was alive, then you couldn't play your role convincingly."

She shook her head. Georgiou was right. If she knew that her father was alive she couldn't be sad.

"So," Georgiou continued with joy, "everything went like a clockwork, you were sad because your father was dead, then you've been kidnapped, although three days without any calls for ransom drive me crazy, fortunately, everything went well."

Alina turned to Dimitris "Is Stelios dead?"

"No, not. Stelios is alive, after three hours surgery and retired, at last. And, believe me, it was very hard to convince him," Dimitris answered by stroking her belly. "And I have hired another one."

"Mr. Kalogerou, you played hard, I must admit," said Georgiou embittered.

"May I ask who you hired?" Alina asked him as she was trying to stop him stroking her belly all the time.

"I hired the best bodyguard ever for my wife and my daughter and I'm not hearing anything, although it was also a little bit hard to convince him, you know. I promised Aris that you are going to sign a couple of books for his girlfriend and for Themis girlfriend. He is, already, outside your room." Dimitris leaned over and gave Alina a kiss on her mouth. Her anger faded.

Alina turned toward Georgiou, "Mr. Georgiou, in the room that they kept me all these days I think that I heard ..."

"Emily! Behind all that mess, even for the fatal injury of your father, was Emily." Georgiou turned to Manos. "Mr. Alexiou, we went to arrest Emily in her apartment. We didn't manage to do it as she committed suicide."

"Dad, why did Emily hated you so much?" Alina asked her father.

Manos was sitting on a chair. He had recovered enough, although he was still very weak. "It's all started several years ago, almost thirty years ago. When I met Emily, I mean professionally, he had come to me seeking for a job. Your mother was gone for over a year in America taking you with her. My father's small dairy factory went very well. There was a very small competition that time. I was the only one with machines. There was also another farmer, a few kilometers away, who had been the husband of Emily, as I learned later, much later. The problem was that this farmer wasn't good enough. He had many debts and in an auction, I bought his farm and his small dairy unit. Some days after the auction I learned that he committed suicide. I didn't know him. I had never met him my whole life. I didn't know that he was married. I didn't know Emily was his wife. I haven't seen her in my life till the day she came to me seeking for a job. I was desperate for a secretary because my business was going very well. I had several proposals from investors who wanted to invest in my innovative dairy unit. I hired her without thinking, or do beforehand any research on her. And the truth was that Emily was a treasure for me until the moment she misunderstood my intimacy. After working together for so many hours, intimacy was something natural between two people. I explained to her that our relationship would be strictly professional. She seemed to accept my decision.

But I was wrong. Emily wanted to revenge me by causing trouble in the factory. Perhaps you've learned about the scandal with Fotiadis. Emily was behind it."

Alina nodded. She knew about that scandal.

Her father continued, "When I learned that she was responsible and she was the one who approached Fotiadis in order to sell him my plans for some new products I fired her. Believe me, it was the most difficult moment of my life. I don't like firing people, you know that Alina, everybody knows that, but Emily was dangerous for my work. She started crying and confided to me that she had a child with disabilities and she needed the job and the money for paying the institution of her son. At first, I couldn't believe her. When I saw the child's birth certificate I reconsider of firing her. She also took me to the institution in order to see her son. I felt very bad. So, I gave her another chance..."

Manos took a deep breath, "... and everything ran smoothly until the moment your mom sent me a letter that you wanted to visit me in Greece. I was so happy. I told Maria everything about Alina and she was happy too, then Emily understood that something new was I my life and I told her also the truth about my daughter. Big mistake."

"Yea, right, you could hide Alina from me in a very effective way," Dimitris said with complaints and without stopped caressing Alina's abdomen.

"Oh, stop complaining, Dimitris. You were an easy target, as long as you had a beautiful woman on your side. The point is that I told Emily the whole truth. That I had married an American woman and I had a daughter with her. I thought Emily would understand me. She was a mother. But Emily saw Alina as a threat. She always believed deep inside her that she could change my opinion and I could fell in love with her. This wasn't going to happen. So when Alina came in Greece, she photographed her. She kept the photos all these years, until one day she saw a ticket to America in my name."

Manos turned to Jennifer, "Yes, Jennifer, I was ready to come to America this time because I wanted to convince you that I still love you very much and still want you by me. Yes, I know that you've told Alina that you don't love me anymore but I couldn't believe her. I didn't believe her. I wanted to hear it from you, that you don't love me anymore and I will disappear from your life. Forever."

Jennifer kissed him on his mouth. "I never stopped loving you. You've stolen my heart years ago."

Manos smiled. "Emily understood that I was still in love with my ex-wife so she started to blackmail me. She was about to give the photos of Alina to the newspapers. That would be a disaster as I had given my word to Jennifer that nobody would learn about Alina. She said that she loves me and she could love also Alina as her daughter. I doubt about that. I told her that I will go to the police and due to her disable son I gave her a month, in order to find another job. After that month she ought to be out of my factory. These were my last words. Then Emily decided to kill me by cutting the brakes on my car. You know the rest."

"Dimitris, how many times did I tell you that I didn't like this woman?" Alina asked him.

"Many times, sweetheart," Dimitris answered still caressing her belly.

"And why she kidnapped me?" Alina asked Georgiou.

"She wanted money. She would leave for Australia with her son. She was a dangerous woman. She thought that your father was responsible for the suicide of her husband. She wrote a note before committed suicide. I sent it to the forensics lab in the Police Headquarters," said Georgiou.

Manos looked at Dimitris, "When are you going to marry my daughter, because I want to get married, too."

Dimitris stopped caressing Alina's belly. "What do you mean Manos? Who do you want to marry to?"

"I want to marry to Jennifer," Manos said with pleasure.

Kalogerou looked at Georgiou, who nodded his head. "Mr. Kalogerou, forgive me, I didn't find the time to inform him about that matter. I had my mind on Emily."

Dimitris took a deep breath. "Manos, you cannot marry Jennifer," he said strictly. Manos stood up abruptly from his chair throwing his crutches away and proceeded towards Dimitris.

"Manos ..." stammered Jennifer, not believing that Manos could walk without any help.

"Jennifer, please stop." He turned to Dimitris in vexation. "Dimitris, I love Jennifer very much and I want to marry her as soon as possible and no one would tell me what to do with the woman of my life if you don't want to tell you what to do with my daughter."

"Dad, please," said Alina.

But Manos was very angry to stop. "Be quiet, young lady, I will deal with you later." Alina didn't speak.

Manos stood in front of Dimitris. "Tell me why I cannot marry Jennifer? Did you ask me if I want you to get marry to my daughter? Did you buy her a ring?"

"Well, Manos, I don't need to ask you about what to do with the woman I love. And yes I bought her a ring which she wore it if you just check her finger, and, Jennifer, I think that you didn't connect quite well the nerves in Manos' brain. And you idiot, you cannot marry Jennifer because you never divorce her. That's why. But if you insist, you can call Christina to make an appointment with me, in my office, in order to have the opportunity to have your divorce first and then you can marry Jennifer again if you want to. However, as your lawyer, I recommend you to take her and go to your house, and I take Alina to my house. Do you agree with that, Dad?"

Manos stopped shouting as he realized that he never divorced Jennifer. "Give me a break smart ash. Jennifer connected my brain perfectly well and, I will take her with me right now and go to my house as soon as you take Alina to yours, as you just proposed... my beloved son," said Manos and turning to Jennifer he kissed her passionate trying to gain all that lost time away from her.

Dimitris took Alina in his arms. Alina was about to say something. "Mrs. Kalogerou, do you have any objections?" And before even Alina answered he kissed her on the mouth. Then Dimitris turned to Georgiou, "Mr. Georgiou, could you please be my best man?"

"That would be a great honor," Georgiou replied full of happiness.

"Thank you very much, sir." Dimitris gave her a gentle kiss, as he didn't want to disturb the baby in her womb.

THE END

Don't miss out!

Visit the website below and you can sign up to receive emails whenever Clairie Saunders publishes a new book. There's no charge and no obligation.

https://books2read.com/r/B-A-NIWDB-UEJBD

BOOKS 2 READ

Connecting independent readers to independent writers.

Also by Clairie Saunders

MISSION SERIES
Mission Accomplished: Love

Standalone
Beautiful Secrets
Her golden eyes